The Door A Jar

Randy Schneider

For Sally

Who encouraged me when the door was ajar…

Once you know love, you can know nothing else.

Table of Contents

Chapter One 1

Chapter Two...5

Chapter Three...12

Chapter Four 20

Chapter Five...31

Chapter Six...41

Chapter Seven 48

Chapter Eight 55

Chapter Nine 59

Chapter Ten...79

Chapter Eleven...91

Chapter Twelve...103

Chapter Thirteen 113

Chapter Fourteen...130

Chapter Fifteen...151

Chapter Sixteen...159

Chapter Seventeen 175

Chapter Eighteen..181

Chapter Nineteen 202

Chapter Twenty..216

Chapter Twenty-One...231

Chapter Twenty-Two 252

Chapter Twenty-Three 272

Chapter Twenty-Four...293

Chapter Twenty-Five 314

Chapter Twenty-Six 331

Chapter Twenty-Seven...340

About the Author

Randy is a storyteller living in the mountains of Colorado. He uses words and stories as a framework to convey the essence of what is.

Chapter One

"I no longer want to be human," I said.

I expected some reaction from him, but nothing. His gaze never wavered. His eyes reminded me of old, worn, and faded blue jeans. The wear of age couldn't hide the fire in his intensity — an intensity that held my gaze captive. Held me captive.

It never occurred to me that I could look away because I couldn't. In any other situation, my gaze would have dropped, waiting for some sort of validation or rebuke. That thought — expecting an audience — passed. No other thoughts were brave enough to surface. Only silence and his gaze remained. Time stopped. The world faded. All that remained was an awareness of emptiness.

A slight nod of his head jolted me back into the moment so violently that my body jumped. He brought a finger to his lips, and his eyes softened. I felt my body let go. My eyes dropped to the table in front of me. I didn't need them to know that he had stood up. Turning effortlessly, he disappeared through a plain door.

The world began to rush back in. Everything seemed both new and familiar. I looked around, taking in my surroundings. The room was simple — far more humble than I had expected. The walls were plain, with no bookshelves, paintings, or pictures. We sat on simple cushions. A small table rested in front of where he had been sitting. "Probably where he takes his meals," I thought. A worn rug covered the floor.

What surprised me most were the windows, gloriously open. Wispy curtains whirled gently in the breeze. A skylight revealed the sky above, where clouds drifted lazily, casting their shadows across the floor.

With nothing else to distract me. I waited.

Waiting was easy. Finding this place, this man — that had been an impossible search. But now, I was here. The door opened again, and he returned, carrying a tray with four jars.

There was nothing remarkable about him. He wasn't short or tall, fat or thin. He wore simple clothes. His brownish hair relaxed casually on his head, neither long nor short.

What struck me was how he moved. Each motion appeared effortless, seamlessly transitioning to the next. His eyes — a clarity that could have easily been missed if one wasn't paying attention.

I had prepared myself for this moment. I had my reasons, my experiences, and my pain lined up to support my decision. But as I braced for the anticipated confrontation, I realized I had no idea what was about to happen.

He placed the tray on the table and sat down — or rather, alighted, on his cushion. Taking a small pad of paper, he carefully wrote a few words before meeting my gaze again.

I took the gesture as permission to speak.

"The last straw was what happened to Leah," I began. "She was brutally assaulted by a man who drugged her and took advantage of her. I could identify him. Everyone in the bar could identify him. The police knew who he was. And yet nothing — nothing — was going to happen to him."

I paused, my voice tightening. "Leah was broken beyond repair. She's gone. But the human animal who did this? He's still free."

His gaze didn't waver. I thought I saw a faint nod of recognition, a silent acknowledgment. But there was no resistance. No rebuttal. No demand for clarity or validation. Just the unwavering, listening gaze.

"Humans continue to decimate the world," I continued, feeling the words push their way out. "They manipulate and abuse others for profit and power, without conscience. I am repulsed by my species. We care for nothing but ourselves, taking whatever we can through violence or greed. And then Leah..."

My voice faltered, but I pressed on. "I can no longer be human."

His gaze shifted to the tray, where the four jars sat next to the note.

Chapter Two

Leah was coming down from a trip when I first met her. At that moment, all she needed was someone to hold her upright so she could get into the cab. The way she leaned into me felt as if she completely trusted me. Her body was warm. I felt something — something different. It stirred deeply inside me. The cab door slammed shut, and just like that, she was gone.

It haunted me. She lingered in my dreams, but it wasn't enough to satisfy the infatuation that had taken hold of me. I might have languished forever fantasizing about this mystery woman, but then, by chance, we met again.

The room was loud and full of people. Through the crowd, I spotted her — the woman — this time with the most attractive man in the room. He was boasting about his achievements and superior physique. Then her eyes met mine. I wish I could say it was magical, but it wasn't. It was another cry for help.

I held out my hand. Her eyes drew me toward her. I had no resistance.

"So nice to see you again," she said as I approached. The "man candy" didn't miss a beat, continuing to weave his tale of superiority for the captivated audience.

There was a flicker of recognition in her eyes, a silent "Where have I seen you before?"

"I was there for the taxi a while ago," I said.

"You sent me home and didn't fuck me. That's unusual." She smirked as we subtly moved away.

"At the time, you had more pressing needs," I replied.

"Ah, a gentleman. Most aren't."

"Is that what you're looking for? A gentleman?"

She tilted her head, maybe from the wine, maybe from curiosity. She looked at me critically, making no effort to hide her assessment.

"Maybe," she said softly. For the first time, her persona dropped, and we both fell quiet.

"What would a gentleman do now?" I asked, my voice barely above a whisper.

"A gentleman wouldn't need to ask," she replied. Then, with a playful smile, she added, "Don't worry, you are a gentleman."

"Dance," she said, extending her hand.

The dance floor was nothing more than a piece of plywood in front of a jukebox. While Leah moved with the grace of silk, I did my best to sway with the deafening beat. Her eyes closed as she rocked and weaved, completely absorbed in the music. I moved from side to side, always watching, maybe even trying to protect her. I liked to think I made her feel safe. But the reality was different — she was always in the moment, always present.

As the song changed, a crowd gathered around us. At first, bodies brushed past us politely, but then they began to bump and move without care. I felt uncomfortable, but Leah? She was lost in the movement, the music, the moment. I had to wrap my arm around her waist just to keep track of her in the confluence.

Eventually, we found a table. There were drinks. Leah picked one up, took a sip, and twisted her face in distaste. She tried another and another until she found one to her liking. It didn't matter that none of them were ours.

She put down the chosen drink, glanced at me, and cocked her head, leaning in close. "I'm probably not what you think. Or maybe I am." Her words hung in the air before she added, "Let's go someplace and find out."

It was likely that she had a tab at the bar, but she didn't seem concerned. She took my hand, and we moved past the jukebox, past the man candy, past the bartender who was mid-argument with a waitress, and finally, out into the night.

Three steps outside the door, she stopped. Eyes closed, she drew in a breath as though it was her very first breath. I closed my eyes and did the same. I was still holding her hand, just in case she vanished again.

The air was cool and heavy. When I opened my eyes, she was watching me. She smiled.

"The first breath is always the best," Leah said. "And every breath is the first." Her chest lifted and fell as she closed her eyes again for a moment.

"I knew an oboe player once," she continued. "He'd say, 'Let's breathe some life into this beast,' and then his music would come alive." She looked directly into my eyes. "Breathing is everything."

I couldn't hide how completely out of my depth I was. She could see it and smiled knowingly.

***

Leah led me through the streets, past vendors and patrons, through lights and darkness, sounds and silence. As we walked together, I began to feel like Leah was leading me into a new life. For her, though, it was just another evening, another breath.

We found a quiet corner in a café and ordered some food and a bottle of wine. As we waited, she took my hand and studied it.

Curious, I asked, "What do you see?"

"Hmmm, odd. I can't say," she replied, her face wrinkling in thought. Just then, the waiter arrived with our wine. I handed Leah the cork, and she breathed it in deeply, savoring the moment. It didn't matter whether it was good wine or bad — what mattered was that we were sharing the experience.

She raised her glass. "To my gentleman friend."

Our glasses touched, and the gentle chime echoed between us. As she took her first sip, her eyes were on me, watching. Self-conscious and slightly awkward, I took a sip as well, grateful I didn't spill.

"How long have you been in the city?" she asked.

"Not long," I replied.

Leah smiled. "Are you staying for a while or just visiting before you head off on another adventure?"

"I came here for work," I explained, "but my fortunes have shifted."

***

After we finished our meal, the bill came, and she nodded at it, making it clear she had no intention of paying. "Hopefully, your fortunes haven't dried up," she said.

"It's not like that," I said, handing my card to the waiter.

When the waiter returned with the receipt, Leah borrowed the pen, scribbled something on a piece of paper, and tucked it away in her pocket. Then, as we left the café, she paused. I could see her biting her lower lip, considering her options.

"Did you have plans?" she asked.

"Dinner and a walk," I replied.

"And then?"

"Probably back to my place."

"Interested in a change of plans?" she asked, holding out her hand.

"What do you have in mind?" I asked as I took her hand.

"The river never asks how it will get to the ocean. It flows where it will and always finds its way home," she said.

Had the street not been a crowded confluence of bodies, I might have thought she was joking. But there was a definite pull, a current drawing us along. In the distance, I could hear street musicians playing, and the crowd carried us forward.

Eventually, the streets narrowed, and traffic slowed. People yelled and laughed loudly. Anger and joy fused into a single symphony. Then, the current opened into the square.

The sounds may have drawn us in, but the smells, colors, bodies, and movement exploded into a celebration of life. She led me to the center of the storm. Unexpectedly, in the eye, there was calm. We sat on the steps below a marble statue and watched. Someone handed us a plastic cup. Leah tasted it and passed it to me. "Careful," she whispered, and within moments, I understood. The world around us began to blur as sounds became colors, colors became smells, and everything blended into motion.

Her hand lifted mine, and we rejoined the confluence. My body moved. Her body moved. Our bodies touched and floated until I couldn't tell which was my body and which was hers. I felt her hand pull me close and lead me out to a side street. Without prompting, we both took a deep breath and exhaled together. I remembered Leah's words: "The first breath is always the best." And she was right.

Chapter Three

Leah looked into my face, and suddenly, we both smiled — then laughed. Not just a quiet chuckle but a full-bodied explosion of laughter. My whole body shook, a feeling I had never experienced before. I was alive. Leah had breathed life into me.

We laughed so hard that we doubled over, then sat down, and eventually lay flat on the cobblestones, still laughing. Both of our bodies heaved with life, but slowly, the laughter subsided. As we lay there, simply breathing deeply. My body tingled, and my mind grew peaceful. I imagined she was feeling the same. Her hand touched mine. The cobblestones beneath us were cold, but her hand made me feel warm. We turned our heads toward each other as if for the first time.

She smiled — not the laughter smile, but a radiant, glowing smile. There was nothing better.

For me, time stopped. Soon, the awareness of the world around us began to return. I could have stayed there, held in her gaze forever. But even the moon waxes and wanes with the pull of the universe, and our souls, too, eventually surrender to the pull of the night.

We sat up and watched the crowd surge and ebb. The music swelled and faded. In the lull between waves of sound, we stood and gathered ourselves. Leah took my arm and pulled me close. Gently tugging on my elbow, she leaned in and whispered, "Take me home."

"Where is home?" I whispered back. Our eyes met, and she was smiling.

"Home," she whispered again, pulling me closer.

It took me a few moments to get my bearings and figure out the way back to my place. "Bit of a walk," I said. Leah didn't seem to mind. Her eyes were soft, and her body gave no resistance.

The night air wasn't cold, but she held me close as we walked. Leah seemed lost in thought, and I didn't break the spell that held her.

When we arrived at my apartment, I opened the door for her. Only then did she let go of my arm and step inside. After two steps, her shoes were off. Standing barefoot on the wooden floor with eyes closed, she took a deep breath. Unconsciously, I did the same.

Leah turned and held out her hand. I couldn't resist — I took it. She led us to the bedroom, somehow already knowing where to go. We lay down together, spooning, and our bodies found a new familiar. I could feel her breathing, and soon, I heard the gentle rhythm of her slipping into sleep. Her body was warm and heavy against mine. She pulled me into her deep stillness, and I didn't resist — not that I wanted to.

***

The warmth of the sun radiating through the window woke me from a deep sleep. It took me a moment to remember there should be another body next to mine. Instead, there was only a warm spot where she had been. From outside the room, I heard movement — cupboards opening, the sink running, the coffee grinder whirring, and then, "Shit."

I found Leah in the kitchen, wearing one of my shirts, hands on her hips, glaring at the coffee machine.

"It won't go," she said, sensing me behind her.

I stepped up and pressed the power button. The coffee machine sputtered a bit, then settled into the familiar rhythm of heating and dripping. She leaned back into me, and I instinctively wrapped my arms around her. We had found familiar again. The first domestic drama of our fledgling relationship had been averted. I took a deep breath.

There was a pause. For me, this was a new adventure, and I had the sense that it was unfamiliar ground for her, too.

"Usually, it's a scramble to get out the door," she said. "Maybe a shower, but never lingering. Lingering makes things uncomfortable — it creates an obligation." Her words seemed to pull her into herself, into memories. Her body tightened.

"No need to rush," I said softly. Her body relaxed. "Stay and smell the coffee."

I tried to make light of the situation, but she tensed again. I let the moment settle before speaking again, more gently this time. "Please stay a while." I didn't want her to disappear again. Her body eased.

With coffee poured, we retreated to the table by the large window, where the sunlight warmed the space. The company rented the apartment for me. It had a modern feel — large windows, high ceilings, everything bathed in neutral grays. "Safe white," my mother would have called it. Even the artwork on the walls stayed safely within the neutral palette. Leah, now quiet, began to take it all in. Until last night, I had been comfortable with the sterile feel of the place. Now, it seemed antiseptic and lifeless.

Leah pulled her knees up into the shirt and sat in a squat on the chair, resting her mug on her knees. We both looked around the room, seeing it for the first time.

"The company rented this for me while I'm here. It's nice enough," I said, breaking the silence.

"Company?" she asked, her voice quick. "Do you have someplace to be?"

"Some calls, maybe a meeting later," I replied. "No rush. You?"

"Same," she said, taking a sip of her coffee. "No rush. I can leave if you need me to."

"How would I ever find you again if you left?"

She smiled. "I have a feeling you wouldn't have much trouble finding me."

"You could make it easier," I suggested.

She seemed to ponder that for a moment.

I got up and went to the second bedroom, which served as my office. Finding a pen, I wrote down my number on a sticky note and returned to the table. "Here, now you can find me."

Leah took the note and stuck it to the table in front of her. With another sip of coffee, she closed her eyes as she took it in. She seemed to breathe it in. The mug lowered back to her knees, and she let out a long breath, her body relaxing.

She looked at me and asked, "What sort of work do you do?"

"Biomedical engineering," I said. "I make drugs, hopefully to help people."

"What brings you here?"

I took a deep breath, pursed my lips, and sighed a little. "The company is building a manufacturing facility here. I've been sent to make sure everything we need is available — land, water, power, people. It was a way to get me out of the lab."

"Sounds important," she said, her eyes narrowing slightly. "Feels like there's more to the story."

"There is," I admitted.

Leah leaned forward. "Wanna spill?"

"I discovered some things about the company a few months ago that made me question everything."

"Like?"

"Like whether I can keep working for a company more concerned with profits than people, even if the drugs I'm developing are meant to help people." I paused, gathering my thoughts. "The diseases my drugs are treating come from chemicals my company produces."

"And now you're here to build a factory for those drugs?"

"I needed to get away from the lab and sort things out. Management knows I have concerns. Sending me here was a way to keep me quiet. The factory will be built whether I'm on board or not."

"So, you came here to find your soul," she said with a smile.

"I came here seeking answers to questions that can't be found in the lab. I hoped I'd find people here with the wisdom to help me answer them."

"And you found me," she giggled. "I have no answers. I'm probably more fucked up than you are." Her giggle turned into full laughter. "I can tell you where to get a good drink or maybe a joint, but that's about as deep as it gets for this girl."

I laughed along with her, partially out of embarrassment. She was laughing so hard she had to set her coffee down to keep from spilling it. Eventually, she got up and went to rinse the mug in the kitchen. Then, to the bathroom. I heard her still laughing behind the closed door.

When she emerged, she was scrolling through her phone with a new sense of purpose. "I know someone who might be able to help you," she said, glancing at me. "Maybe we could grab lunch?"

I shrugged and nodded in agreement as she tapped away on her phone.

Chapter Four

"Breakfast?" I asked.

She looked down at the shirt hanging on her, then back at me. I got the hint and started looking in the refrigerator. Normally, breakfast was whatever was left over from lunch or dinner the past few days. Not finding anything too appealing, I turned to the pantry.

I found a box of cereal — it looked kind of like granola and was probably left by a former tenant. I looked at the ingredients out of habit and, finding nothing to worry about, I shook the box. Leah looked up and shrugged her shoulders in acceptance.

With bowls and granola on the table, we sat down to eat. Just then, the phone buzzed.

"Great," she said, looking at her phone. "Ben is in town and can meet us for a late lunch. Okay?"

"Sure," I said.

"The pub is down the street. We can walk." She picked up the sticky note with my number and entered it into her phone, then looked around for a pen. Not finding one, she went into my office and wrote the pub address on the sticky pad. "If I'm not back by 1 o'clock, I'll meet you at the pub." She placed the sticky note on the table, looked at her phone, and then at me. "Need to pick up a few things." Her fingers tapped vigorously on her phone. One final tap, and she looked at me again. "You can't miss Ben. Ask at the bar if you aren't sure."

With my shirt still hanging off her shoulders, she slid on the pants she'd worn the night before. Looking down at herself, she gave a huff of resignation. Leah pecked me on the cheek, collected her bag, and was out the door before I could say anything.

***

She was right — I couldn't miss Ben. I'd waited as long as I could before heading out. The pub was further than I'd thought, but I still arrived a bit early. It was a nondescript, stone-fronted building sandwiched between a bodega and a laundromat. Inside, it took my eyes a moment to adjust to the dimness. To my surprise, everything was quite orderly and clean, not the dive I'd expected. The bar itself was a massive sculpture of carved, well-worn wood. A few people, who I assumed were locals, sat at one end. High-topped tables framed what could have been a dance floor. That's where I saw Ben.

To say Ben was a large man would be accurate, but not large in the American, overindulged way. He was simply huge, with large hands and an enormous head displaying piercing green eyes. His body matched his hands and head, and long, curly, dark hair draped down his shoulders. He was halfway through the largest plate of nachos I'd ever seen. When the door opened, a flash of light caught his eye. He looked at me, smiled, and motioned me over, sliding a chair out with his foot. Ben carefully wiped his hands on his napkin before offering his hand to me.

Ben was in the business of finding things for people. Things that may or may not be legal. You might say he knew people, he knew everyone. He had connections in every corner of the city, maybe even the country. He wasn't a part of darker organizations nor the authorities, but he knew them, and they knew him.

Ben nodded at the bartender, who was aware of my entry. The nod must have meant "all clear." Two beers arrived before I settled in my seat.

"Thank you," I said as I sat down. Ben was grinning and nodded.

"What brings you to our corner of the world?" he asked, turning back to his nachos.

"You know the factory being built north of the city?" I replied.

He nodded. "I know of it. Lots of moving parts. Some kind of drug factory."

"Yes," I confirmed.

Ben had a method of using a knife and fork to eat his nachos, folding each softened tortilla chip into a perfect nacho sandwich. It was fascinating to watch.

"Leah said we should meet," I added.

Just as Ben mentioned her name, the door opened, spilling brilliant light across the bar. Amidst the light was Leah, still in my shirt but with a skirt and a new bag. Ben wiped his hands and stood, waiting for her eyes to adjust. Leah saw us and headed over. She breezed past Ben and pulled me into a passionate kiss. Startled, I drew her closer and closed my eyes.

As she relaxed, I loosened my grip. Ben had a confused look on his face as she flitted over to give him a hug. Confusion turned into a smile. The bartender, without needing a nod, had already set a drink and another chair for Leah. The bar seemed to take on a new energy; even the locals noticed.

"I was just asking why you think we should meet," Ben said to Leah.

"He's looking for wisdom," she replied with a smile. "And you know everyone."

"Yeah, you might say I know wise guys."

"Not that kind of wise guy," Leah laughed, touching his arm gently.

Ben looked at me. "If not wise guys, what kind of wisdom do you need?"

"A crisis of conscience," Leah said, glancing at me. "Talk to Ben," she nudged.

I took a breath. "The factory will make drugs to help a lot of people."

"That's a good thing," Ben nodded, returning to his nachos.

"Yes, it is," I continued, "but the illness the drugs are for is caused by chemicals the same company makes."

"So, the same company causing the problem is also the company solving it?"

"Yes and no. Not everyone will get the drug, and it may not reverse the damage already done. People will suffer and die."

"Maybe you should tell someone," Ben suggested.

I explained, "It's not that simple. Those chemicals are everywhere: in food, packaging, water filters — you name it. Stopping production would require a massive global change and a lot of money. More than likely, the chemical effects would linger for years."

"Any chance you're wrong? That the benefit outweighs the harm?"

"No. I took it to my boss. He asked if I liked my car, my apartment, vacations — my life. He said the money had to come from somewhere. That's when he offered to send me here, to keep me away from others. Keep me from asking more questions."

"No easy answers," said Ben.

"Part of why I came here, to find clarity. I may be part of the solution, but I'm also part of the problem."

Ben looked at Leah. "Usually, I am on the other side of this coin. You know, making the crooked seem straight."

From the bar, one of the locals came over and tapped Leah on the shoulder. He had a muscular build. A dark jaguar tattoo was on his arm. Its face bared its teeth on his forearm, and the jaguar's paw reached down to the top of his hand. The tail looped up and around his neck.

"Hey honey, how about we get away from this freak and geek show and have some fun? You look like you need some wildcat energy."

"Don't think so," Leah replied. Ben caught the bartender's eye and gave the briefest of nods. That was all it took. I saw the bartender's arm drop below the bar and grab a bat.

"Rodger, this is your last warning. I told you before. Leave the ladies alone. Now you're out," said the bartender

"Just telling the lady she's way out of their league." He shouted back, still looking at Leah.

The bartender was at his side. There was no doubt that if there was a scuffle, who would prevail. Roger backed up, sizing up the bartender, then Ben.

"Not a fight you can survive," said Ben

Roger retreated, spitting on the floor before he left.

Ben patted the bartender on the back, and they smiled at each other. "Sorry, friend," Ben said.

"Had it comin'," he laughed back.

Ben looks at Leah, then at me. "Some problems are easy to fix. Some aren't." He scratched his face thoughtfully. "Some people come here looking for a shaman or a spiritual master. Those guys give you a show and take your money. You need the real thing."

"There's a man. The shamans steer clear of him. Sometimes, he's in the city, sometimes not. I don't know his name," Ben said. "I believe he has a place near the old city, where the Jungle meets the fortress wall."

Leah nodded. "All the doors look the same."

"How will I know which is the right one?" I asked.

"Don't know," said Ben. "That's just where I think he lives."

Leah smiled. "You have a knack for finding what you're looking for. Maybe when you walk down the street, the right door will open."

We laughed, and Leah blushed, finishing her drink.

***

I took the hint and headed to the bar to settle up. The bartender wasn't having it. He waved me off with a smile and a nod toward Ben.

Ben turned to Leah. "Small favor?"

Leah nodded. Ben pulled out a small package wrapped carefully in a brown paper bag. A string was tied around it, holding it together and sealing the contents from unwanted viewing. He handed the package to her. Leah knew better than to ask questions.

"Bar on 7th, you know the place," said Ben, meticulously folding the last of the nachos. "They're waiting for it and know it's coming. Ask for Jack."

Leah set her bag on her seat and pulled out a few clothes. She nestled the package into the bag and placed the clothes on top. Patting the top of the bag, she smiled at Ben.

"You're the best," he said.

"Back at 'cha," she winked. Both of them looked at me.

"Good luck," said Ben, holding out his monster hand. "I'll let you know if I have more for you."

"Thank you, I appreciate that."

Leah took my arm as we left the pub. The moment we stepped outside, the light forced me to close my eyes. I took a deep breath, and I felt Leah do the same.

"Quick errand to run. Meet you at your place. Let's eat in."

"Okay," I said. "Sounds good." After a peck on my cheek, she spun around and started down the street. "Whose cooking?" I asked.

"Not me," she said, laughing to herself.

"Okay!?" I shouted back, realizing that I needed to get some dinner.

Neither of us noticed that Roger had been just around the corner waiting and was now following Leah.

***

Leah's small errands kept her in a circle of people who paid well for discreet services. She never asked Ben for compensation, and he never offered. Ben's stamp of approval opened many doors. The relationship benefited them both; Ben couldn't go anywhere unnoticed, but Leah could slip in and out anonymously.

The bar on the 7th wasn't far, but Leah decided to walk. The last 24 hours had set new feelings and opportunities in motion. The impulse to know what lay ahead fought with her resolve to live in the moment.

As she passed through a park, her phone vibrated with a new opportunity. Helping Ben was already paying off. She pocketed the phone and refocused on her errand. She didn't notice Roger following in the shadows.

At the bar, Justin poured her a glass of wine with a smooth, practiced smile. Leah smiled back. "Looking for Jack."

"What would you say if I told you I don't know Jack?" he teased.

"I'd say you don't know jack shit, but Jack is expecting me and could jack you up," she shot back with a grin. He nodded toward the back of the bar.

Leah headed to the back of the bar, and Justin turned, watching her glide across the room; a hand with a tattooed jaguar's paw dropped a white pill in her glass.

Leah quietly knocked at the back door. It opened to a large man smiling down at her. She handed over the neatly wrapped package. He wasn't Jack. He was an associate, and seeing him would have to suffice. She'd wait for an all-clear or for an envelope to take back to Ben.

Chapter Five

Sitting down at the bar, Justin shot Leah another million-dollar smile. It wasn't the first time she'd thought he could be a good time. She also knew he had several kids with several women, and that killed the romance for her. She took a drink of her wine. Then another. Something tasted off, so she smelled it and looked at the glass. Justin noticed and came over.

"Doesn't taste right," she told him.

Justin sniffed the glass and frowned. "Not sure," he said, dumping the contents in the sink.

"Something else?"

"Sure, can you handle water?"

"Rust pipes, want something stronger?"

"Water," she said, smiling.

Justin set a glass in front of her. "Try this one," he said, still wearing that million-dollar grin.

When Leah looked down, the room began to swim. It took effort to grab the glass and drink.

"Oh, shit. Justin, call me a cab and hand me a pen."

He handed her a pen and some blank paper from the register. He then pulled out his cell phone and speed-dialed for a taxi.

Leah wrote down the address to the apartment so she could hand it to the taxi driver.

Justin gave her a concerned look, "you okay?"

"Don't feel so good," she replied weakly.

The bar phone rang, and Justin answered while watching her the whole time. "Got it," he said after a short pause. "Jack is happy. The cab's on its way. You okay?"

Leah steadied herself by gripping the bar. "Just need to get home, thanks," she managed, giving him a faint smile. Then she noticed two arms folded on the bar near her. The top arm had a jaguar tattoo, the paw reaching down the back of his hand. Her blood ran cold. She grabbed her phone and quickly tapped the screen, then glanced out the window to see if the cab was there.

Not yet. She wondered if she'd imagined the tattooed arm and chanced a look. There was an empty spot where she'd expected Roger to be. A wave of relief hit her, but then the realization struck — if he was here, she didn't know where he was hiding. The room spun faster. She knew she had to get outside.

The door was close by, and she summoned her resolve to move. But her legs felt like lead. It took all her concentration to will her legs to move, then her body. Step by step to the door.

Outside, the cool air of the evening hit her, jolting her awake just enough. She saw the yellow of the taxi and stumbled toward it.

The door opened, and hope rose in her chest. She could feel the paper with the address crumpled in her fist as she reached for the door. It swung shut. An arm grabbed her waist. She didn't have to look, she knew.

Leah tried to scream, but no sound came out. Panic wouldn't work. She realized if she was going to survive, she had to stay focused.

Leah closed her eyes and let the arm lead her, forcing her body to go limp. She felt him struggle to keep hold. They turned one corner, then another, and finally, he let her drop onto the ground. She realized they were in the park.

The feel and smell of damp earth filled her senses. Despite being dragged deeper into the park's depths, she felt surrounded by aliveness. With her eyes closed, it was easier to focus. She could "see" herself from the outside. She watched as Roger paused, probably checking to see if she had any fight left. She kept her body lifelessly limp. He prodded her with his boot.

"Not so tough now, bitch. Freaks and geeks can't save you here. I know you want to party."

With no response from her, he lifted her over his shoulder. Though Leah was petite, he struggled to carry her, muttering curses as he did. He brought her to a clearing, shielded from the park path and street.

The cool earth beneath her restored some lucidity. She tested her muscles, trying to see if she could move — maybe run, maybe fight. Her muscles barely responded to her request. Her left hand still gripped the crumpled paper with the address. She heard Roger fumbling with his belt, still muttering to himself as he moved closer. Her heart pounded faster.

She felt her skirt and underwear sliding down her thighs. He moved himself over her. She did the only thing she could. She opened her eyes and locked her gaze onto his face.

It startled Roger. He jerked back and instinctively threw a fist at her head.

She sensed the impact and pain, though they felt distant. He recoiled, shaking his hand in pain from where he'd struck her. Enraged, he reached for a large rock nearby.

***

"Okay?!" I shouted back, realizing I needed to get some dinner for us. I watched her head off down the street — a cute skirt, my shirt, boots, and a bag. There was a certain stagger to her step, and when she popped on her sunglasses, she took on an air of celebrity. Her hair was short-ish with a streak of lavender, blending in perfectly with the crowd of younger people filling the street. Soon, she was indistinguishable in the early evening crowd.

I took stock of my time. Leah was walking for her errand, so I assumed it was nearby. I probably had about an hour to pull dinner together — not a lot of time to express any culinary excellence. Still, several nice restaurants were available on the way home, and I briefly considered them. Then I thought of my grandmother, who would've been disappointed if I didn't cook for Leah. Grandma's voice was enough to convince me that I could pull something together quickly for the two of us.

Thinking of what was in the apartment, I decided a quick stop at the market was in order. Near home, there was a square filled with farmers' stands, each piled high with fresh produce. The market wasn't like a supermarket; instead, it was tucked along cobblestones near an old church and some government buildings. From the main street, it was a hidden gem only the locals seemed to know about. A flourish of color tucked between the stone and concrete of the city. Each stall overflowed with vibrant produce, the vendors watching attentively.

Usually, I'd take my time to browse each stall, talk to the proprietor, and then pick up a few things. I stopped at the first stand I saw with fruits and vegetables. It was shaded by a multicolored blanket. An older woman sat amidst bags of vegetables, her tan, wrinkled face framed by earthy gray hair. I quickly pointed to greens, radishes, cucumbers, and anything that could make a simple salad. Her eyes twinkled as she carefully picked each item, placing it in a bag.

"Good, good," she murmured each time she added something. Every time I shopped at this market, I marveled. Back home, the same produce, if I could find it, would cost double or triple and wouldn't be nearly as fresh. Bags full, I walked with purpose toward home.

When I finally got back, I immediately set to work, washing and chopping the produce. Before long, every counter space was covered, ready for assembly when Leah returned. Checking the time, I expected Leah any moment. A quick shower was in order. I didn't hear the phone chime.

In the shower, I realized I didn't have any wine or drinks aside from water. I'd have to make a quick trip to the corner. Then I thought about candles and music. The ideas piling up made me cut the shower short. Dressed, I looked around the apartment — it was acceptably clean. I picked up my phone.

Everything stopped. A text: "Man wth cat ttoo." Then another: "fnd me." They were about half an hour old. The hurried wording made me think she was texting in a rush, which intensified my sense of urgency. I texted back, "Where are you?" and tried calling. No answer. No response. I thought for a moment. The bar was on Seventh Street, but I didn't know the exact location. It was close to the pub where we had met Ben. Running was my best option, so I bolted out the door, phone in hand, hoping for an update. It crossed my mind that finding Ben might help, but I had no way to contact him. I headed for Seventh Street.

The sun was setting, and the city was coming alive with people escaping from stuffy rooms, ready to taste the night. I remembered the crowd from the night before and realized I was running against the current. I hugged the edges of the street, dodging and weaving through the throngs. Shops were closing, tables and displays popped up on the sidewalks. Small lines began to form outside restaurants and bars. The smell of fried food filled the air, and musicians were staking out corners. Laughter, music, and the hum of conversations swelled as I moved along.

Finally reaching Seventh Street, I slowed to a quick walk, peeking into every bar. It felt futile. Some places had long waitlists and wouldn't let me just "check the bar." I described Leah — small, short hair with a lavender streak, skirt, bright bag — to the bouncers. Some gave me a flicker of recognition, but none had seen her that evening. I asked if they'd seen a man with a jaguar tattoo on his arm. I told them his name was Roger. They hadn't seen him either.

I paused, scanning the street. Young people with colorful hair and tattoos filled the scene. Aside from the pull she had on me, Leah could've been right next to me, lost in the crowd. I spotted an old stone building across the street, clearly a bar. It stood apart — no line, no bouncer. Up the street was a busy intersection leading to strip malls and new high-rise buildings. This building, an edifice of the past, felt like it had to be the place. I stepped inside.

The bar was quiet, with patrons keeping to themselves. Televisions scrolled highlights and news, though no one was watching. I went up to the bar and was greeted by a bartender with a million-dollar smile.

"What'll it be, buddy?" he asked.

"I'm looking for someone. Have you seen Leah?"

"We're all looking for somebody, buddy. But if you're looking for a drink, I got you covered."

"She was wearing a dress shirt and has a lavender streak in her hair," I pressed.

"Not ringing any bells, buddy. Maybe you should try down the street." The million-dollar smile persisted.

"It's important," I insisted.

"It always is," he said, pulling a draft for another order.

I glanced out the window. Nothing but people passing by. Across the street, past the corner, was a dark alley — a dead end.

Frustrated, I turned back toward the pub where Ben had been. Checking my phone, I saw there was still no word from Leah. A lump grew in my stomach. The crowd outside had thickened in the few moments I'd spent in the bar. People laughing and yelling barely covered the sounds of traffic.

Music would weave its way between their bodies in search of a listener. The smell of perfume and cologne mixed with cigarette smoke as neon lights washed over the crowd, casting it in colors of lust and art.

Pushing through the hordes to the quieter side street, I crossed over to find that the noise faded with every step away from the main strip. The gravel path of a park met my feet, and my footsteps echoed in the quiet.

Chapter Six

The moon hadn't risen yet, and shadows stretched out from the trees in every direction. Even faint city sounds barely reached the park. Only a few steps in, and I felt I'd entered another world. My every footfall was audible, each twig, snapping like a gunshot in the quiet. The shadows turned this new world to an eerie gray. I sensed movement. I stopped.

Then, a faint ping. It was barely discernible, but in the stillness, it caught my attention. I followed the sound to a faint glow off to my right. Quietly, I crept toward it. It blinked off, only to ping again a moment later. Leah's phone. I picked it up, recognizing my missed call on the screen.

I pocketed the phone and crouched in the clearing. Whatever had been moving before was now gone or hiding. My eyes adjusted to the dim light.

What had been a void of darkness ahead turned out to be a dark ravine. Trees clung to the side and their branches canopied the stream below. The undergrowth spilled over the edge, hiding any descent. I moved closer, peering down.

There, among the shadows, I spotted a body. I recognized the shirt.

"Leah!" I called, my voice echoing.

No response.

My heart dropped, the urge to race down overwhelming. But I couldn't find a clear path down the steep, slick embankment. Frantically, I skirted the edge, looking for any way to reach her. The body lay still. Flashing red and blue lights flickered in the distance, reflecting off the creek below. Rescue teams were making their way toward her.

I watched as they approached the body. When they turned her over, their light revealed blood where her face had been. I recoiled, unable to look away as they carefully wrapped her in a bag. There was no attempt to revive her. She was gone.

They carried the bag back up the creek toward the red and blue lights. I heard people shouting and then doors closing. The lights stopped, and silence fell over everything. I don't know how long I sat there, looking into the void. A hollow sense of loss filled me, leaving me numb.

Gradually, faint sounds of life started to find my awareness. I had forgotten that, not far away, there were people, music, and food. It reminded me of my evening with Leah just a day ago — how alive and seen I felt, how my life had changed in an instant when I gave myself over to this strange, elusive woman. And now, she changed my life again.

From nowhere, the thought of Ben at the pub flashed into my mind. I heard voices approaching. This was a crime scene now. I needed to leave.

Steering clear of the human sounds, I found my way back to the path, then to the sidewalk that led to the street. Leah's phone buzzed in my pocket, and I fought the impulse to check it. The sidewalk found a streetlight that illuminated my way to the next corner. It was familiar, and not far ahead, I could see the pub. Unlike 7th Street, there were few people, mostly couples. There were no old men playing music, no tables with jewelry or drinks or food. All those sounds were in the distance. A police car with flashing lights raced by, unnoticed by anyone.

When I entered the pub, Ben was not at the table where I had hoped he would be. There were still locals sitting at the end of the bar, but Roger was absent. His ejection must have been permanent. The bartender nodded in recognition.

"Ben?" I asked.

He shook his head, just as another police car raced past the window. He glanced outside and then caught my eye. "Know where I might find him?"

The bartender considered for a moment, then picked up his phone. "He'll be here soon. Drink?"

I thought for a moment, then asked for water. I found the table we had sat at earlier and noticed a television silently spilling images across the room. The programming switched to a reporter standing by a bridge. The crawl across the screen read, "Big Cat loose in the city, one dead." I looked at the bartender, who wasn't watching.

It didn't take long before Ben arrived. He nodded at the bar in thanks, and immediately, the bartender filled a beer glass. Ben stood beside me, watching the TV.

"Wasn't a big cat," I said quietly.

Ben sat down just as his beer arrived. He looked at me, his green eyes steady. I wondered if he knew.

I opened my phone to the text message Leah had sent and set it on the table. I waited. Ben read the message, then looked back at me.

"You found her."

I nodded. "Too late." Tears welled up, and I began to cry. His large hand rested on my shoulder, offering silent comfort as I shook.

When I looked up, I saw a look of concern. I mistook it for compassion.

"Somebody has bought his protection," said Ben. My face contorted in confusion.

"No way the police would search so quickly unless they were tipped off," he continued. I remembered the movement in the park when I first arrived. It could have been Roger or someone covering his tracks.

"The story was crafted to eliminate an investigation." Ben removed his hand from my shoulder. "Be careful what you say and who you say it to. If someone comes to talk to you, it may or may not be the police. You know who killed her. That makes you dangerous." He sat back on his stool and took a drink.

"Understand, to these people, life is cheap," he said. I took a moment to absorb his words.

"But Leah…" I trailed off.

"Leah lived on the edge, an easy target." His words felt callous. "She was like fireworks — brilliant, then gone, and forgotten."

I began to understand. "The only person who values your life is you," he said. "And if you want to stay alive, you need to face up to the facts."

"And you?" I asked.

"As long as I have value to the powerful, I am safe." He paused, contemplating his words. "But the winds of power can shift, and my fate could be the same as Leah's."

Leah was a faceless pawn to the powerful. Governments, corporations, and organizations rely on the weak and the marginalized to maintain power and profits. The indigenous were massacred or enslaved at their whim. Then, slaves were traded, killed, or worked to death. Only the powerful could keep death at bay, though even for them, life hung in a precarious balance.

We both sat in silence. The screen continued to scroll the lie of Leah's death as if repeating it enough would make it real.

I pulled Leah's phone from my pocket and set it on the table. Ben looked at it, his face unchanged. With a swift motion, he brushed it off the table, then crushed it under his boot. He bent down, picked up the remains, and folded them in half with his bare hands. He left the mangled device on the table and then looked over at me.

"You may have saved both our lives," he said, relief softening his features. "You are full of surprises." He paused. "Thank you."

Now, nobody would know what was on her phone. Her secrets — and Ben's — were safe. We shared a mutual trust.

Chapter Seven

The pub was quiet as Ben leaned in close. "The man I told you about has been seen in the city. He's managed to live on the fringe and remain alive. You're crosswise with many powerful people now. You know too much for your own good. He might be able to help you."

Ben explained that the city walls had been built long ago to keep its inhabitants safe from invaders and Indians and the jungle. Over time, infirmaries and barracks were built into the walls for the injured and soldiers. As wars and commerce changed, the buildings were abandoned, only to find new life with artists, families, thieves, and criminals who had little means and big dreams. The conformity of the facade kept them safe. They kept the white doors and removed the house numbers. Some burrowed through the thick city walls to the forest, either for a quick escape or access to resources outside.

"That's where you may find him," Ben said.

It was late when I finally left the pub. The street was empty. The market where I'd bought food for dinner was shuttered and covered. Back in my apartment, the counters were still covered with the dinner we'd never have. The bed felt cold. The idea of sleep haunted me as I lay down. I spooned the memory of Leah and what could have been, only to be awakened by reality, over and over again.

The knock at the door was unexpected. Two men in uniform flashed badges at the door and asked to come in. I was still drowsy, needing coffee as they stepped in.

"Have you heard about the woman attacked by a big cat last night?" the older one asked.

"We found your address written on a scrap of paper she was holding." They waited for my response. I thought about Ben's words, questioning if these were real police or not.

"I had a date with Leah last night. She never showed. Was she the victim? Is she dead?"

"Sorry to inform you this way. We have a couple of questions."

I sat down, putting my head in my hands. "Did you know her well?"

"We just met," I said. "How does this happen?"

"Can you tell us where you were last night?"

I gestured at the kitchen, the counters still full. They looked over, taking note.

"I was cooking dinner," I replied. "When she didn't show, I walked around the neighborhood in case she got lost. I gave up and must have fallen asleep waiting for her."

"Did she leave anything here?" It seemed like an odd question.

"Like I said, we just met. Nothing here."

They looked around, trying not to make it obvious, but there was nothing to find.

"Do you know any of her family? Anyone we should inform?" I shook my head. Our time together had been so short that I had no idea about family, where she lived, or even what she did. I remembered her asking me to take her home. For her, home wasn't a place; it was where she felt safe and loved.

"We'll let ourselves out. Here's a card with our number if you need to contact us."

I took the card. It looked official, but everything still felt off. I locked the door after they left.

I spent the rest of the day in a haze. At some point, I cleaned up the kitchen and went for a walk, hoping to clear my head. It didn't help. I checked my email; the company had scheduled a site visit for later in the week. I reviewed invoices for equipment — everything seemed in order.

On the kitchen table was a newspaper I'd picked up on my walk. The headline read: Big Cat on the Loose. Deep within, an article warned young women of a rapist slipping drugs into drinks and following them home. The suspect was described as muscular and tattooed, preying on women alone at bars. To a casual observer, the two stories would be unrelated. But it wasn't hard to see how one might cover for the other.

I thought about Ben's comment — that someone had paid for Roger's protection.

The thought that a rapist — and most likely a murderer — was freely wandering the city, looking for his next victim, turned my stomach. Even more troubling was that he was being protected. Lives were being ruined at every turn by people with impunity, and not just by my company, or organized crime, or rapists. It was everywhere. The lust for money, power, and control was pervasive, and no one seemed immune from its lure.

On the back of the newspaper, a map highlighted the tourist and trendy spots in the city, dramatically marking the fortifications on every side. Finding the "white door" barracks wouldn't be impossible. I decided to narrow down the possibilities by reading some of the city's history.

After mapping out the most likely places, I ordered some Chinese food, satisfied with my plan.

When the delivery person arrived, I decided to ask about the white doors.

"We don't go there; it's very dangerous," they replied, eyes shifting nervously.

"But where is it?" I pressed.

"Near the forest, by a big gate. Don't go there — it's dangerous," they warned again.

I handed over the cash for my meal, feeling a strange unease. As I handed over the bills, I couldn't help but wonder how many people had died — or would die — to keep money circulating so that I could pay for dinner. It left me feeling dirty somehow. After I ate, I snapped open the fortune cookie. "To the true seeker, the door will open." The words bolstered my resolve.

It occurred to me that a taxi might refuse to take me where I wanted to go, so I checked the bus schedule and found that stops existed near my target area. I began making a plan: leave early, bring water and snacks, and prepare for whatever I might find in this "dangerous" place.

The bed brought no solace. I thought of Leah and how she died, replaying every detail of my encounter with Roger, searching for something I may have missed. I thought about Ben, and about the night Leah and I spent together. The bed felt empty after just that one night, as if something significant had been taken from it.

I thought about this mystery man everyone feared. How could he possibly help? What was I about to get myself into? Would I even find him, and if I did, what would he look like? What price would I pay for his wisdom?

The more I thought about it, the more disturbing everything became. It wasn't just my company and its questionable ethics — it was more than that. Rapists and murderers moved through the world with impunity, no different from my company, no different than governments. I realized that I might never be able to reconcile myself with the world as it was.

I tried to focus on the good people do and how we help and care for each other. But as I did, I realized that so much of that "help" was just another way to extract money or gain power. I began questioning my own motives. Eventually, my mind wandered back to love. I realized that I had only really experienced love in those moments when Leah and I laughed together freely, without expectation. At that moment, I understood "home." Home was love, and the only person I had shared it with was gone.

I reflected on home, love, and a longing to feel held. Sleep finally came, gentle and deep.

Chapter Eight

The morning was abrupt. Street noises drifted in, drawing me from the depths. Birds called out, greeting the sun, their sounds filled with morning delight. Disoriented, I shook off the fog of sleep and went straight for the coffee. As I did, a memory surfaced — Leah, wearing my shirt, giving the coffee machine a glare. The pantry still held the granola, and the fridge was stocked with the greens and vegetables I'd planned to use for our dinner.

With coffee brewing and granola soaking, I gathered my things and reviewed my plan. "Weak," I muttered. I had no idea where I was going, who I was looking for, or what exactly I wanted to accomplish. Thankfully, I had made a list: water bottle, map, bus fare, and food. I checked each item off. I had also prepped a rough itinerary based on the bus schedule, and I still had an hour before I left.

What does one wear to meet the city's most feared spiritual figure? I settled on a simple button-up shirt, comfortable pants, and sturdy shoes, knowing I might be walking for hours. I double-checked my phone for any urgent work matters but found nothing pressing. I stowed the phone securely, taking only the cash I thought I'd need and tucking a credit card into the headband of my hat.

After breakfast, I noticed a wave of nerves. Perhaps coffee wasn't the best idea. I filled the water bottle, took a deep breath, and left, relieved that my door had a code lock, so I didn't need to carry keys.

It would take three buses to reach the top of the street I hoped was the right one. The first bus was new and smelled fresh. The driver was sharply dressed, and most passengers had earbuds in, focused on their screens. I simply watched the neighborhoods, parks, and churches pass by. People got on and off until my stop, where I disembarked.

The second bus was neither new nor old, smelling faintly of perfume and cigarettes. The seats were worn, and the passengers included children and elderly folks carrying bags of goods. The driver seemed to know everyone, exchanging brief greetings with each. Smiles and laughter filled the air as we passed by modest homes. As we traveled farther, the yards grew less tended, and some houses appeared abandoned.

The third bus was on its last legs. The seats were stripped of cushioning, and young people crowded the back, playing loud music and smoking. The scenery outside turned grim: dilapidated buildings, dust-covered parks, and fenced-off lots. My stop was the last before the bus looped back toward the city center. A few people remained on board as I stepped off, their heads lolling in the heat.

Ahead, I saw the old fortification wall, with a gateway carved through it to make way for a road. The road was paved, but the area beyond remained cobblestone. Through the gateway, dense foliage arched over, forming a natural canopy.

Much as described, one side of the street nestled into the protective wall, where white doors lined up in uniform rows. The windows above were open to catch the breeze, but no one was visible. Only a few elderly men sat on doorsteps, smoking. As I walked, I could feel unseen eyes watching my every move.

I hesitated to ask the old men for help. Who would I tell them I was looking for? There were no house numbers, and even if there were, I had no address. I took a deep breath. It was the first. My heart pounding, I took my first step, then another, hoping I would know what I was looking for when I saw it.

Suddenly, my mind flashed to lying on the street with Leah, laughing until we cried, the warmth of her hand in mine. The memory went from magical to miserable. It solidified my resolve. I kept repeating in my mind, *Don't let her die for nothing. Don't let her die for nothing.*

At a break between buildings, I saw a glimpse of the perimeter wall beyond. Water trickled from a drain at the base, flowing over strands of green algae. The massive stone wall stood imposing, overgrown in places. The white doors continued, every street appearing identical to the last. I walked street by street, moving slowly, always aware of the eyes following me. But I found nothing. At the end of the row, a strip mall appeared, with a busy street. I'd reached the end of the white door gauntlet, feeling both relieved and disappointed.

I took a deep breath, drank some water, and turned to face the doors once more. "One last shot," I told myself.

About halfway back, I paused to rest, sitting on the curb. As I looked back down the street, a door opened behind me.

A man stepped into the doorway and nodded at me. I nodded back. He left the door open as he stepped back into the room. I took a deep breath and followed. He sat down and invited me to do the same.

Chapter Nine

My gaze dropped to the tray with the four jars and the note. The jars were old jelly jars with lids. It looked as if each jar was empty. I glanced up and saw him watching me. He nodded as if he knew I wanted a closer look.

"You'll have to choose one," he said quietly as I inspected each glass. Again, I caught his gaze as I reached to touch a jar.

"May I?" I asked, and he nodded. There were no differences that I could discern. The note simply said, "PURE WATER."

"This one," I said, looking to his face for affirmation or challenge. Again, a nod.

He handed it to me along with the paper. It was cool to the touch and had some weight; I assumed it was the glass. Whatever was originally on the lid had worn off, leaving only specks of color and scratches. It was now just a jar—a jar that held my future.

"Take some time," he said. "When you are ready, find pure water that has not been touched by metal or plastic. Fill the jar at least half full. You can drink it then or wait until you are in a familiar place."

"What will happen when I drink it?" I asked.

Silence. His chest rose and fell as he met my gaze. Another breath passed before he replied, "I can't say."

He collected the remaining three jars and placed them on a shelf behind him. As he stood, his eyes caught sight of a bee that had flown in through the window and was now navigating the room. From another shelf, he retrieved a saucer and a small jar. Moving gracefully across the room to the open window, he set the saucer down on the sill and poured some liquid from the jar. Within moments, the bee found the saucer and perched on its rim.

"Sugar water," he commented. He watched the bee carefully, and when it flew back out the window, he poured the remaining sugar water back into the jar and returned everything to its place on the shelf. Then, he quietly resumed his seat on the cushion.

"How will this make me stop being human?" I asked. "Could I die?"

He watched me with the same attention he had given the bee. This time, his gaze did not drop, and the intensity behind his eyes deepened, revealing a complexity beyond my understanding.

"There is no guarantee," he began. "Once you begin, the journey's path is your own. It cannot be directed or explained — it can only be known and only through experience."

I looked down at the jar. It appeared empty. I wanted assurances. I wanted to know what to expect. I was about to leave with nothing more than this jar, and I found myself grinning at the absurdity of it all. My future was now held in this glass jar, yet it was a complete mystery. I realized that this, too, could be a dead end in my search. The jar could be just a jar. He could be just a man. Perhaps there was no real way of letting go of my repulsive humanity.

"Will I see you again?" I asked, still rolling the jar between my palms. The room dimmed slightly as a cloud passed by. When I looked up, he was carefully choosing his words.

"It is possible," he said, nodding slightly as if agreeing to something only he understood.

"Do I pay you?"

A soft smile spread across his face, and for a brief moment, I thought I saw the hint of a blush. "That is very generous of you," he said. "But the journey will cost you everything." He paused, closed his eyes for a moment, and then added, "That will have to be enough."

His words and demeanor surprised me. I looked back down at the jar in my hands. My mind buzzed with questions, but the answers could only be found in this jelly jar.

I bowed my head slightly. "Thank you for your time and attention."

He returned the bow in acknowledgment. As I stood, so did he. He motioned toward the door. Stepping outside, I took a deep breath. It was becoming a habit.

I looked up the street to the rows of doors. If you didn't know what you were looking for, you'd never find it here. It would have to find you.

Heading back up the street, I boarded the bus back to civilization. The ride back seemed to take much less time, probably because I was deep in thought. I was starting back home, literally from the end of the line. It seemed suitable that this new journey would begin from the dregs of the city. I didn't board an empty bus. The day was warm, and the buses had air conditioning. A few passengers congregated underneath the blowers and seemed to know each other. The bus driver didn't seem to mind. At least on the return trip, the noise from the back of the bus was gone. In the quiet, I watched out the window, keeping to myself, occasionally looking at the jar in my hand.

Before I boarded the last bus, I looked around for something to eat. I was back in the heart of the city. The sidewalks had trees for shade, and cafes and restaurants were sandwiched between shops. Apartments lifted themselves above the tree line to see the distant harbor. Across the street, a manicured park with deep green grass hosted people walking their dogs or running for exercise.

I stepped into a glass-doored establishment and immediately felt the heat of the day fall away. Well-groomed servers with matching aprons glided between tables, serving equally well-groomed customers. The hostess smiled and showed me to a table. A doe-eyed server took my order, and my body settled into the plush chair. I remembered the first time that I was able to afford to eat in a place like this. I had just cashed my first real paycheck and took myself out to dinner. I remember thinking, "Now this is living." Every part of the experience fed my senses both then and now. I was being lulled into a sense of complacency — effortless pleasure.

The dining room opened into an atrium above me. Sunlight bathed me in warmth but not heat. Large plants bordered the space. I closed my eyes, and the experience continued. Smells from the kitchen delighted my expectations. Quiet music, barely audible, caressed my soul. I leaned back into the chair and soaked in luxury. When I did open my eyes, movement across the room beside the huge pots of plants caught my eye. For a moment, I saw Leah watching me, moving past the fronds and leaves. The sunlight highlighted her lavender hair. She moved like a dancer walking onto the stage. Her eyes fixed on me. I blinked, and she was gone. The doe-eyed server was walking toward me, smiling and holding a perfectly balanced tray in her hand. I felt the glass jelly jar and put it on the table in front of me.

The illusion faded. How easy it would be to leave the jar on the table when I left, stepping into this life of pleasure. I had the money. The cost wasn't tangible currency. I felt like I was betraying Leah and myself.

"Everything tasting okay?" she asked.

I smiled and nodded. "Yes, thank you," being perfectly compliant to the norm. The meal was sublime, but it left a bitter taste in my mouth. I couldn't wait to get out.

When I got on the bus, I realized how easily it was to be anesthetized and accept a life of emotional mediocrity. When I got to my apartment, it screamed, "You are so important! More important than those shacks at the end of the bus line." I put the jelly jar on the table as a reminder that I wasn't.

I checked my phone — evidence of my affluence — and saw that a driver would pick me up in the morning. My guide left a message: "It will be rural; bring water and clothes." The project manager in the States sent me a detailed list of observations that they needed. I had my own agenda, too: find pure water. I packed two of everything and wrapped the jar carefully into a shirt nestled in the middle of my daypack. Prepared and emails sent, I worked my way through the leftover salad greens in the refrigerator. As the heat broke into the evening, I could hear the city coming alive. On another night, I would have gone to experience the life of the city. Tonight, I sat on my balcony and looked toward the jungle that seemed a million miles away.

The driver and guide showed up on the street just minutes before our appointed time. I was already waiting, having eaten the rest of the granola and salad. Our ride was more off-road-ready than comfortable. The driver was a younger man with thick black hair and sun-darkened skin.

My guide was a bit older and dressed professionally to make an impression. He saw my daypack and smiled.

"Good to see you're ready," he said.

We loaded up — driver and guide up front and me in the back. Beside me on the seat was a worn rug sack and extra water. Behind me, tire chains rattled their warning. When I asked, I was told that there may be mud.

I learned that the driver got his name, "Chongo," from his ability to climb any tree. My guide was Jorge, but he told me to call him George. After the expected pleasantries — "How long have you been in the country? Great weather, eh?" — I was told the ride to the site would take at least an hour, maybe longer. Being content to watch and listen, Chongo and George started a very animated conversation. I caught bits and pieces; I was pretty sure that they didn't think I understood. For the most part, they were right. Their conversation went from girls, girlfriends, and wives to jobs and money. Eventually, they started talking about the alleged jaguar attack a couple of nights before. Chongo was wary that a jaguar could have made it into the city. He had hunted them in the jungle and was sure that the noise of the city would have been a deterrent. George was savvier, thinking that the police must have had good reason to claim it was a big cat.

The conversation turned when Chongo described the jaguar as a spiritual beast. He speculated that a shaman had shapeshifted.

"Why would a shaman kill a young woman?" George wanted to know.

Chongo went silent. George didn't press him and stayed quiet. We rode that way for the better part of an hour.

The road went from very well-maintained pavement to what could be described as a country road. We left the city in traffic, which eased to a few cars and then to very occasional passing by. The city gave way to farms that gave way to hills and valleys. Signs on the side of the road first advertised modern conveniences, and eventually, hand-painted signs pointed to food, water, or fuel. Eventually, any signs of modern convenience ended.

Dirt roads sprouted off the pavement with just two tire tracks to delineate the path from the fields they traversed. Every road ended in the dark of the jungle surrounding us. Ahead, mountains grew so high that I couldn't see the tops through the windows. Droplets started to bead on the hood of the vehicle. I heard Chongo say something about mud.

I was told by my boss that this location had been selected for several reasons. First, the water was plentiful and pure. It had a naturally desirable pH, which was one of the things I was supposed to check. Second was cost; the government wanted to bring more technology to the area and had nearly given the site over for free.

Along with the property an agreement that residents in the area had opportunity for employment. Finally, the company would have to upgrade the infrastructure — roads, power, and essentials. The other unwritten but well-understood part of the agreement was that there would be no questions asked about the manufacturing or methods.

Ben was right. The right palms had been greased. The right contractors had been lined up. All that was left was for me to approve the location with actual "eyes on" to determine feasibility. The reality was that regardless of my approval, the project would probably move forward. Nobody wants a chemical factory in their backyard, even if the drugs were perceived as helping people.

We turned onto a dirt road; it was maintained better than most. We passed several homes that were built from existing materials in the area. The rain never materialized into a problem, and we drove right up to a farmhouse.

George explained that the farmhouse was abandoned. The farmer who lived here had died, and his family was more interested in the money than working the land. The house sat where I expected the factory would be built. It was on a small knoll that overlooked a valley with a stream and steep hills on either side. A dense forest rose up the hill. George said that the entire valley had once been forested but was cleared for livestock. I shuddered to think of the work it took to clear the land.

***

I pulled out a tablet and started with my observations.

"How far are we from the city? How long did it take to get here?" I asked. "Is there another town close by, maybe farther down the road?" I took pictures of the farmhouse and barn. Somebody had moved heavy equipment into the pasture in anticipation. I took pictures of that, too. I looked, and a single electrical line emerged from the forest and connected to the farmhouse. It didn't continue down to the homes we passed.

George laughed. "Somebody probably said there was electricity. I think there's a small water wheel by the creek."

"I'll need to look," I said. George shrugged in acceptance. "I'll also need to walk the cleared land to get an idea for the engineers and architects." It was likely that all of the necessary measurements had already been taken and plans were ready.

George lifted his hand toward the forest, inviting me to head up the path. I paused and pulled out my phone. No signal. I made a note on my tablet. I checked the elevation with my GPS and took more notes on the tablet. Up the path, we crossed an old, barbed wire fence — again, pictures and notes. There was a brief transition between the cleared land and the jungle. In the short time the farm had been vacant, the jungle was doing its best to reclaim its former glory.

We were in the sunshine and then in the jungle — one world to the next. Not just the light, but the sound changed. The smells changed. Our path, once a trail up the hill, was being reclaimed. Vines and branches liberated themselves into the clearing of what had been the path. George reached over his head and pulled a machete out of his pack. He used it to gently push the new growth out of our way.

I could hear water long before I could see it. The smell changed from earthy compost to clean and organic. I couldn't tell how George could find his way until I saw the wire draped through the trees. He followed it to a pool where the jungle gave way to crystal-clear water.

"They built the pool here just below the wheel," he said. I looked up to see water running down a sheer rock face and, beside it, a water wheel. There was a narrow set of steps running beside the wheel and a shack where the wire ended.

We climbed the steps carefully. The dampness made the moss feel slick. The shed was empty. Someone had claimed the mechanics that had been there before, or maybe the jungle just expelled them down the creek. Above the shack was another pool.

"Look, they built this to divert the water," George said, pointing to a channel with a rudder that could control the water to the wheel. It was ingenious.

At the far end of the pool, water streamed down the rock face.

"Anything above us?" I asked.

"No, just jungle." I set my pack down. I used some vials and a test strip to verify the pH. Then I pulled out the jelly jar and held it against the moss on the stone, letting water fill it up. Replacing the lid, I slid it back into my pack. George watched, having no idea what the water was for.

We paused to take in the spot. Butterflies danced around the mossy rock face, traversing between the damp moss and the brilliant flowers dangling just above the water. Higher into the trees, other flowers of gold and red watched as if awaiting their turn to be visited. Stones jutted from the sides of the hill, damp from the moisture coming down on every side. Roots crawled across the stones and lifted themselves into the trees, where birds feasted on fruit and insects.

George dropped his pack and pulled out a couple of apples. He offered me one. He saw the look on my face.

"They travel better than bananas," he said.

"Magical," I said, looking around.

George smiled. "I'm surprised that the farmer didn't build closer to the water," I said.

"Water everywhere," said George. He paused and looked at me, considering his words. "The Indians who lived here considered streams like this to be the heart of the jungle. This is like the aorta of life, starting deep in the mountains and bringing life to the earth."

We sat for a moment. I pulled out my tablet and brought up a set of plans for the area. There was a pipeline clearly marked on the plan, diverting water from somewhere near where we sat to the factory. Even if the diversion returned, it would be well downstream. The pipeline was like diverting the jugular from the body and allowing it to die. I didn't have the heart to tell George. I closed my eyes and took a deep breath, Leah's legacy. I tried to imprint every sound and every smell into my memory. I watched every bird, every insect, every flower. All of this would eventually be gone — for money. I realized that although the drugs my team developed would help people, they would kill this part of the forest.

We threw our apple cores deep into the woods. I suspected some ants or birds would delight in the delicacy. We backtracked down to the farm and fences and took a circuitous route back to Chongo and the vehicle. He was resting in the shade outside the house. I took a few moments for more notes and pictures. I considered how to best present the data. If I made it look too remote, they might kill the project. Or maybe if I made it look too pristine and beautiful, they would reconsider. Reality intervened; it didn't matter if it was remote or beautiful. What they cared about was money. What I would say didn't matter.

When we got back in for the ride home, I noticed a tarp covering something in the back. More than likely, Chongo had taken the opportunity to select a few choice items from the house. I couldn't fault him. An opportunity not taken is an opportunity lost.

Back on the main road, we headed back home. George and Chongo exchanged a few words, and I saw Chongo look in the mirror at me.

"Food?" said George. It was well past noon, and the apple had carried me through, but I was hungry. I nodded.

We took a turn and drove down parallel tracks to a house. The walls were stone, covered with white lime, and the roof was rusted tin. Flowers lined the porch, and a garden peeked around the side with rows of vegetables. Two skinny dogs greeted us, their tails wagging violently. A plump woman wearing an apron and a worried look watched from the porch. Her face changed when she saw Chongo — a brilliant smile and open arms awaited us all. Adjacent to the living space was a simple room with several tables and chairs. A fan hung from the giant timbers holding the roof, moving the air; the breeze from the window was far more effective.

As we sat down, I noticed a child running out to the garden, the dogs giving chase. Another young woman brought us water. Each plastic glass was a different color. I could smell the fire that was heating the pot of soup. Through the door, I saw the child return with okra, corn, peas, and beans. The older woman hastily washed the produce and added it to the pot. From the windowsill, she grabbed a loaf of bread and brought it to the table. Chongo broke the end off and handed me a piece. The child brought butter, soft and warm, and sat at the table with us. Soup bowls and spoons came to the table. Napkins cut from old rags were neatly folded for each of us.

The whole time, Chongo and the women chattered away in a dialect I couldn't understand. George was very entertained and listened. He finally leaned over to me. "Distant family." I assumed he meant Chongo.

"The men are off working. Something to do with the new factory."

When the soup was ready, everyone came to the table. Two children sat beside me, watching me closely. Chongo turned to me. "Everything came from the land. Came from here." The older woman spoke to Chongo and looked at me. Chongo, then George looked at me, too. "She says you have a sadness in your heart. The soup will help."

"I lost a friend recently," I said. "It was very sad," Chongo repeated to the older lady, who motioned for me to eat some soup.

"Her soup helps everything," said Chongo.

I dipped my bread into the broth and tasted it. It was unbelievable. Every spoonful held some new flavor, vegetable, or herb. She was right. Every part of my body tingled with rejuvenation. The heaviness in my heart lifted, and I felt myself begin to laugh with the children next to me. They were playing a game I couldn't comprehend. At the end of each phase of the game, they would erupt in contagious laughter. When they laughed, the dogs would bark and howl. The women would shriek and squeal. I felt alive again.

As life pulsed back into my body, I wished that Leah could have been here. I was reminded of our laughter and her warmth.

Laughter subsided, and the older woman looked at me with compassion in her eyes. She nodded and smiled. It was probably the best meal I had ever eaten. Stepping away from the table was one of the hardest things I had ever done. It was time to go.

I touched George's arm and made the universal signal for money by rubbing my pointer finger and thumb together.

"They won't take your money," he whispered. "You can leave it under your plate, and they'll find it later and be grateful." So, while Chongo said goodbye, I excused myself and placed all the cash in my wallet under my plate. Handling money after such a pure experience gave me a dirty feeling; it was the only gift I thought I could give at the time.

The ride home had a lightness to it. George and Chongo laughed as Chongo told stories about the family. The conversation lulled. I asked Chongo about hunting jaguars. George shot me a glance. Chongo didn't take offense.

"Hunters come and pay big money," he said. "It is very dangerous, so we use dogs to chase them into a trap. Then the hunters are safe to shoot them."

We all went quiet for a moment, reflecting on his words. "We only hunt the jaguars who have killed someone. They are sacred to my people." I nodded with new understanding. George and I locked eyes, and I let the subject drop.

"When will they start building?" asked George, changing the subject.

"Not sure," I said. I knew that the process had already started, but actual construction would be the last part of the project.

"More people will come?" asked Chongo.

"Yes."

"Many people?"

"Yes."

"Auntie should build a hotel." We all laughed. The shift in thinking had already begun.

Back at my apartment, I put the jelly jar on the table and downloaded all of my notes from the tablet to the computer. I started my report. Along with the pictures and elevations, I included the distances from necessary infrastructure and the lack of accommodations for both food and hotels in the area. I ended my report with the observation that although the water running from the mountains was pure, diverting that water in appreciable amounts would be devastating to the local flora and fauna. I suggested wells be drilled to protect the area and make the water source more sustainable. It was a shot in the dark.

Chapter Ten

When I finished, it was dusk. I could hear the city coming alive. I went to the kitchen and realized I wasn't hungry. On the kitchen table was the jar. I thought about tearing off the lid and drinking it down right here and now, but I decided against it. Instead, I took a deep breath.

"This dance belongs with Leah," I thought.

I took a moment to consider what could happen. I had no idea. Would I be returning tonight? What if I died? There was no way to know. No way to prepare. I took a few moments to put my work affairs in order. I put my phone in the charger and left my wallet on the nightstand. I turned out the lights and looked around the apartment. On the table, the jar was illuminated by the moonlight peeking through the window.

"An omen?" I thought. There was no way to know.

Before I left, I thought about telling someone what I was about to do. Nobody would understand. Most sensible people would have attempted to talk me out of it. It strengthened my resolve. I left with the jar in my hand.

I knew exactly where I was going. I headed toward the pub where Ben was most likely devouring nachos and beer.

I didn't stop. The park was dark and quiet. The threat of a jaguar had deterred visitors. I found the clearing where I first saw Leah's body and sat down. The moon was rising, casting shadows of gray across the area. Below me was the creek where her body had been too far down for me to reach. I set the jar down in front of me, sitting cross-legged on the sparse grass. My heart was beating.

I took off the top and took a sip. It tasted like water. I drank the rest and set the jar down, replacing the lid. Nothing. Not knowing what to expect, there was an initial feeling of disappointment. I had hoped that whatever magic was going to happen would happen quickly. I took a deep breath.

So much had happened in the last few days: meeting Leah, finding her, and losing her again. I had never felt so close to anyone as I did that night. I looked at the jar. A warm feeling rose within me. The day had been hot; the cool of the evening hadn't set in yet. The moonlight seemed to strip the colors from the foliage around me. My heart rate slowed, and I could feel my pulse strong and steady in my limbs.

Soon, the heat was too much, and I took off my shirt. I was thinking about Leah, and I laid down on my side, curling as if spooning her again. I felt myself drifting into a dream state, but I wasn't asleep. I could hear the creek lulling me in, the water flowing. The water lapping against the rocks. It made a subtle but different noise when it flowed against the downed trees. I could smell the water, the scent of clean running water mingling with the stagnant pools that held teams of water striders.

Every tree had a smell, and every smell had a feel. I could feel the bushes on the edges of the clearing and the grass as if I could feel each blade. Then, movement. Ants were striding across the ground and climbing into the trees, leaves bending slightly and brushing against each other in the slight breeze.

My legs spasmed, and my body rolled. Movement. The urge to be hidden took hold, and I crawled to a tree near me. I put my hands on its bark and leaped to a large branch. My tail swung to maintain my balance.

"I have a tail," I thought. It would be my last thought.

I sighed deeply and reclined on the branch, my belly resting against the bark.

From the branch, I could see the whole of the ravine that bordered the creek. Without much effort, I could see the rest of the park. What was once dark was now very clear. An awareness replaced my thoughts. The array of life around me took on an immersive quality. I could smell old blood, old death from Leah's body just days ago. I could smell new death lingering in the bushes where a house cat had found a bird.

I could feel movement. Every leaf, blade, and bug transmitted its movement, and I could feel them all. At first, it was overwhelming, but it became normal. I felt attached to everything.

I felt the heavy footsteps before I heard them. Hearing and feeling were one and the same. The voice was familiar. It was muttering something. The words meant nothing to me. I sat perfectly still as a man dragged a woman into the clearing below me. The whole of the park could feel their intrusion. Waves of sound and smells and feelings flowed across every leaf and blade.

I watched and listened. The woman was alive but unresponsive. Her eyes were open but unfocused. The forest hummed with a memory from days before. A heavy sadness whispered a melancholy song in the breeze.

The man moved with methodical memory. He stripped her from the waist down and pulled off his shirt. The tattoo on his arm caught my attention. A memory with no substance came from somewhere inside me. He was unbuckling his pants, staring at the woman, and muttering to himself. He didn't see me as I quietly lifted myself, preparing for the attack.

All of the forest felt me leap. I landed with both paws on his back, buckling his knees and dropping him to the ground. Face down, my jaws clamped to the back of his head and neck. I could smell him urinating on himself. His body writhed, and his arms reached back, struggling to grab anything that might save him. My jaws clamped harder, and I felt a pop. His arms dropped. I bit harder, and I could feel his heart racing. I put the weight of my body on top of him and waited, knowing that the struggle would stop.

The entire forest could smell his blood. Its liquid would find its way to the water below us. Insects were moving in. The grass waited for the body to be moved. His body went limp, and his bowels discharged. Death.

I dragged the body from the clearing closer to a large tree. He was too large to devour now. I would have to stow the body for later, to get it off the ground. He was too heavy to lift all at once. Biting into his shoulder, my teeth severed the ligaments that held the arm. With a quick pull, the arm came loose, the tattoo now irreparably severed. The other arm came loose the same way then I devoured the thigh. Still heavy, I dragged the body into a fork in the tree. The arms became an offering to the forest.

The woman was still lying motionless in the clearing. She was neither dead nor sleeping. I could smell her fear. I laid down next to her, our bodies touching. I let my tail drape across her leg, and I watched for danger. I felt her let go of the fear. The forest watched over both of us. One life was enough for tonight.

My body was completely at rest. One might assume that I was sleeping or dreaming, but that would be inaccurate. I was listening to the songs of the forest. It was an unending melody of triumph and loss, life and death. It whispered truths that cannot be spoken and revealed beauty that cannot be seen. The beating of my heart added to the melody. The shallow breath of the young woman beside me joined in harmony. The water called to me, saying, "You must come, you must come."

In the distance, the jungle called to my heart.

"Come, it is not safe there," it breathed into the night.

"Tonight," I hummed back, "I must wait for this precious life to awaken."

It took time for the body to stir. The forest waited with me. I felt her body move before the grass did. Still, it quivered underneath us as she did. A groan broke the melody of the night. The chirping of the crickets paused to listen, only to begin again when the groaning subsided. I gently rolled my body away from hers to watch from the trees. Her eyes moved and fixed on the sky above us. Branches gently swayed in the breeze, and I could see her watching, then awakening. She sat up with a start. Still groggy, she swayed even while sitting. She rubbed her face with her hands. Looking around, it was obvious she both knew and didn't know where she was.

The events of the evening flooded into her mind. Panic set in as she looked around. She saw the blood and recoiled. Gathering herself, she ran.

It wouldn't be long before humans would descend on the clearing. The forest braced itself for their arrival. Hints of dawn bordered the horizon, highlighting the space above the buildings and trees. I climbed down the tree and made my way down the ravine to the creek. The foliage on the banks was thick. The canopy above us made light a precious commodity. Each leaf grew large to catch the bits of sunlight that sprinkled through. Moss held moisture to the ground, covering the rocks and keeping roots safe. The route down to the creek that seemed so precarious to my former self was simple for me now. I could see, more like feel, my way through. I easily leaped from stone to felled tree to low branches to creek bed. The water of the creek was cool to my feet. I could feel the spongy mud between my toes. I walked upstream toward the jungle, toward safety. I bid farewell to this pocket of forest. The urge to claim it with my scent passed. It was never mine to begin with. My home was calling to me.

My paws moved silently through the water. Small ripples were the only evidence of my passing. I moved slowly, carefully listening, feeling with every step. I moved with purpose and strength. What my eyes could not see, my body knew. The creek was narrowing, and the deep ravine gave way to an old stone bridge. The bridge had been abandoned; its once stout construction was now too feeble to carry traffic. Brave pedestrians and the urban wild would occasionally use it as a pass-through to avoid the depth of the ravine. It had man-smell and the tired feeling that comes with age and neglect. The bridge marked the gateway from the park to the city. From here, the ravine ran through the city. The park was one of the few spaces that the jungle had reclaimed. The rest had succumbed to the perils of modern civilization.

As soon as I emerged from the darkness beneath the bridge, the challenge of my journey from the forest became more obvious. The thick foliage that had concealed my movements gave way to bare dirt and concrete retaining walls. Moss and vines spilled over to reclaim what had been there for centuries before the city. It was a futile battle that was being lost. The water, once free to meander its way to the ocean, was now channeled, moving swiftly and making progress difficult. I had to forgo the water and its subtle camouflage and walk along the concrete embankment. The faded concrete gave little cover, increasing my purpose and speed.

The whispers of the trees and water were more difficult to hear. The noise of traffic ahead of me made me strain to hear the voices of the plants and the navigation from the water. The feel of the living forest that embraced me was replaced by the putrid smell of exhaust. It was the smell of commerce. The affirming scents of the ferns and hosta were covered by the consuming stench of sewage and rotting trash. It was the smell of death — not the death that brings new life, but the sterile death from which nothing would grow or thrive.

The sun had risen high enough to be seen above the buildings. It was warm enough that within minutes, the wet prints left by my paws evaporated. I would occasionally escape the heat by swimming in the channel. The current was strong enough that I had to paddle furiously with my legs to keep from being carried back. I hugged close to the concrete walls, seeking out the cover of shade whenever possible. Above me, at the top of the walls, were sidewalks. I could hear the mechanical clicking when lights changed at the intersections near the bridges that carried traffic across. The smells and sounds of people moving through their day as they crossed the hot pavement filled the air. They smelled of sweat and perfume, neither of which sang to me; they hid the wisdom of the water and earth.

In the sanctuary of the darkness under bridges, I would stop and listen past the traffic, smelling beyond the asphalt and gasoline for the forest. I assessed how much farther I had to go by the effort I had to use to hear its call. Occasionally, a large stone would peek out of the water and whisper to me, "Careful, brother, not far."

It was a relief when the noise of traffic began to subside. Sheer concrete walls gave way to stone and masonry embankments. There were places where the water had eroded its man-made retention, and plants sprouted. Some small trees had taken hold, and their roots began the difficult work of unseating what man had built.

The day was now hot and bright. I was finally able to climb the embankment and see what was above. The apartments and large buildings that provided shade over the canal were gone. There were small homes with fenced lots separating them. Sidewalks were uneven, as nature either moved them with the shifting of the earth or roots had lifted and heaved them out of the way. Some of the homes looked abandoned, their man-smell now accompanied by the musty scent of rotting structures. Close to the canal was a large tree in a yard overgrown by neglect. The house itself was quietly resisting the pull of gravity, losing the battle. The giant leaves concealed the network of branches beneath. I found cover — a large branch suitable to rest on and low enough that I could observe everything around me.

Rodents had found the house and brazenly moved around the exterior. Wild grasses and weeds with thorns barely concealed car parts and furniture that had been cast out of the house. Every type of crawly creature was using the cast-offs as homes, food, or cover from predators.

Sparse traffic would occasionally speed by without noticing the microcosm of deterioration. I heard people walking by, talking without noticing. A small dog wandered into the yard, looking for something to eat. He was busy sniffing out rodents and didn't notice me watching. He came close, and I took him as a snack to feed my nap.

I was careful not to sleep too deeply. I could hear the creek. With less traffic, it was singing again. The whispers of the grass and the trees were not the same as they had been in the morning, but they were a welcome change from the noise of the city.

Chapter Eleven

The report of blood in the park by a hysterical woman was first met with skepticism by the authorities. They had dragged a body from the park just days before; the blood could have been from the earlier incident. It was early in the morning when the dispatch supervisor decided to wait for the light of day to send officers to the park to investigate. He was well aware that the jaguar attack was fabricated. He took the woman's contact information and created a turnover log for the next desk supervisor to respond to.

It was noon before the next supervisor sent officers to interview her. She had waited for them at home. A phone call found her, and she had decided to drop into the local pub to calm her nerves. That is where she met the police. Sitting together at the bar, they asked her what happened the night before.

She recounted her story. "I went out for a drink and met a man," she said. "He was muscular with the tattoo of a jaguar on his arm. Soon after meeting him, I felt tired, and he offered to help me home. He suggested we walk through the park. Then I remember waking up — blood next to me. I ran home and called the police."

A large man with green eyes sat alone at a table, listening to the story. The police said they would go and look in the park. Ben knew that there was a good chance they wouldn't investigate. A few hours later, with nothing better to do, one of the officers walked through the park. He didn't expect to find anything. He knew that Roger had been warned to limit his activities after they found Leah's body.

The officer smelled the residue of a bowel evacuation, thinking somebody had simply relieved themselves in the park. Then, he nearly tripped on an arm. The call was made. Crime scene tape cordoned off the area, and dogs were brought in. The body was found. There was no doubt this was a real jaguar attack.

***

The creek told me about the dogs before I heard them in the distance. It was time to move. The daylight would not provide much cover. My dark pelt was suited to move through the shadows of the jungle. The sun was high, and the shadows were limited along the deteriorated banks of the creek. I had to move quickly, requiring me to take chances. Masonry walls narrowed, forcing my path.

The water ahead warned me of the metal bars that obstructed my passage. The outer wall of the city had been fortified to prevent attackers from entering. Metal bars barred me from escaping through the water. I quietly climbed to the street with an arched gate that would lead me to freedom. To either side of the arch were narrow streets with perfectly spaced white doors — no shade. Sparse traffic moved in and out of the archway. I waited, hugging close to the only shade available. I crouched, listening. The sound of the cars differed depending on the direction of their arrival. They sped past, leaving dust in the air behind them.

The lead dog found me hiding. His barking alerted the hounds that were still down by the creek. He knew better than to attack me. I countered his incessant barking with a growl, baring my teeth as I crouched, ready to defend myself. He yelped when I made him pay for getting too close. His body fell into the water and swallowed him. The barking of the pack was not far off. I sprinted through the arch into the jungle and up the nearest tree. The dogs were now in hot pursuit, surrounding the base of the tree.

I leaped silently to the wall. In the darkness of the jungle, they didn't see me move and stayed below. I moved clandestinely, keeping low and moving slowly. I knew it wouldn't take long for them to figure out I wasn't there. I knew they would track me from the base of the wall. Men would not be far behind.

I could feel the jungle now. It wasn't just the smell or the cover of its darkness. There was an undeniable feel it projected, like the familiar sense of home. Its embrace awaited me. On one side of the wall was the earthy safety I longed for; on the other, the putrid man-smell of death.

The jungle whispered, "Listen."

Dogs were approaching from the other direction. I had two choices: the jungle or the street below. My eyes could see into the darkness of the jungle, a trap — a barred cage with a dead rabbit. It had the smell of death and man smell. Men were positioned at the side of the cage, ready and waiting. Choosing the street, I dropped down between the structures and hugged the building. No cover — completely exposed. I heard a sound and stopped. Anticipating danger, I crouched to defend myself.

A door opened.

In the entryway was a man. His eyes were familiar. He stared into mine. No fear. He stepped aside, and I followed.

The room was familiar, like a distant dream. It wasn't the jungle, but it was welcoming. There were cushions on the floor. He slowly sat on one and watched me. I carefully surveyed the room. My tail moved silently behind me, keeping me aware of any movement to my rear. He had pulled the curtains to darken the room so I could see. I checked every corner for threats. He remained still. In the darkest corner was a blanket. I would not be seen; that is where I hid.

He didn't move. I didn't move. The hint of an evening breeze whispered itself into the window, "Rest." I let my body relax. In the distance, I heard the dogs come close and then move farther and farther away. Footsteps of men followed behind them.

I could have escaped through an open window. The jungle was just a few meters away. Instead, I accepted his hospitality, at least for the moment. With my belly full and my body safe, I felt the call of sleep. Darkness would soon conceal my exit and lead me back.

I sensed him move and leave through the door almost silently. The floor beneath the blanket was cool but not inviting, like cool moss or grass. The breeze carried both the life of the jungle and the death in the city. Neither had the feel of danger.

***

The heat of the sun through the skylight awakened my body. The light was too bright for me to see, but I could tell I was alone in the room. There was a haze in my mind. I only

95

half-realized that I was naked. I could smell something edible in front of me. It took a few moments to see a cup with steam rising gently into the room. Beside it, a bowl of something warm like porridge with spices and a hint of sweetness.

I sat and lifted the cup with both hands and sipped. It was earthy. I could feel its warmth coat the insides of my body. After several sips, I picked up the bowl and smelled it. A wooden spoon invited me to taste it. It was warm but not hot, with a myriad of flavors that were completely new to me. At first, the new flavors caused me to pause, but my body couldn't resist. I ate and drank, moving my blanket out of the sun before I laid back down. Deep sleep awaited.

I dreamt I was back in the lab. We were distilling the process needed to mass-produce the new drug. We carefully mapped out each step of the process. Each change to the molecular structure was scrutinized for precision and optimization. When we reached the end, I printed the expected molecular structure to verify our results.

A new lab assistant with a lavender streak in her hair came into the lab as the team was celebrating our success. She asked why we were celebrating, and I held up the finished structure, verifying the result. An odd look came over her face. She opened the folder she was carrying and pulled out a similar structure. At the top of her page was a red header used by the preservative/chemical side of the company. I examined them side by side. They were nearly identical. The process to produce the offending chemical was identical to the cure.

I realized we were still making poison — maybe a more effective one. The thought woke me up.

***

The light in the room suggested that it was morning. Beside the blanket were neatly folded pants and a shirt. I realized I was naked under the blanket and reached for the pants. They were simple, light-colored fabric with a tied waist. I'd seen them in the market by my apartment. I rolled the legs up a few turns like I'd seen the Indians do. The shirt hung on me but fit well enough.

The door opened. I felt it move before I saw the movement. My host appeared and smiled at me. He sat down on his cushion.

"Toilet?" I asked.

"Of course." He motioned to the door and said, "Straight through."

My body didn't need any additional instruction. I was up and opening the door.

There was a hallway to my left and another to my right. Ahead, I would pass into and through the old wall of the fortress. The inside of the massive wall had been carved out and shored up with stone arches. The room was small, but the arc gave it size. Through the room was another door that opened to the jungle beyond the city. I passed through the door. To my right was a small shack, like an outhouse with a hole to squat. That was all the invitation my body needed as it let loose with violence. Politely, it was a bowel movement; realistically, it was a total purge.

Finished, I stepped out and pulled on a rope just outside the door. The whole floor flooded down the hole that flowed into a sewer line. Ingenious, I thought. Whoever installed the sewer line knew there was no way they could plumb the fortification wall, so they converted the outhouses.

In less of a rush, I paused to look into the jungle. Just outside the door, discretely arranged, was a garden. Plants nestled in between branches and roots. A footpath wandered through the undergrowth, with stones carefully placed to provide access but not intrude on the plants that grew naturally. Trees ascended to the sky, and the canopy resembled the arches of a cathedral. Vines climbed the trees and let their flowers and leaves dangle above. The ground was covered with old leaves and branches that had succumbed to time. I could hear water gently running, babbling to itself. I didn't dare investigate more than a quick look.

Back inside the arched room, the atmosphere was cool. I imagined that in the heat of the day, this room was very pleasant. Strangely, though the walls were thick stone, the room felt light, like sitting in the shade beneath a tree. There were simple mattresses on the floor and a table with chairs. It was easy to imagine that a family might escape the heat for a siesta or other activities. It was cozy and inviting.

The hallway between the arched room connected to rooms on either side. I could smell a kitchen on one side. It occurred to me that not all of the doors on the street opened to distinct homes. They combined behind the facade for a more accommodating living space. I could imagine that the original barracks could have been entered individually and that the passages provided both access and cover, depending on the needs of the moment. The structure could have easily been both an infirmary or a prison with minor modifications. Someone hiding from authorities could have easily entered one door and traversed up or down the street unseen. The back door was a simple door that also looked like every other door in the hallway.

I opened the door and stepped back into the room. He was still there. My relief must have been obvious. He smiled. The room was different than I remembered. The colors were more subdued than I recalled. I didn't remember that the room had a scent — not just the smells coming from the kitchen, but the walls and the floor had a smell that created a feel. The cushions had a scent that contributed to the ambiance. The blanket in the corner had a smell that caught my attention. It was my scent and not my scent… Beyond the quiet of the room were the sounds of life around us. I could hear a dog walking up the street. I could hear movement in the adjacent rooms. Then, there were the sounds I cannot describe that pulled my attention back to the jungle.

I did remember the cushions on the floor. Instead of sitting down on the one I had before, I moved between them. I made a small circle around the room. I became aware that I was smelling the room by pulling air gently into my mouth. I could taste the room that way. The movement had the added benefit of orienting me; it was a feeling I had never experienced before. I found a cushion that felt "right" and moved it to the space in front of him. I arranged myself as I sat down, very aware of my location in the room.

"Good morning, and thank you," I said.

He smiled and nodded. "You're welcome. Good morning." He paused.

Until that moment, it hadn't occurred to me how I had gotten back to this place. I looked around and remembered that I woke up without clothing. I glanced at the shirt and pants, and I must have had a confused look.

"Give it a moment," he said.

"Dogs," I said.

"Yes, dogs."

"Door," I said.

"Yes."

"You were in the door."

"Yes."

"Danger." I closed my eyes to memories that didn't translate into images. "It's a blur."

"Understandable," he said.

He remained quiet. I was processing what was unprocessable. I searched my memory for the last clear thought. I was in the park. I drank from the jar. Everything after that was images that were both images and not images that made no sense.

"How long was I asleep?" I asked.

"Several days."

A gentle knock at the door, and it slowly opened. A woman's face peeked around the door.

"Ah, breakfast! Come in, come in," he said happily. "Hungry?"

I took a moment. I wasn't sure. My body was sluggish, and my mind was still foggy and lost, trying to recollect the days before. He could sense my hesitation.

Chapter Twelve

The woman wore the same traditional dress and blouse I'd seen in the market. She had a bright smile and clear eyes. She moved gently with a tray in her hands. Her hair was pulled back, with a few stray hairs creating a vaporous halo around her face. Her skin carried the color of the sun — luminescent and smooth. Her hands were supple and strong. She handed over the tray, glancing at me and giving me a quick smile when our eyes met. Her retreat was as effortless as her entry. The door clicked into place as it settled into its frame.

"Here, drink this. I will help. It comes from the herbs of the forest. It settles the mind and awakens the body."

The cup was warm, and the smell was familiar from my awakening the night before. I took a moment to breathe it in. Its warm essence helped lift some of the fog even before I drank. Its warmth gently brought the urge to eat.

"Beans and rice," he said, handing me a bowl and spoon. The bowl, like the cup, was earthen, with simple designs etched or painted on the outsides. The spoon was carved from wood. The sides of the bowl were lined with plantains, and there were fresh herbs sprinkled on top. It was a simple meal.

We ate in silence. It was a welcome diversion from the fragments of my memory. I closed my eyes as I sipped from the cup. It was like the moment when Leah and I breathed our first breaths together. It was the first time I really tasted it. Taste wasn't just flavor; it was an immersive experience that pulled smell, feel, and connection all together. It wasn't just that I was sipping something tasty and warm; it made me feel warm and connected.

The beans and rice didn't just taste good; they felt good. I devoured every last grain in the bowl.

"I don't remember how I got here," I said.

"I understand," he said. "Clarity may come with time. What is past is done. Seeing the ripples of the past may unlock your experience."

"What happened to my clothes?"

"You left them behind."

"Behind?"

"Yes, behind."

"Where?"

"I don't know."

"Came here naked?"

"In a sense, yes."

I felt something inside grow warm. I became quiet, and my eyes narrowed as my head tipped down. I could feel a growl. It came from a place of anger that wasn't anger. I felt more confused and vulnerable than afraid or angry. I remembered growling before.

"Did I growl at you?"

"No," he said. Then paused. "There is something that you might find interesting. It might help. Do you feel okay walking?"

It seemed like an odd question. "Yes, where to?"

"You'll see, but first, are you interested in taking another jar?"

He stood and retrieved the tray of jars from behind him. He set it between us. Three jars left.

"I'm still not sure what happened with the first," I said.

"Do you feel any different than you did before?" he asked. It struck me as odd. I thought about it.

"I think so."

"Is that enough?" he asked.

Another odd question. "I'm not sure," I said.

"Pick another jar and take it with you. You can decide later what to do with it."

I agreed and selected the middle of the three jars. He held out his hand, and I handed the jar over to him. He picked up a glass pitcher, filled the jar, and replaced the lid.

"Pure water," he said.

He put the tray back on the floor behind him. He motioned for me to stand up, too. He took a look at me — barefoot, unshaven, and clothes that hung off of me. He smiled and disappeared through the door. He came back with some sandals and the woman who had brought in our breakfast. He motioned for her to look at me. Her whole face smiled, and she brought her hand to her mouth.

He said something to her that I couldn't understand. She looked at him and spoke back. Looking at me, she asked, "Can I help you?"

I was looking down at myself, not sure what she meant. "Yes, please," I said. First, she unrolled the legs of my pants and carefully rolled them again. Now my legs were even. She lifted and snugged the waist before adjusting the shirt.

She put the sandals on the floor and tapped my left foot. I put my left foot down, and she adjusted all of the bindings to fit my foot. Then, the right.

She stepped back to size up her work. I could tell she was satisfied, but just barely. I looked myself over and realized I did look better, but probably not suited for a social event. They looked at each other. In the absence of disapproval, I was acceptable.

"Ready?" he asked.

"Guess so," I replied, still not sure where we were going.

***

I followed him through the door into the hallway. We took a few steps toward the kitchen and stepped inside. The room was bright, but there was no light fixture. Light seemed to stream in from everywhere. A wood-burning stove had water simmering, and another pot probably contained what remained of the beans and rice. A simple counter displayed small piles of leaves and vegetables being prepared for a later meal. He grabbed a woven bag with a shoulder strap and placed the jar inside. From a bowl on another counter, he selected a few pieces of fruit, eyeing each one for ripeness before adding them to the bag.

We left through the jungle door.

"This is the herb garden," he said, walking up the path I'd seen before. He moved around the foliage and behind a wall of stacked stones. A pool. Water burbled from a moss-covered wall. A trickle overflowed into a small stream that returned to the jungle. My eyes adjusted. The water was perfectly clear. A game trail came just to the edge, where animals could come and drink. Birds rested on the rocks and moss to drink and bathe. Hammocks hung on the edges of the clearing.

"This is where we get our water," he explained.

I bent down next to the pool to sip the water while he watched me. Mud oozed up over my sandals and between my toes. A moment of recollection washed over me. My body remembered the feel of the mud, the sense of cool water splashing onto my legs. I touched my lips to the surface of the pool, the smell of water and leaves mixed into a familiar organic brew. The mental image was gray and muted, but the memory was vivid in every other way.

I stood up and noticed a cup hanging from a string next to me. "Next time," I thought. The water was refreshing and sweet.

"I could have gotten my pure water here?" I asked.

He nodded. "Why didn't you tell me?"

"It is important that you find your own way," he replied with a slight chuckle. "Also, you didn't ask."

He turned and headed back down the path, and I followed. Beside the door, opposite the outhouse, were carefully carved handholds to scale the wall. He effortlessly climbed to the top. I followed. It was much harder than he made it look.

From the top, the actual size of the wall became more apparent. It had been built wide enough for rooms to be safe below. The rooms were for food or water storage. I could see where the building on the city side of the wall was attached. The ingenuity was impressive.

Stovepipes breached the roof invisible from the street. There was a path along the wall that was private; residents could come and go completely unseen.

***

We walked along the ridge of the wall, which was well-worn from years of use. The ridgeline of buildings crested the hill bordering the city. On the other side lay the jungle — so thick that we would have struggled to move through.

Outhouses occasionally jutted from the wall. No other paths ventured into the jungle.

The heat of the day was rising. I kept glancing over at the shade of the jungle. At first, I just wanted to escape the heat. But then a longing arose, different from merely seeking relief. It was a desire to rest in a safe and familiar place. The longing lived within me; the pull to be in the jungle was subtle, inviting, and real.

Walking the wall gave us quick access to the borders of the city. We traversed over the archways that had been carved out for paved roads. The rows of white doors changed to small homes — some abandoned and others occupied by squatters. It was obvious when we reached the incorporated neighborhoods. Suddenly, power lines and gas meters appeared. The homes looked fresh and maintained. Eventually, our walking path on the wall yielded to a park with green grass and sidewalks. Without the jungle, I felt inexplicably exposed. Unconsciously, I hugged the edge of the park where a creek arced its way toward the harbor, flowing down and through the old city.

We reached the end of the park, still following the creek. We stopped to take a break by the water. He opened the bag and pulled out the fruit. He offered me a choice, and I accepted the mango. It was sweet in the way that only a fresh mango can be.

***

We watched the water for a moment. I could smell that it was losing its earthiness. The mown grass had a homogeneous smell that was dull in comparison to the jungle. The sounds of urban life drowned out the babbling of the water and the rustling of the leaves. Voices of children rose against the sound of traffic ahead of us. It took keen awareness to listen beneath all of the noise. I shut my eyes to focus. Images raced through my mind. Something about the water. Then, "I have a tail" was the last verbal thought before the blur.

"I am not sure what is happening," I said. I could feel him listening.

"I had a tail."

"Yes."

"It was long and black," I realized aloud.

"Yes."

I thought about it for a minute. "I was a jaguar."

"Yes."

"How is that possible?"

He remained silent. My mind started to spin. "Am I turning into a jaguar?"

"No," he said, but it felt qualified and hesitant.

"Why?" I asked.

"I can't answer why," he replied. "It will reveal itself to you." He paused. "That is why we are walking." He started to get up and looked toward the street where the park ended, surveying the area before stepping back onto the path.

A thousand questions exploded in my brain, and I stopped listening to the water and smelling the grass. I stepped back onto the path to follow.

Chapter Thirteen

Completely captivated by my thoughts, I blindly followed. We made our way to paved streets and sidewalks. Shops sprang up with parking lots and traffic signals. The heat blasted up from the concrete and down from the sky. All the cars that passed us by had closed windows, AC blasting, and music blaring. Pedestrians sprinted from air-conditioned shops to air-conditioned cars. Intersections slowed our progress but ahead were green trees.

When we finally made it to the shade, we found ourselves in a cemetery. We walked up a rise, carefully minding the headstones placed in neat lines and rows. We crested the rise to see a long circular driveway and a pavilion. Lines of parked cars signaled a funeral was about to start. People were slowly making their way to an open plot where a casket was prepared to be buried.

We walked closer and stopped in the trees, close enough to observe but not be part of the proceedings. People congregated near a woman and two small children. The woman was wailing. A priest stood nearby, reading quietly as people arrived. Beside the priest was a portrait on an easel. It was a photograph of Roger.

Images in my mind began to string together — still gray and muted. My body remembered in ways my mind could not. "There was a woman," I thought. "She was in trouble." I closed my eyes.

I felt my paws on his back. I felt the snap as I bit his skull and neck. I smelled what he released as he expired. I tasted his thigh. His body was in several pieces when I pulled him into the tree. The woman was safe.

For a moment, panic struck me. I was a killer. My mind flooded with guilt, and my body responded. I thought I was going to vomit. My legs wobbled beneath me. I put a hand on the tree next to me to steady myself. The tree welcomed my touch. It hummed the song of the forest — of life and death. I knew this song. It touched me, awakened me. I took a deep breath. It was the first.

For a moment, I saw the situation from the perspective of the tree. It didn't care. Death was a part of living. The only ones who cared were gathered around the coffin. I watched as the priest spoke. The woman who had been hysterically wailing was now subdued. Her children sat beside her, mostly uninterested. A man stood behind them, hands on the backs of the chairs. He looked like an older version of Roger.

He patted the boy's head and placed his hand on the woman's shoulder. She touched it in acknowledgment.

As the words finished and bonds were reaffirmed, the casket was lowered into its resting place. One by one, people filed by to either place a handful of dirt in the hole or drop a rose; some dropped money, and others poured from a bottle. At the end of the line stood a woman in dark glasses and gloves. As she passed by the coffin, she spit.

People left. Workers filled in the rest of the hole with shovels. The rest of the world continued on. A breeze rustled the leaves on the tree, and I felt it touch my face. We sat silently for a while. I remembered other funerals I had attended. I recalled the sense of loss. No amount of grieving changed the situation. Eventually, the grief would work its way through, and life would carry on.

I looked over, and our eyes locked. His pastel blue eyes held compassion. A gentle smile graced his face. "I don't remember everything," I said. "I remember enough to know how he died and that the woman was safe." His gaze never wavered. "There is more, but I can't find the words. It's as if his death had nothing to do with me or Leah. I thought that justice would somehow be appeased. Instead, justice has nothing to do with it."

My eyes dropped back to the grass. The blades where my hand had been were straightening back up. A part of me watched with wonder as I felt them stretch. He pulled another piece of fruit from the bag sitting between us. He handed me the strap.

"Are you okay to go home?" he asked.

"Home?" I replied, recalling Leah's request.

"If you follow this street next to the creek, it will take you into the city. I believe that is where you are staying."

"Yes." Until this moment, the other world didn't exist.

"This street follows the creek into the central part of the city," he said, pointing down the hill. "Are you okay to go home?" he asked again.

I nodded, now a bit apprehensive about leaving him behind. I looked into the bag. Inside, I found some fruit, and the jar already filled with water. "Will I see you again?" I asked.

He smiled, and his body reflected the smile, too. "Probably."

"Is it always like this?" I asked.

"Explain," he replied.

"Did you become a jaguar?"

"Different journey," he said.

"This jar?" I asked.

"A mystery," he replied.

"You don't know what this jar holds?"

"No."

"You didn't know I would become a jaguar?"

"No."

"Do you know what will happen to me?"

"No."

"You don't know the outcome?"

"No."

"Why am I doing this, then?" I asked aloud, but mostly to myself.

"To come to terms with your humanity."

I fell silent. He was right.

"I don't know your name," I said.

He considered his words. "Only humans have names."

I had no response. I stood quietly for a moment. "What should I call you?"

"Friend."

That would have to be enough. He looked toward his path home.

***

I walked close to the water. I listened carefully to hear it burble and flow. Each step closer to the city was another step further from the jungle. Soon, I would be enveloped in a world where nothing was natural. Even the trees and grass in the city came from somewhere else. It had its pull on me, too. It was familiar. It was my bubble that was safe and predictable. Until I experienced the jungle, I had no idea that my bubble was death. On reflection, a part of me knew that was why I came to the jungle.

A street sign caught my eye. It was Seventh Street. I turned, and before long, the street looked familiar. I walked past the bar with the bartender, who had a million-dollar smile. I knew the park was a few streets away, and I kept on going toward the apartment.

The apartment was familiar and foreign at the same time. It was like stepping into a time capsule and seeing everything differently now. I put the jar on the table and snagged a piece of fruit before powering on the phone and computer. Among the plethora of messages was a notation on my calendar that I was to be on a call in an hour.

I shed my clothes and started the shower. Even after shaving, I didn't look like myself. The water in the shower eased me back into my strength. A focus came into my mind. I moved, knowing what I needed to do without expending any additional effort. It wasn't long until I was ready, and the call came.

The video froze a few times and finally found continuity. I could see my boss with the company CEO at a table, both watching the monitor.

"Good evening, son," said the CEO. He called everyone son or dear.

"Good evening, sir."

"It's good to see you in one piece. We've heard there was a jaguar attack in the city."

"One piece for sure," I replied smartly.

"When we didn't hear from you, we thought we should call."

"Thank you, sir. I'm quite alright."

"Been busy?" he asked.

"I took the opportunity to explore the rainforest. You know, the jungle."

"I remember; we encouraged you to explore and learn more about the place," said my boss.

"Yes, sir."

The older man, the CEO, spoke next. "We had hoped that sending you to the wilds of the jungle would bring some perspective. The jungle is a dangerous place. It's eat or be eaten. Kill or be killed. That is why we are building the factory — to be the first to the market and stronger than our competitors."

"I understand, sir."

He continued, "We are expanding the project to include more product production and an R&D facility."

"I'm not sure there are enough people in the area to increase production," I said.

"We're thinking bigger than that," he laughed. "We plan to build housing and create a small village for our employees. It will be more cost-effective than expecting people to commute."

I tried not to think about the implications of this plan.

"We will need someone to head the research and development department. I was hoping you would consider the job."

"Sir?"

"You will be close to the jungle, where lifesaving discoveries are made every day. You could make a real difference in the world."

At any other moment, this would be the offer of a lifetime. Today, I saw the hook that would forever keep me in the world of death. I could do research, but I would also be making poisons.

I smiled. "That is very generous, sir. I will consider it."

"We are still crunching numbers and going over the data you sent us. Good work."

"Thank you, sir."

"Be careful down there. I was talking to one of my good friends, and his son was killed by a jaguar a few days ago. Terrible thing. I knew him when he was younger. He was a good man."

"I'll be careful, sir."

An arm reached for the camera, and the call ended.

I sat back and sighed. Then I took a deep breath. I let my eyes close. My mind began to drift through the last few days. It was too much to process. There was no conclusion or spiritual truth that could wrap everything up neatly. I experienced the sublime and the horrifying. I was both weak and strong. The order of my life had given way to chaos. It was ugly and dirty. I was born, and I died all in a few days. For no particular reason, tears came.

My body shook, and I wept for a very long time. Everything welled up inside of me and begged to be felt. Each memory, every success, and every failure brought tears. I grieved. Finally, just tears. Tears that let me sleep as if for the first time.

I dreamt of being a jaguar. I rested in the safety of the jungle. She shielded me so I was safe and alerted me whenever danger was present. In turn, I lived in harmony with her. I hunted to keep life in balance. I never took more than I needed, and she never let me starve. What was left of my kill was consumed by her other children and eventually returned to the earth. I was not the master of the jungle. The jungle cannot be mastered.

I dreamt that I was a jaguar dreaming of being me. To the jaguar me, living in a box away from the earth was completely out of sorts. Sitting in front of a computer was unnerving. The idea of money was intriguing, but I spent money on useless distractions. The jaguar me see the fear I lived with. I was afraid of everything. The jaguar me had never known fear before. Fear was reserved for those moments of last resort when I needed every ounce of strength and courage to survive.

When I woke, I was struck by the thought that the last few days could have just been a dream. I mused on the idea. How and why would I dream of something so fantastic? I was on the sofa. The room was bright with the morning sun. I had slept late, and my body was stiff. I could feel something scratching my skin. I found a receipt. It must have fallen out of Leah's bag.

The receipt was from the cafe where Leah and I had first eaten. She looked at my palm. I remembered. Then she scribbled something on the receipt.

"Your palm says that you will avenge my death."

My blood went cold.

On the table sat the jar. Not a dream.

The jaguar me was not alarmed. He observed my agitation. I laid down again and closed my eyes. It was too late to dive back into dreams. My mind was beginning the monumental task of finding purpose or meaning in what I'd remembered. It was a fool's errand to try to make sense of it all. His calm became my calm. Everything had moved with a flow of unseen intention. Even this moment was part of that continuum of experiences. I let my mind wrestle with the continuum while the rest of me foraged for something to eat.

As expected, I would have to go out for food. I picked up the pants and shirt off the floor, grabbed the bag, and headed out the door. The jaguar me was ready for the hunt. The market beside the church was the best place for me to go. I started at the top of the street and wandered past the stalls, scouting for my next meal. The familiar smell of rice and beans pulled me close. I found the street vendor, sat on the curb, and devoured it.

I realized that I was wearing the pants and shirt from the day before. Something in me thought I should have my own and return what I was lent. It was a new hunt. Stall after stall was selling clothing, most of it modern, much of it emblazoned with the logo of the maker. I found a stall selling traditional clothing. I started looking through the piles of shirts, each one individually wrapped in cellophane. It was easier for tourists to pack them that way. The woman minding the stall was watching me. She reached over and touched my bag.

"Yours?" she asked.

"From a friend," I said.

She looked at me, tilting her head and squinting just a bit. I felt watched. I met her gaze. The feeling of strength and confidence rose in me. Unconsciously, the jaguar me was subtly letting himself be seen. She nodded and reached below the table. She brought out several pairs of pants and some shirts. None of them were wrapped in cellophane. Each one carried the scent of the person who hand-stitched the fabric. Truly made by hand. She held up several shirts to my back before she selected one. Then she tried the pants, holding the waist to mine. Finally, happy with her choice, she folded them neatly and handed them to me. I reached for my wallet. Her hand found my arm, and she simply nodded, "No."

I gave her a questioning look back.

"From a friend," she said, smiling.

I nodded in gratitude, not sure what had just happened.

The jaguar in me was ready to explore. I would need provisions. I hunted for food I could carry without much trouble. Fruit was the obvious choice, along with some bread and water. The fruit was colorful to my eye, and I let it entice me. I'd point at something that looked colorful, and the stallkeeper would carefully make a selection before handing it to me. I would hold it and smell it. Almost everything was new to me. Even my snacks would be an adventure.

In a separate stall was a honey vendor. The jars caught my eye, just like the ones on the tray. Each jar had a piece of honeycomb dripping with amber ambrosia. I bought one and stowed the jar in my bag.

With my bounty carefully gathered, I started my journey back to the apartment. Lost in thought, I floated through the streets.

The outside world faded to the thoughts of Leah. Her essence and the weight of her words lingered. They left more questions than answers.

I spotted the cafe where we ate that night. I sat down and ordered a coffee. I let the coffee cool while I watched people pass by. The lull allowed my senses to blossom. The jaguar me observed without thought. I witnessed everything with different senses; even the coffee took on an earthy complexity. Answers would have to wait.

I had the sense of a hunt as I explored the city. Before, the city had distracted me from the mundane parts of my life. Now, I observed everything like it was the first time. The jaguar in me knew to stay aware to stay alive. The hunt meant sustenance or safety or danger. Every smell, sound, and vibration were worth exploring. The jungle embraced all her children; the city was cold and stale. Even more reason to remain alert.

I wandered down to the docks. The water in the harbor was murky and dark. I smelled oil and diesel. Warehouses added the smell of decomposing fish. To my amazement, if I focused, I could smell the grass of a nearby park. The song of trees called me to their glorious shade. I felt less exposed. The trees provided an escape if I needed it. The farther away I moved from the water, the more I could smell the city. The scent of Decay dominated despite trees and bushes planted near buildings and in parks. The sound of a bird was a rare occurrence.

Completely unaware of time, I noticed that the sun was fading, and I could smell the city transitioning to evening. I made my way back toward the apartment. Getting home, I put the honey jar next to the other. The staleness of the air conditioning felt like death. I opened the door to the balcony despite it still being hot outside. The breeze still held the decay of the city but brought with it the possibility of rain. And the sounds — not the constant drone of motors, but of people and their distractions.

I showered and sat down to relax. The human part of me was letting go of being awake. The jaguar part was more alert with the sun going down. I let my guard down. The jaguar me began to investigate the rest of me. My body slept. The rest of me was more and more awake.

Morning came with a sense of release and a longing for the jungle. I wondered what the day would hold. My human me was aware of work responsibilities. The rest of me was willing to explore the unexpected. Live in the moment. The balcony door was still open, and the sounds of the city waking were building. Above the din, I heard a bee investigating the apartment.

Unconsciously, I opened a jar for the bee before going to the bathroom. When I came back, the bee was drinking. I realized that I'd opened the water jar instead of the honey. I watched the bee resting on the table. The open jar called to me. Jaguar me could not resist the call. I drank.

On the sofa, the jaguar embraced the human side. Though drifting, I felt safe and strong. Laying down, I felt the bee land on my wrist and crawl to my hand. It stopped moving, and it curled into a ball in my palm.

Chapter Fourteen

I am a honeybee. All I feel is love. I feel love for my queen. I feel love for my swarm. I feel love for every flower.

There is only the queen. The queen is both the queen bee and the swarm; they cannot be separated. There is no me. There is only the queen and love.

I awaken from the palm of my hand. I fly through the door in search of flowers and nectar. I don't go far before I can smell the nectar from a flower garden on another balcony. The flowers shimmer in a translucent radiance, signaling that they are fully in bloom and full of nectar. Each flower welcomes me, showering me with pollen. I hum to her to tell her she is beautiful. She blushes and lets me drink her nectar. It is mutual love. I leave her, promising to come back.

"My best to the queen," she shouts as I fly to the next.

The dance plays out again and again and again.

I drink my fill and head back to the hive. No matter where I am, I can always feel the hive. Inside, I always know where home is. I am free to make note of where flowers are blooming or about to bloom. I watch carefully to see the brilliance of their translucence as an indicator. I never think about the flowers I have visited; instead, my memory is a map.

I reach the hive and fly in through a crack in an old standing trunk. I am greeted by the swarm and share my nectar. We sing together, celebrating the harvest. I dance to show where my flowering friends are. They dance to me where they find other lovers awaiting a visit. As we hum, I can hear the queen. Her voice welcomes us home. She sings songs of gratitude and encouragement as we leave again.

The jungle is easy to negotiate. Depending on the season, we can fly to the canopy and delight in nectar kissed by the sun. Other times, we travel distances to find orchids hiding in rotting logs. The jungle is constantly changing. Every time I fly out, I listen for blooming flowers, sniff the air for direction, and finally watch for the translucent radiance that invites me in.

Today, flowering herbs call to me; I fly to a place I knew when I was other than a bee. A pool lined with herbs by a wall that borders the jungle. On the other side of the wall lives another world that could be nectar lucrative but dangerous.

I rest on the mossy bank of the pool and drink sweet, pure water from its edge. The herb flowers are small but succulent. I have to visit many. It is tiring work, but it is a labor of love.

I fly up and over the wall. A window is open, the curtain gently flowing in the breeze. I recognize the man inside. I fly about the room, and he takes note, pouring some sugar water in a saucer. I fly to the saucer and drink as he watches. I fly over, land on his shoulder, and hum. I am surprised that he hums back. I fly to his other shoulder and hum again. He hums back. I fly around him as he goes back to his cushion and land on his arm. He watches as I fly around him again, lingering in front of his face. He smiles. I see two jars behind him on a tray and land on one.

I take off and fly around him, only to land on the jar again. I do it again. He smiles and picks up the jar. I fly to his shoulder. He stands and walks through the door into the hallway.

"Come look!" he says, and the woman appears. He holds up the jar and tilts his head toward me. She brings her hands to her cheeks and smiles with her whole face. Out the back door, up the path to the pool. He sets the jar down next to the pool. I fly around them both, landing on the jar lid and then flying around them again.

She cups her hands and holds them in front of her. I land and dance on her fingers as she squeals with joy. I hum to her fingers like I would to flower petals. I fly around them again before heading back to the hive.

At the hive, I recount my adventure in song, humming and dancing to the delight of the queen and the swarm. Others sing of the beauty of the sun from the canopy, while others sing about a field of lavender past the safety of the jungle's edge. Just as I am about to leave again, an arm reaches down through a hole in the top of the trunk. The alert goes off, and we all scramble to protect the hive. The gloved hand breaks off a part of the hive and retreats, with hundreds of us in pursuit. The thief is wearing thick clothing, making it nearly impossible to sting and defend the hive. Many try. I fly into the face and am repelled by a net. After a few desperate moments, the queen calls us back to safety, lamenting that our hive is vulnerable. She is considering moving. We all assure her we will protect her and move with her if we have to.

It is getting late, so we all return to the hive. Home. The queen sang songs of far-off lands with translucent flowers that could not be counted. She recounts the heroics of those who have fallen. We hum together with the chorus of her song. We make sure the junior bees are fed and safe. We seal off the last of the full combs and prepare to sleep.

The rest of the jungle anticipates the night. Moonlight caresses the leaves, casting shadows on the ground. Some flowers fold up for the night. Leaves fall gently to the ground, covering creatures as if putting them to bed. Nocturnal hunters begin moving through the trees and across the jungle floor. In the twilight, before everything is settled, is the best time to hunt. At the last of the day, creatures hustle to find safe shelter, making them easy to find and hunt.

From the hive, I can see the moon through the hole in the trunk. Its song is a loving lullaby for us. The trees and the plants move along in unison. The queen adds her voice, and we hum together, making it a symphony of loving reverberation. We welcome the night, and the night welcomes our rest.

We hear the sun long before its light cascades across the hive. We welcome the first rays of the sun that spill onto the jungle floor.

We prepare for our day. If we are going to move, we will need more honey, more food for the workers and drones, and more food for the junior bees. We all know what we need to do, and as soon as the sunlight peeks over the horizon, we are off. We hum our love for the queen, and she sings her love for us, urging our safety and hoping for a plentiful day.

It isn't hard to find my way back. On my way, I take note of landmarks that could mean more nectar when the balcony gardens finish blooming. The sun guides me into the city where I was before. I greet the blooms on the balcony, flirting with them and drinking deeply. New blossoms shimmer and welcome me with pollen. Finding the open door from the day before and flying in. I fly around the room; it is familiar — not because it has flowers, but because I have been here before. On the sofa is a man; I land on him, and he doesn't stir. Something inside of me recognizes him. At that moment, I feel love for him. At that moment, I realize he is part of the swarm. He is part of me. Somehow, we are inextricably connected, like I am connected to the queen and to the swarm.

I land on his chest. His breathing is even and quiet. It draws me in. I begin to rest, and the feeling of sleep washes over me. Strangely, so does the feeling of waking up.

***

The morning light washes across the room, touching my body. I can feel its warmth. I welcome the feeling. On my chest is a honey bee, lying there quietly; I can feel its hum.

135

Gently, I use my hand to hold the bee as I sit up. He nests into my palm. With wonder, I watch him resting, breathing gently. I feel love.

I feel only love. There aren't words that describe this love. Gently, he awakens, and the two of us take each other in. He crawls up my palm for a better look. For a moment, I see myself through his eyes. He recognizes me as a different shape, but we are one and the same. He knows me, and I know him.

He is hungry; the nectar he has harvested is a prize for the swarm. He instantly knows what I am thinking and crawls to my shoulder. We go to the kitchen and make sugar water, pouring it into a saucer. He flies down and drinks slowly, humming. I feel his gratitude. It welcomes me back to the swarm. In my mind, I can hear the queen thanking me. Not a thought, more like music in the distance. My heart soars, and I whisper back, "Thank you." It sounds like a hum.

He looks at me. I can hear him hum back, and I burst into tears.

"Acceptance without reservation. Love without condition. Connection without expectation."

I catch a tear in my palm. He flies and tastes it. Salty. I know what he is thinking.

"What is this?" I feel him ask.

"I have never been a part of a swarm before," I think, letting it translate into a feeling. "There is only the swarm," rises inside of me. He flies to my forehead and touches it with his antennae. I instantly see the queen. I understand that he has to go back to the hive. My heart breaks.

"I am nothing without love," I think. "I am nothing without the swarm, the queen." He alights on my shoulder. I drop my ear close to hear him humming. "It was a love song." I hum back as best as I can through tears.

My friend, my heart, flies out the window in search of translucent lovers. I know the dangers he faces just to return to the hive.

"Be well, be safe," I whisper.

I go to the balcony and look out across the city toward the jungle. It is calling me. The jaguar in me longs for the safety of the jungle. My heart longs for my swarm, my tribe. The human me is losing any resistance to the pull of my heart.

Hunger brought me back to the room. I opened the honey jar and tasted the honey. It was familiar. I was from the hive. I was horrified that I bought honey from the thief. I took another dip with my finger; I couldn't help myself. It reminded me of the hive. It reminded me of the flowers and the moon. It made me hum.

I reached for the bag and found fruit. I bit into the bitter flesh to find a sweetness surrounding tiny seeds that burst as I chewed. My eyes closed, and I experienced both gratitude and satiation. When I finished that one, I tried another. Completely different but no less incredible. I sat down on the balcony floor and took a bite out of each fruit. I left the uneaten portion beside me for ants, bees, or birds. I sat for a while, and a bright yellow bird with dark spots and a sweet voice landed beside me to select a favorite before flying off. Another bird with a lavender streak down its tail landed close enough that I could have touched it. She watched me carefully before snagging another and then flying off.

I washed the clothes I had been lent. I thought about it and hand-washed them in the sink with simple bar soap. My precious handmade attire had probably never met a modern washing machine or detergent. A part of me wanted to preserve the sanctity of the gift. It was a loving gesture. I cried again while washing and hanging them over the back of a chair to dry.

The day was maturing. I could tell from the heat coming from the balcony door. I couldn't bring myself to close it. It felt like closing myself off from everything that was now important. I checked my phone, mostly out of habit. Back in the States, my team was successfully making plans to bring our work to market. The marketing team was busy making statements about the miracle drug that would soon be available to anyone. Bean counters were sending spreadsheets with projections of profits. The machine was humming along without me. Nobody seemed to notice that I hadn't responded. Aside from the video call, nobody asked about me at all. The CEO did send me an article with the latest rainforest discoveries and the potential profits from the research.

Feeling restless. I showered and put on some clothes for the evening. Outside the door, as I stepped onto the street, I closed my eyes and took a deep breath. It was the first of the evening. Leah had no idea what she had awakened. With my eyes still closed, I parted my lips slightly and breathed in, smelling the air. The air was humid and close. The asphalt, having been heated all day, was giving off the essence of petroleum and sulfur. Trash containers in the alley were also letting go of the vapors that had been stewing all day. Diesel and gas fumes hung in the air. I could smell the people passing by. Some smelled like cologne and money. Others smelled like fruit going bad. Still others had a musk that clung to them. Someone smelled like soap.

I kept my eyes closed and listened. Evening traffic was thick and slow. It had the sound of frustration and anticipation. Voices were everywhere, speaking to imaginary listeners. Around the corner, shopkeepers in the market were closing down their stalls for the evening. Neon lights sparked and gasped before humming and glowing. Street vendors were setting up tables or tuning up instruments, anticipating an influx of potential customers.

Then I heard a bird. I opened my eyes. On the ledge of the apartments behind me was a single bird chirping. I realized what I wasn't hearing: the melody of water running freely in a stream, the sound of leaves rustling in the breeze, the voice of the jungle calling me home, the voice of the queen singing us back to the hive. The sounds of the city were a poor substitute.

I couldn't help but listen with my new ears, smell with my new sense of smell, see what I could not before, and feel.

Always before, I had a destination. For Leah, the moment was the destination. I let the moment dictate.

The crowd around me was moving toward the square where Leah and I had spent the evening. I let the confluence carry me. Bodies were close. Each one moved with a rhythm unique to itself. Unlike the hive, everybody had a singular mission of its own. The bees had a singularity of purpose. No motion was wasted. Every movement was in concert with all other movements. In the confluence, the only commonality was that we moved together. At the square, the confluence exploded in every direction. The stream of movement gave way to an ocean of sensation. Everything called to my attention.

The smell of street food mingled with the smell of bodies. Multicolored lights from the signs above the restaurants and bars cast eerie shadows across the crowd. Music from hucksters and venues throbbed a dissonant competitive beat. Shouting and laughter filled the spaces where the music couldn't. The drone of traffic provided a backdrop. The movement was everywhere. My senses were overloaded. I retreated to a corner. I took a deep breath, not to feel more, but to settle myself.

Nights before, this experience had made me feel alive. It broke a spell that had held me living but not alive. Tonight, my senses awakened, and the intensity numbed me. A different spell was being broken. I closed my eyes and leaned against the stone of the building beside me. I felt its coldness; it was real and solid. I let the chaos be outside of me. Inside, I was aware of my body. The awareness of my body brought me to the beat of my heart. I could feel my pulse in my hands and feet.

I remembered the feeling of water. I remembered the sound of the hive. My heart remembered these things. My heart longed for them. I could feel mud squishing between my toes and the crackle of leaves as I walked stealthily across them. No light could be as beautiful as the translucent leaves of a flower pregnant with pollen and nectar.

In the crowd of people, I was alone. In the jungle, I was connected to everything alive. I stood somewhere in the middle, with no way to reconcile the two.

I could smell the earth. I welcomed it like a lover welcomes their beloved. It was a kiss, a caress that lingers past the moment. I opened my eyes and looked at the sea of bodies. I felt no love. I let my heart guide me down the alley.

I reached the grass and walked barefoot, slowly, feeling every blade touch my feet. The sounds and smells of the square were now carried by the breeze as a distant reminder. I found a tree and touched its bark. It was rough to the touch. My fingers felt the bark give slightly, acknowledging my touch. I looked to see if there were flowers in the branches. Not in the trees, but in planters lining the grass, meticulous rows of flowers patiently waited for tomorrow's sun.

I closed my eyes again and imagined water, clear and cool. Instantly, my senses could feel water nearby. I was drawn to the possibility when I came to the edge of the ravine. Now, the smell of water was tangible and real. At the edge of the ravine, urban maintenance gave way to the wild. I walked through the brush to look over the edge. It took a minute for my eyes to adjust as I looked into the darkness. Then I could see the water.

I looked for a path down over the rocks and moss to the water. Nights before, I had abandoned my urge to climb down. Tonight, there was no other option. I found a trail made by something feral. It meandered through the trees and made its way down to the water's edge. The trail was used by smaller animals, and I had to crawl under the thick foliage. Stems with tiny barbs pulled at my clothes. I was undeterred. When I got to the water, I stood in its coldness.

My toes felt the mud. I smelled the moss hanging from the trees and the bitter smell left by the leaves and barbs on my clothes.

I began to remember. The memories weren't images; they were sensations. The water spoke in burbles of the path I took to the jungle. I remembered lying next to the helpless, guarding her. I remembered the whispers of the trees. I sat on a rock, my feet and now my hands in the water. I listened to the whispers of the trees.

"Welcome back," they breathlessly whispered in the breeze.

I closed my eyes and let gratitude fill my heart, my only way to respond. I let the wild reveal its secrets. I could smell old death. I could smell dogs that had searched the area. I could smell life. Decomposing leaves and trunks were sprouting fronds and seedlings. I could feel the sides of the ravine hanging with moss and ferns. The air here was very different from on the street. The breeze shed the putrid smell of decomposing garbage and asphalt. It was replaced with the sweet smell of fauna. Fallen leaves succumbing to the earth lent an organic sweetness.

I let the memories come and sink into my heart. When I remembered the trap and the dogs, the trees shuddered. The song of the queen brought a stillness of recognition. The door opening and the cushioned floor had them all on the edge of their roots. The hand that invaded the hive drew gasps, and the water momentarily turned cooler.

Then the trees remembered back. They let me see the jaguar. His clear eyes pierced the night. He gently found rest in the trees; his tail wrapped around the helpless until she stirred. He walked with power and confidence, following the water to the jungle. The jungle was always there, calling, welcoming me back home.

I sat on the rock, feeling the past flow by with the water. The whispers that lulled the revelry became a melody. I could feel the song in my body; my body vibrated with the rhythm. I let the rhythm sink into my bones. It was the rhythm of the jaguar prowl, the rhythm of the hum in the hive, the rhythm of the water lapping against my ankles. I listened with more than my ears. The rhythm of the earth was even in the drone of traffic and the music of the square. It was subtle, quiet enough to be missed unless you listened carefully.

I let the melody surround me. It found its way into my soul. It was the melody of the queen — the longing that drew me to the jungle. The reason my tail wrapped around the helpless. The face of the woman in the market. The feel of Leah's body against mine. It was love.

Once you know love, you can know nothing else.

A breeze moved through the ravine with a rush of warmth. "There's more," it said. The leaves rustled in agreement. A stillness came; everything stopped moving. The water striders floated on the surface, motionless. The water rested. A reverence descended upon everything in the ravine. The rhythm felt in the silence.

The sounds of the city never stopped. The city was oblivious. It was the doorway I would have to pass through. I sat on the rock for a while, no longer overwhelmed. I knew that I would have to make my way back through the city. I knew I had to drink from the next jar sitting next to a pool at the edge of the wall of safety.

I sat on the rock until my body was ready to move. The aversion to the city became just an annoyance. I walked in the water, my shoes in hand. It was dark, and my feet had to find their own way. Trees, ferns, huge leaves, and moss bordered my path. Ahead, I knew there was an old bridge that marked the end of the wilds of the park. Next to the bridge was a path that led back to the sidewalk bordering the park.

I was heading back to the apartment. Tomorrow, I would leave the city again. I bypassed the square where the locals were imbibing into the evening. My route took me past the pub. As I rounded the corner, I saw a huge man standing outside. Next to him was a small woman. He handed her a package and kissed her forehead. I could see her body smile. She headed toward me, and as she passed, I saw her face — sweet with a look of determination and focus. I looked back, and the large man was watching me.

He waited as I approached. Ben's green eyes pierced the distance between us. He held out his hand and pulled me in close when I grasped it. He smelled like cigarettes and beer.

"I was about to go in for a bite and a beer. Join me?"

Any apprehension was quickly dismissed. I had no fear. "Sure, thank you," I replied.

The bar was fuller than before. Ben's table was waiting for us. By the time we made it to the table, beers were on the way. I took a sip. It tasted numb. I set it aside.

Ben was watching me carefully.

"You know that Roger's character was attacked by a jaguar," said Ben. "From what I hear, it was a real attack. The city is on edge."

I knew it was an invitation. I sat quietly.

"Same park where Leah was found," he said.

Ben made eye contact. I didn't budge. "There was a woman. Police interviewed her right here in the bar." He leaned forward just a bit and dropped his voice. "She'd been drugged. He was about to rape her, and the jaguar killed him." Ben paused.

"After the interview, she acted like there was something she didn't say. It bothered her. So I asked her if there was something else."

Ben leaned even closer.

"She said the jaguar guarded her until she could leave. It laid right next to her." Ben sat back and crossed his arms.

I watched Ben with the quiet intensity that the jaguar gave me. "Then I found out that your company had paid for his protection."

We sat in silence. The bartender brought a burger for Ben and looked at me with a questioning look. "Water, please," I answered.

"Somehow, I think you know all of this," said Ben.

It occurred to me that I hadn't seen the news for a few days. It felt like a trap. "Sorry, haven't seen the news for a while. Work stuff," I replied.

Ben smiled and reached for his burger. The cooked meat had an acrid smell. I was glad when the water arrived.

"Some of the locals think it was a shapeshifting shaman taking care of business. You know, like a sheepdog runs off a wolf."

His eyes didn't move from my face.

"Did you ever find the guy at the edge of the city?" asked Ben.

"Been meaning to do that," I said. We both knew it was a lie.

Ben bit into his burger, and its juices dribbled down his chin. He put the burger back on the plate and caught the juice with his napkin. He was nodding his head like he understood.

"You know, I went to see a shaman once." He was grinning as he took another bite, wiping his lips with the napkin again.

"Told me I had a spirit animal."

"Really? Which one?" I asked.

"Don't remember. Probably a gorilla, I think."

"I was sure you were going to say jaguar," I quipped.

We laughed.

The laughter subsided. "Good to see you, Ben. Stay safe," I said, getting up.

He held out his hand. "You as well." His eyes held more questions. I let the love of the bees rise to mine so that he would feel seen.

"Your company has grown the project, I hear," he said as if inviting me back to the table.

I nodded. "What I hear too." I smiled and moved to the door. The air outside was an improvement, but still heavy and noisy.

The apartment was a refuge for the moment. The warm night air did its best to remember where it came from. I sat on the balcony, feeling past the confines and chaos of the city to the place where the wind originated. It carried the scents of all the lives it had touched, sharing them, then adding my scent to the story and moving on.

I found a blanket and curled up. The balcony was my tree branch, and the apartment was my hive. Rest came easy and gently.

Chapter Fifteen

I dreamt of the jungle. I followed the crystal-clear creeks over stones and falls to the ocean. They sang to each other in the sounds of the waves and the rustling of the leaves. I sat on the beach listening. There was a sense that I had forgotten what I was looking for. At the time, it was incredibly important. Now, it was a trifle, somehow lost.

Morning came to the balcony in subtleties. The sky gently lightened until the stars were awash in the brilliance of the sunrise. The quiet drone of the city grew louder with the pulse of commerce and technology. As the sun hit the side of the building, I heard air conditioners jump to life. Too warm to sleep, I sat up to watch the world waking up.

I am leaving the city today. A part of me wonders if I will come back to this apartment. The rest is curious about what will happen next. Just in case, I make sure the pantry and refrigerator are empty of anything that could spoil. The clothes are hung, and the dishwasher is empty. I unplugged the computer and closed it. Finally, I set the thermostat and closed the place up. I sat on the sofa to take stock. Would I need money? I was going to the jungle with only a vague idea of direction. The third jar awaited me. What of the fourth?

I put on my new outfit and placed the loaner in my bag with the jar of honey. I decided to take what cash I had on hand to buy some breakfast, maybe a coffee. Life on the street was gaining momentum. I found a street food vendor with beans and rice. I added coffee to my order. As I sat and ate from a Styrofoam box with a plastic fork, the absurdity of food in plastic made me pause. Even the coffee in the paper cup with ink and a plastic top made me feel removed from the pulse of what is natural. I was sitting on concrete with cars whizzing by. The square and the church were both stones brought from distant places. I watched a bird checking bits on the ground. I slid my nearly empty container a meter or so away and watched to see if the bird would find it.

The bird was like everyone else, just trying to survive. It occurred to me that only the most aggressive could survive here. Even the top of our proverbial food chain struggled with disease as a result of our technology. I thought of Leah and Ben hustling to scratch out a living. It strengthened my resolve. I passed by the honey vendor on my way to the street. An older woman now manned the shop. There was no way that she was the honey thief. She was just trying to stay alive another day. I fought back the urge to knock the cart over or to say something.

I knew the way. I didn't need to retrace my steps to the cemetery. I didn't need to follow the stream. My sense of direction came from my experience as a bee. I looked up to see the balcony of flowers. I remembered them as glowing and translucent. My eyes saw them as red and orange. I knew that there was a park with flowers in regimented rows up the street. The rows made visits very efficient. I could smell the flowering trees at the far edge of the park. I took off my sandals when I walked on the grass. The blades tickled my feet at first, and then the feel of the grass unfolded unseen mysteries. I could feel the remnants of irrigation and the evenness of fresh mowing. They vibrated with traffic, and I could feel that traffic to my right was much heavier than ahead. The air carried the smell of rain, reminding me of the jungle. The sun warmed the scents of the city.

Ahead were more stone buildings than apartments with businesses. Flowers were gathered together on balconies or in pots. I remembered that this area didn't offer much to the bees. The concrete was warm to the touch but didn't hold any interesting stories. The sandals provided relief. A bus passed by, and I didn't even consider it.

I didn't have to look to know when the city transitioned to homes. I could feel the change. It smelled different, and the flow of traffic was no longer a continuous drone. I was able to fly over walls and through spaces when I took this path before. Now, I had to be a little creative to negotiate the obstacles that ground dwellers face. A few dead ends and some circumnavigating brought me to the city wall. I found a street that had been bored through. On the other side, homes lined the road. At a bridge, I stopped. I smelled the water. It had come from the jungle. I knew I needed to head more to my left.

I walked barefoot up the stream. The water was cool. A bit of a shock when I first stepped in, but it became a welcome reminder. Grasses grew on the banks of the stream. Fences on both sides kept the path obvious. Shrubs and then trees lined the sides. Finally, the jungle.

There was a very small pool around the spring that produced the water. The sunlight danced across the surface. Birds flew from branch to branch above the water. Tree roots surrounded the pool, protecting it from eroding. The hive was close. If I closed my eyes and listened carefully, I could hear the hum. I didn't need a map from here.

Before I found the hive, the bees found me. They flew and landed on my head and shoulders. I held out my palm, and the bees would dance, wiggling back and forth. I knew the dance. They were directing me to the hive. I found the hollowed trunk where the queen and the swarm lived. I saw how it was possible to climb another downed branch and reach into the hive. Part of the old trunk had collapsed leaving a hole down into the hive. The fallen trunk created a perfect bench to sit on. I reached into the bag and brought out the jar of honey. It had been stolen from the hive. I opened it and set it beside me. Bees flew into the jar to taste the honey and harvest it back. I sat and watched the bees come and go. They would fly around me and land on my head or shoulders, greeting me and welcoming me back.

I realized that the hive could be protected from thieves and weather. I hummed as I thought about it. I moved slowly and found a round stone about the size of a softball. I climbed the broken branch to the top of the hive. I stopped and hummed a bit louder. I wedged the stone into the hole in the trunk. I made sure that nobody was injured when the stone descended into the hole. I took a second stone and gently tapped the first into place, securing and sealing the hive from the weather. The bees all came out to watch when I tapped the stone down. They clung to my clothes and hair. They stayed clear of my hands and the stone. Once in place, they would fly down to inspect my work. I gathered several more stones and gently placed them, capping the hole. Then, I summoned all the strength I had and pushed the branch to the side. I rolled it several times and heard it crash, splintering into pieces.

The hive would be safe from thieves, predators, and rain.

I sat on the ground in front of the hive, bees circling me. I could hear the queen. Gratitude in her heart. I could feel the love. It warmed me deeply. A tear dropped to my cheek. Two bees carried it to the hive. I waited until the jar was empty and then put it back in my bag.

I knew my way to the pool. Not from any remembered map, but another part of me was familiar. I felt strength and confidence rise in me. I moved slowly through the jungle. It was thick with growth. I could sense where animals or men had passed through and followed the paths they made. It afforded me the ability to smell the jungle again. There was a sense of coming home, a welcoming that rustled through the leaves. I took my sandals off and let the earth touch my feet. The earth molded itself to my passing. Shortly, I was at the familiar pool. On its edge was the jar and a wooden plate with bread and fruit. I sat at the edge and watched. I could see the door, and it was closed. The wood fire oven was barely smoking. My eyes were slightly unfocused as I watched for movement. Ants marched across the leaves that covered the dirt and then climbed to the trees. Birds alighted on the mossy edges to drink or bathe. I could hear the slithering of a snake or a lizard off to my right. I was safe.

The bread and fruit were a welcome treat. I dipped the jar, third jar, into the pool and drank. I set the bag with the clothes and empty honey jar closer to the door. I could feel the jungle calling to me.

I looked around, and a path leading into the jungle drew me in. I walked the path, trusting where it was leading me. The further in I went, the more my senses awakened. The earth touching my feet and the heaviness of the air fed my desire to go deeper. I began to hear the forest like I had as a jaguar.

Dense trees opened up to a stream that was rushing from the hillside. It was wide enough that the bending of the trees still allowed sunlight to sprinkle the earth. Where it touched, orchids bloomed. Part of me looked past the brilliant pinks and whites to see the translucent shimmer that would seduce the next bee to pass by. I followed the stream until I came to a set of falls. The mist from the falling water painted rainbow arcs across the pool. Against the hill stood an ancient tree overlooking it all.

Such a beautiful spot; I sat nestled in its roots, leaning against the trunk. The feel of the tree bark was familiar. I watched and listened to be sure I was safe. The jungle began to whisper again. "Welcome home." The water lapped at the edges, burbling the same.

The bark of the tree gave gently to my weight. I was aware of it touching my back. I had the sense of the tree being aware of me touching its bark. The awareness of insects climbing and the breeze blowing above. Vines wrapped and clung, climbing to the sky. Birds rested in the branches. I could feel all of it.

I could sense all of this without thought. All sense of time evaporated. I am the pillar of the forest. I reach between earth and sky. I breathe with the light. Inhale in the daylight and exhale in the darkness.

I am a tree.

Chapter Sixteen

There is a sense of something larger. A continuity. Words fail to adequately express the entirety of the experience. There is only now, the present. In the present, I am still the seed that fell to the ground, carried by a bird, and then washed down a stream before coming to land here. In the present, I am still the sprout that breached the bed of decaying leaves on the jungle floor. I am the sapling that struggled to find light beneath the canopy of more mature trees. Their roots sustained me by passing water and encouragement. We are connected.

If my trunk were bored to count my rings, I would still be experiencing every ring. I am experiencing every flood, every drought even now. I feel every boring insect that breached my bark and every bird that nested in my branches. I am every leaf still catching sunlight and every leaf that has fallen. I am the seed growing, awaiting it's time to fall or be carried away. I am the log that will fall under the weight of the vines girdling my trunk. I am the decomposed wood that is eaten by termites and beetles.

I experience all of my life in every moment. In my heartwood, I am the tree that produced my seed and the trees my seeds will produce.

There is a song that is sung by the jungle. I feel the rhythms of the song in the breeze and in my roots. I have no voice of my own. I have no lyrics to sing. Together with the monkeys and birds, the streams and the rain, the leaves and the breeze, we sing. It is not a song of words. It is the song of life. We breathe our songs into the spaces between us, binding us together.

Together, our voices reveal without prejudice. What is heard is real. The song carries the sounds and scents of life and death in its melody. The smell of new death cannot be forged or hidden. Males and females cannot conceal their hormones and pheromones. Territories are marked and re-marked indelibly by their keepers. The heat of the day and the coolness of the evening are the refrains between verses. The humidity and the rain are a subtext to the melody. The song requires no interpretation, and everything is listening.

I felt a bird land on my limb. I could feel its tiny feet grasping the twig. As the bird moved, the twig shook and swayed. It is a small bird; I can tell by its feet and movement. The tree has never seen a bird, only felt them come and go. My human mind holds an image of a bird. A sense of curiosity takes hold. Just as I have never experienced life as a tree, the tree has never experienced life through eyes, ears, or smells.

I gently open my eyes to see a brilliant yellow bird on a twig. A sense of wonder races through the trunk and branches. I feel it. In our collaboration, the tree is experiencing life through me as I experience life as a tree.

I let my body draw in a deep breath. It is the first. With the breath comes the smells of the jungle — too many to attempt to identify. Then sound. I feel the roots of the tree microscopically vibrate, and the roots of the plants around us do the same.

I look around and see the stream and pond. I am used to seeing; the tree isn't. My eyes are moving too fast. I close them and start again. I feel the bird, and now another bird is sitting on the twig. I gently open my eyes to see both birds. The association between the feet gripping the twig and the bird now coalesces. I close my eyes and feel the mist from the water hitting the rocks beneath us. I open my eyes to the mist and the pool. I feel the "aha" and the vibration in the roots. And I close my eyes again. I feel the sunlight on one side of my trunk and the coolness of shade on the other. I open my eyes and see the transition. Leaves confirm the warmth of the sun and the coolness of the shade.

A rustling of the leaves nearby reveals beetles rummaging. I close my eyes again, hold the image of leaves and beetles, and smell the essence of the jungle floor. The tree responds with a sense of living acknowledgment, a knowing that one day we will be lying on the soil, decomposing and being rendered by insects. The burble and flow of the stream is interrupted by almost silent paws. A jaguar surveys the oasis and jumps up into the tree. It comes to rest on a branch overlooking the pool. I watch motionless. The tree responds with familiarity, having felt the jaguar before. My body has a sense of awe when seeing the jaguar. The tree senses my awe, and curiosity arises.

My eyes close, and I let myself remember. At first, it is confusing to the tree. There is no sense of the past. The image in my mind doesn't translate. I look at the jaguar and let the memory become an experience. I am, again, the jaguar. I feel the tree reaching into my senses as I am feeling the jaguar in me. We sense the forest differently now. We are aware of the danger and of food. Each scent is not just a life-giving way to life; it is an opportunity to eat. Smell isn't just a revelation of what is; it is also how life is sustained. As the jaguar, I hear the song of the forest. The song alerts us to our surroundings. It sings of opportunities and dangers. It welcomes us. The tree feels the call of the jungle in a different way than ever before.

A rustling of the leaves. I gently open my eyes to see a small peccary foraging near the tree. He is unaware of the jaguar. The jaguar is very aware of the peccary. The song of the jungle includes the measured breath of the jaguar and the rustling of the leaves. The peccary comes close to the tree, and the jaguar drops. We watch the brief struggle before the peccary submits. The sound of the struggle is now part of the song of the jungle. The smell of fear weaves itself into the song. Blood drips to the leaves, changing the sound. There is neither a sense of victory nor lament. A life is surrendered, and another continues. Then, a stillness descends. The hunter carries his conquest to a safer space to eat. We sense him leaping to a branch in another tree.

A bird grasps an extended twig, and I let my eyes be drawn up to yellow and orange. The tree has no memory of the vision of the birds before and again vibrates with the excitement of seeing a bird for the first time. The sound of another bird calling catches our attention, and I look to see brilliant red with the voice of an angel. The tree has no experience with hearing. I can feel the confusion.

"Vibration," I hold in my mind. The tree senses when the earth vibrates; it feels the force of the water against its bark when the stream floods. There is a vibration felt by the leaves in the breeze. Thunder announces the rain by shaking the jungle. This is yet another vibration that is new and wonderful.

I look to the canopy above. Between the leaves, the sky. Against the sky, clouds and birds flying. I see bromeliads blooming. I remember how the bees see the flowers, translucent and vibrant, and hold the image in my mind. The tree knows only the vines that climb and attach themselves to our bark. It knows the weight of the vines weighing against its branches. The image brings a new perspective. Ants crawling up the trunk find refuge in the blossoms. I look around and realize how much life relies on the tree. I let gratitude fill my heart.

To my surprise, the tree knows gratitude. It feels gratitude differently. I know gratitude as an emotion. The tree feels gratitude when its roots are wet. It feels the relief and gratitude of a cloud passing over in the heat of the midday sun. The tree expresses its gratitude by sharing with the trees around it. It holds tight to the roots of its neighbors so that they all stand against wind and storms. The binding of the roots holds water and earth for new trees to be established.

When the heat of the day cools to the evening, there is a shift, like a sigh. The exhale to the nocturnal world begins.

The floor of the jungle grows dark long before the sun sets. Steam rises from the earth as the damp, cool air descends. The air is thicker, and the organic, earthy smell it carries is thicker, too. The tree feels the pull of the sun toward the horizon. The leaves at the top of the canopy bask in the changing light. I can feel their warmth when the sun still kisses them before they say good night. I can feel the coolness on the undersides as the weight of the evening settles.

Some birds are bedding down for the night. Their sweet calls to the sun echo and are repeated in a sing-song mantra of hope for the sun's return. Other birds swiftly hunt for the flying insects the cooler air brings out. In the gray area between the day and the night, the hunter and the hunted stalk and evade each other. The world of color acquiesces to the world of sensation. Not devoid of life but awakened in a different way. The tree doesn't sleep but does draw into itself. The movement of birds or monkeys in the branches disappears. Even the flow of insects crawling on the bark slows. The weight of the vines remains. Leaves no longer using the sunlight to support the tree rest limply in the breeze.

Even in the seeming stillness of the night, life and death still dance together. Under the watchful stars, the drama of survival takes the stage. The cover of darkness is a myth. The song is woven together by night sounds and rests between breaths.

The jaguar walks with the night. I feel him surveying his territory. The trees all feel the jaguar. He walks softly, and he knows the movements of the creatures that are his prey. The jungle gives way to him as he moves. The jaguar knows the rhythm of the jungle, and his own heart beats in time.

I allow myself to breathe into the song of the jungle. I relax, letting go of all that I know and feel. I find myself at home here. It is the heartbeat of the earth, the rhythm of life, the song of the jungle, a lullaby that washes over me. I am already a part of it.

The tree knows all this without knowing. It rests without resting. This simplicity of existence intrigues me. Life integrates itself into an exquisite interplay of extremes. Everything has its season indelibly recorded in the core. Seasons are never forgotten. They are a living depth to the moment in which we are alive.

I reflect on my own experiences, conveniently stored away as memories. My cognition of time creates the sense that, somehow, the past is finished and over. I see how, like the tree, I am still living out what could be called my past.

Leah is no longer with me, but her impact is a ring at my center that continues into the present. Less tangible is the realization that all of this is also a ring in the making, folding into the current moment.

At first, I thought that my perceptions were somehow more complex and advanced due to my cognition. I begin to realize the honesty and transparency the tree is revealing. I let go of the past and recognize the rings that surround my heartwood. The past is no longer dead but alive in the moment and for every moment.

The jaguar returns in the cover of night to rest in the branches above my human body. He is unconcerned with the form sitting at the base of the tree. We feel the warmth of his body against our bark. If I focus carefully, I feel the beating of his heart. His belly is full, and he is unconcerned with the movements around us. He listens for danger instead of food, knowing that the jungle will alert him if danger comes close. He simply needs to listen. His eyes close; he doesn't need them to feel the stars or the gentle breeze. A brave ant crawls across his tail, only to be flung to the earth as a reward for his bravery.

The ant now needs to be careful and avoid the nocturnal predators awaiting him. He skirts the water's edge before finding the scent of a familiar trail to the nest. The coolness of the stream pulls the heat from the air, cooling the breeze. It carries with it the scents of the night surrounding the pool.

The morning unfolds itself to the leaves in the canopy. Sunlight brews the phytochemicals in the leaves, sending an awakening influx to the rest of the tree. The trunk stands a little firmer and draws more water from the roots. The surrounding plants awaken to the subtle change and begin to unfurl their blossoms and leaves. Birds begin to welcome the sun with sounds of gratitude and relief. They sunbathe at the highest levels before flying down again in search of breakfast.

The sun plays against the surface of the pool, sending snippets of sunlight to the trunks of nearby trees and the leaves of the earthbound plants. Even the jaguar is highlighted in the sun. He feels the sprinkles of warmth and relaxes into the branch. The sounds of daylight now surround us. The tree is curious to hear through me as insects fly past. Even the stream sounds different. In the distance, I hear a thumping sound. It is regular, with pauses. I cannot conceive its origination; it simply contributes to the melody of the song.

My body feels a different song. I could sit as the tree from seedling to decay, experiencing every moment with fascination. My body pulls me to another awareness. The sunlight started the life processes of the tree; my body needed movement and food.

I experienced what could be called a separation from the tree. But the tree shows me a different reality. It experiences the separation of leaves that drop to the earth but never feels separate. The leaves continue but in different forms. They are still integrally connected despite the apparent distance. Like a leaf or a branch that is no longer physically connected to the trunk, I am still part of the tree. I will always be part of the tree, and the tree will always be a part of me.

I come into my body and take a breath; it is the first. My movement is slight. The jaguar takes notice before resting heavily back into his perch. Perhaps, like the tree, he senses me as a jaguar; I am no danger.

I look with my eyes to see water, colors, and movement. Then, I close my eyes to let the experience blossom with sound and smells. In the moment, there are no thoughts; they are unnecessary. I feel the aliveness of the earth and the life that springs from it. Water takes on a new sense. I drink in its sound and smell. It revives me as if I were actually drinking from the stream. Unconsciously, I dip my hand and let its liquid life spill across my lips.

I smell the plants near me before I look to see their colors. I hear the birds call and fly past me before I look to see their colors. I look at the flowers before letting my vision see them as the bees do, in translucent glory. At my feet, smooth round seeds lay waiting in the rocks. I pick a few up and put them in my pocket. The thumping sound again calls my attention to its part of the song. Strangely, it sounds like a beacon calling me. I rise to walk toward the sound, my path winding along the stream back to the pool. I already know the way.

As I walk, I can feel my way past the obstacles. The hill invites me to climb before the water crashes over rocks. The water reveals stones that take me past thorns. The jungle is my guide, and I am learning to trust it. In a moment of weakness, I deviate from the wet stone set before me and choose a different route across a fallen log, only to find a dead end — beautiful and impassable. Mossy stones hold orchids as water flowing down the embankment makes any passage impassable. The orchids are safe from any traffic or danger. They delight in the spa of the moss and the spackled shade. I pause to marvel at their sacred beauty before recognizing that the jungle is a much better guide than I am.

The thumping stops. It is no longer a necessary beacon. My guide will take me to where I am supposed to be. A path leads me away from the water and through a thick grove of trees. The thumping starts again just as I begin to see the pool outside the wall. The thumping stops. A man and woman sit just outside the wooden door. They are looking at me before I see them. He has a stone the size of his head, and he is smashing flax leaves to release their fibers. The woman sits beside him, rolling the fresh fibers between her fingers to make a thread. I can smell the smoke from the wood stove rolling over the roof and the wall.

Both nod in acknowledgment and smile. His glance shifts to a wooden bowl of rice and beans sitting on the edge of the pool — a welcome sight. The woman disappears through the door and returns with a mug of warm, thick brown liquid. She hands it to me as I get closer. She notices my clothes and smiles, nodding in approval. I sit at the edge of the pool and cannot resist letting my feet slide into the water. The mug has a warm, bittersweet taste that hugs my throat as I drink. The beans and rice taste equally earthy; their warmth and bulk are welcomed by my body.

I am becoming more familiar. I can see more herbs and plants growing in the outcroppings of the stones. Other paths discretely connect the pool to the jungle so that its inhabitants can share in its bounty. Stones strategically lead to a hammock still hanging between trees overlooking the pool. There is an entry where one could bathe, sitting on rocks rather than mud. Even the clearing where the two resumes working has moss and plants between the stones that make up a casual sitting area. They work together in silence. The thumping of the stone keeps time with the threading and rolling of the strands. I watch, mesmerized by the efficiency of motion, before it occurs to me that I could help.

I stand back up and slide my feet back into my sandals. Empty bowl in hand, I approach and ask, "Can I help?" They both look up and smile at me.

"We're almost finished," he says. He stops for a minute and looks me in the eye. "The ocean calls. Would you like to come with me?" he asks. He breaks our gaze and looks at the last jar, now sitting at his feet, then meets my gaze again.

I had forgotten about the last jar. There was no hesitation. "Yes."

"Then rest; we'll leave in a while," he says, going back to his work.

The thumping of the stone against the log, releasing the fibers, became the background to the melody of the jungle. I trace the stones to the hammock and rest quietly. It was then that my mind sprouted thoughts. The ocean, the last jar, a journey — everything was a mystery. My mind tried to unwind the puzzle. In the midst of the unknown, the mind seeks out fear like a moth to a flame.

There was no way to know what was about to happen. My body now accepted the void of unknowing. My mind perseverates on the potential danger. I had been drawn out of my shell of safety and security. Leah challenged me to live beyond my expectations. As a jaguar, the jungle was my eyes and ears. It called to me. Its song drew me close and whispered when food was close and warned me of danger.

The hive. The queen held me in love. Every flower tasted like love. The tree lived all its life in every moment, always knowing the inevitable, welcoming its place in the world.

In contrast, my mind is only concerned with itself. The musings of an insecure mind remind me of fallen leaves rendered stiff and lifeless by fungus and time. Eventually, these thoughts will decay into compost, from which life begins anew.

A bee rested on my shoulder. We sat together. The tree held the hammock. The hammock held me. I held the bee. I wouldn't have been surprised if a jaguar were lurking nearby, watching and listening. The melody of the jungle became more interesting than my thoughts. The sing-song of birds played against the breeze. The quiet of the pool had ripples from the drips coming off the moss. The bee heard the call of flowers adorning the pool and took flight to find them. The hammock groaned as the tree swayed in the breeze. The thumping stopped.

I looked. The woman held a ball of twine in her hand. She looked at him with a questioning gaze. He nodded, and the ball was dropped into the bag beside him. He added a jar to the bag. They both looked over at me.

"It's time," he said.

Chapter Seventeen

I dismounted from the hammock and started down the stone path. They disappeared into the door and reappeared by the time I reached the clearing. They layed out our provisions for the trip. We would both be carrying shoulder bags. A simple hammock wrapped itself around a change of clothes and a few sundries. The ends were then drawn together with a twist, and the whole thing became a sling pack that draped over my shoulder. My bag had the last jar and a bottle of water. There was a small bag of rice and beans, leaving plenty of space for anything else we would need on the trip.

We geared up with our slings and bags. The lady took a step toward me, her face a radiant blossom. She placed a hand on my chest and smiled. Then she took my hands in hers, still smiling.

"I enjoyed your visit, especially when you came as a bee," she said, laughing.

"Thank you for your hospitality and kindness," I replied, smiling back, not quite sure what was appropriate at this moment.

She turned to him, and they embraced like old friends do. As she pulled back, they simply let their foreheads touch just above the brow line. They stood, heads bowed and touching for a moment. I felt the forest vibrate. Then stillness. The song of the jungle paused in the briefest of ways. It was a moment of recognition that could easily be missed but was now reverberating in the melody. The stillness unfolded between them, filled with the unspoken. Nothing needed to be said. Both smiled and looked at me.

Bewildered by the experience, I must have been staring. It took a minute to register that they were looking at me, jolting me back into my body. My head snapped slightly, and my eyes blinked. I took a deep breath; it felt like a first.

He motioned with a nod toward the path by the pool. I followed behind. I didn't need to look back to know she watched us disappear into the jungle. I could feel her watching. I knew that other things were watching. I could hear them in the song; their eyes were mixed into the melody. And now, a man I only know as a "friend" and I was part of the song too.

A thought interrupted my listening to the jungle song. "I must be crazy," I could hear myself thinking. "I have no idea where we are headed and what will happen when we get there. I don't have money, a phone, or even identification." I stopped walking. He noticed and stopped without looking back.

"You can stop this madness now and go back to the apartment, go back to the life you know. That is the smart thing to do. That is the safe thing to do."

I felt a hush and heaviness in the air around me. I was glad he wasn't looking. I would have run if he were. Instead, my hand dropped into the bag, and felt the jar. Without words, there was a curiosity. "Don't you want to know?" an urge deep inside my gut. "What if you die?" I heard myself recoil at the idea. "What if I don't?"

I stood still. I should say, I stood in stillness. "This is madness; you will die," it was my voice. Then I remembered the tree. I was dead already and alive already. "Maybe there is a part of me that needs to die," I thought, "so that I can be alive." The voice went quiet.

I thought about looking back, then chose to take the next step. Then the next, and the next. He was moving ahead of me. He was adept and agile, moving through the trees and brush. I was slower and had to work to keep up. The struggle fired my passion. The harder I worked, the further away the thoughts of stopping became. It was obvious I wouldn't be able to keep this effort for a long time. I stopped watching to learn his secret. His movements appeared effortless. He could see steps ahead. It was a dance. By the time his foot reached the ground, he was prepared for the next and the next. I stumbled to find my step every time. I tried thinking about what I should do, where I should put my feet, and where I should grab. It was more exhausting. Then I listened. I could hear a rhythm. Steps syncopated with movement. The movement became the propulsion for motion. Motion became the collaboration of my body and everything around me. The collaboration was a silent awareness of the fluid interaction. Then, the path was obvious, and my progress was effortless.

***

We stayed close to the water. The stones were slippery with green, slimy moss, inhibiting any traction. The water was cool on my feet and felt good. Any deviation from the water meant climbing through the brush and slipping on the mud. Whenever he stopped for a moment, there was a harvesting of fruits or greens. Occasionally, he would kick the earth and use a stick to produce a root. Each prize was carefully inspected and placed into his bag.

He was keeping an eye on me. I was slowing down. My heart was beating; sweat ran freely down my face and body. I was tired; really, I was exhausted. There was something organically empowering about the fatigue. We stopped to rest. His denim-blue eyes watched me as my chest heaved with gratitude for the moment. He handed me a large fruit the size of a child's football. I looked at it and back at him. He smiled and held out his hand. I handed the fruit back. He pounded it against a rock, rotating it slightly between strikes until it broke in half. Dark brown seeds encased in liquid flesh peeked out of the cracks. He split it in half, then peeled a seed and put it in his mouth.

I peeled one off for myself. The flesh was sweet and stuck to the seeds. I had to use my tongue and teeth to peel the seed away. At first, I thought that it would take a thousand seeds to make any kind of meal, but soon, I could feel my body absorbing, and the feeling of hunger dissipated. We finished the first and ate a second. He dipped a jar in the water and drank. I did the same.

"Cacao," he said. "It will help if you feel tired." He handed me several small balls the size of a large marble. "Coffee beans," he added. The effect of the caffeine began to take hold, and I felt energized and ready to try again.

"We are heading this way," he said, pointing behind him. Everything in that direction looked uphill. "Don't worry; it gets easier."

The look of relief on my face was obvious. In the moment of pause, I began to have questions. I watched as he dipped a bandana into the water and washed his face. It didn't feel like the right time to ask.

Behind me, in a place that felt like a million miles away, was a computer, an apartment, and a warm shower. Would I ever go back? I felt like I already knew the answer. Months ago, my life had a definite direction. I was prepared to follow the prescribed recipe for a good life. Something diverted my path. The protocol was no longer practical. The expected outcome no longer assured happiness and fulfillment. This new path promised neither. Now, I was just trying to keep up, scrambling toward the unknown.

Chapter Eighteen

He tied the bandana around his neck and adjusted himself on the large stone where he sat. His eyes closed. I followed suit, grateful for a moment without exertion.

The sound of water engulfed me immediately, and the smell of earth and leaves filled my senses. I had stopped listening in my exertion, but the melody of the jungle was welcoming. It had a sweetness that brought me comfort. The leaves rustled high above, and birdsongs harmonized in the air. Life. Everything was alive to me again. I took a deep breath. Every breath felt like the first. Each breath was life, and each exhale was death. I was born and dying in each moment. The realization landed hard in my gut, and my body stiffened. He noticed the change in me, and for him, it was the signal to move again. For me, it was a door opening and closing at the same time. It was time to move.

The stream we were following grew smaller and smaller. The stones on the bank were dry, and it was easy to negotiate a path from stone to stone. The canopy raised higher above us, and the thickness of the forest floor began to thin. It was now possible to walk with only minor obstacles to detour our progress.

The song of the forest now included the crunching of leaves beneath our feet, along with the humid air hanging below the canopy, perfumed by the bromeliads basking in the speckles of sunlight. I could hear something else moving, causing the leaves to shuffle. I felt no fear — perhaps because the sounds were becoming familiar or maybe because he was just a few meters ahead of me.

The climb through the jungle required all my focus and concentration. Now, as our progress became simpler, I realized how easily I could be distracted. I had to keep looking to see where he was and ensure I was following. The lesson from the peccary returned to me: it was a lesson I could accept easily now or with some difficulty later, I assumed.

Ahead of me, he made constant progress. He would pause when I did, but just far enough ahead that conversation would be difficult. When I rested, I looked around and was amazed at how much my surroundings had changed. The sides of the stream were now buffeted by grasses, and sunlight danced carelessly on the ripples of the water. The soil on the banks baked dry yet spongy enough to hold our footprints, felt solid beneath me. Butterflies flitted along our path as if the parting of the thicker grasses would reveal pristine new sources of nectar. Our footsteps now no longer broke down what had settled to the dirt; instead, life sprang back every time our foot lifted.

He had taken note too. He stopped. Standing beside him, I watched as he looked in the direction of the sun, looming heavier in the sky. Clouds moved with purpose as soon as they peeked over the ridge. Wisps betrayed the direction of higher winds. We were on the edge of a gentle bowl carved out by eons of breezes sent down from heights. Just over the edge of the bowl was a protected respite from the winds and weather. A few trees added to the protection on the lee side. There was a clearing where we set our bags down. He unwrapped his hammock and carefully unpacked what was rolled inside. I did the same.

"We will rest here for the night," he said. He nodded to his left, where an old tree with a burn scar had a crack below the char. "You will find things to make a fire. We are welcome to use them; just be sure to replace what we used and perhaps add some more."

In a covered space below the black scar was an assortment of dried twigs and leaves. I gathered a handful of each. In the center of the clearing was a bare spot with several flat rocks. Had he not been sitting there, his hands cupped and blowing an ember to life in a nest of hair and leaves, I would have missed it. I set the twigs and leaves into a nested pile in the center of the rocks. I could hear the crackling of the embers catching while he gently set his nest on top of mine. He cupped his hands for protection while the smallest of flames began to devour the kindling. We would need more wood.

I ventured past the rim of the bowl back toward the small stream. I gathered what I could find that was dry, remembering that I would need to replenish the hidden stock. The forest had plenty of wood for our fire; finding what was dry was another story. It took some time and several trips before I was satisfied we'd have enough.

The fire was now alive and consuming everything we fed it. Small chunks of wood became glowing coals. While I was collecting wood, he pulled the roots he'd dug earlier from his bag and washed them in the stream. He set them on the rocks beside the fire.

He fashioned a pot out of a banana leaf, using a wooden bowl to define its shape as he folded and tucked, then bound the pot. He filled it with water and set it on a small flat stone beside the fire. Every few moments, he would rotate the rock and the banana leaf pot so a different side was exposed to the fire. On another leaf, he tore apart the greens of leaves he'd been collecting. He carefully pulled the stems and ripped the leaves into squares. He wrapped everything up and set it close to the fire.

I made sure all of our water containers were full, save for the one last jar. I began to notice subtle signs that this was a known place to rest. Each of the stones for the fire ring had a perfectly level space to set pots. There were worn nubs on the trees where hammock straps had been tied and retied. The hiding spot for kindling ensured there was always dry stock for fires. A few steps to the rim of the bowl, and you could see anyone walking up the hill or the hill beside us.

The smoke from the fire rose to the tops of the trees and was ushered invisibly into the sky. I watched as he hung his hammock perfectly between two trees, protected by the rim of the bowl and still visible to the fire. I did the same, taking note of how to use the weight of the hammock against itself to bind it to the tree.

"Have you been here before?" I asked, startled that words came out of my mouth.

He looked around the clearing and behind the face of the stone that created the rim of the bowl. He nodded his head. "Very possible," he said.

He was seated close enough to the rimstone that he could have leaned back. Beside him was a carved mark in the stone: two lines crossing, making a simple "X" shape. He noticed my eyes looking past him.

"Safe place," he said, pointing to the mark.

"Is that how Shamans know where to stay?" I asked.

Instantly, a smile found his face. "I suppose they could stay here, but most wouldn't."

"Then who?" I asked.

"Travelers like us," he said.

"I thought you were a Shaman," I said.

His smile beamed again. "No, I am not a Shaman."

"But..." My eyes dropped, and my face must have wrinkled. I could feel my eyes moving back and forth as if searching for something. "Then who?"

"I am the one who opened the door," he said. "A Shaman uses his skills and knowledge to affect an outcome." It felt like he was looking right into me. "He prays for the weather or uses herbs to heal the sick. He is the source of wisdom for those who seek it." He paused. "I am not a Shaman."

"Then?"

"You were at the door, so I opened it."

"Why did you open the door? Not once, but twice?" I asked.

"You were seeking solace, peace," he said. Pausing, "It is like this place; it is solace for those who seek it and unseen by those who don't."

"The jars?" I asked.

"You might think of them as doors awaiting you to open them. But they are just jars," he said.

"If you aren't a Shaman, then what are you?" I asked.

"A friend," he said.

"Then," I hesitated. "You're not a priest or teacher or spiritual guide?"

"If I were a guide, there would have to be a destination," he mused.

"There isn't one?"

"Not really." He was smiling again.

He turned the makeshift pot again. It was starting to bubble. He stood and retrieved his bag. He pulled a smaller bag and took a few handfuls of rice and another handful of beans, putting them into the banana leaf pot. Then he covered the pot, tucking the edges in to seal it.

From the edges of the fire, he retrieved the roots. He smashed them into the bottoms of our bowls. The other banana leaf had steamed greens. He mixed them in the bowl before handing me one. The other he held in his hand as he sprinkled something dried over the top. He motioned, and I held my bowl out. When the dried herbs met the wet heat of the greens and tubers, smells exploded.

The simplicity of the meal was surpassed by the perfection of flavors. It was like nothing I had ever tasted. The first bite shocked me with its complexity; the second and third continued to build the intensity.

"This is really good," I said, mumbling with my mouth still chewing.

"Hit the spot," he agreed.

I was watching him. "If you aren't a Shaman or a teacher, how do you live?"

"I'm not sure I understand the question," he looked up.

"Do you have a job?" I asked.

"Oh, I see," he said, wiping the corners of his mouth. "Right now, being your friend is keeping me pretty busy," he joked.

"It's appreciated," I said.

"I don't have a job like you are thinking," he paused. "I think we have different ideas of survival," he said. "I don't have a car, a house, or a mortgage or bills. Those things would require me to have a job."

"How do you survive?" I asked again.

"Just fine," he said. "I don't need those other things. They distract me." He paused again. "Those are human things; I thought you didn't want to be human?"

"That's fair," I said. "I haven't figured out how not to be human, I guess."

"You figured out how to be a jaguar," he reminded me.

"At the time, I had no idea what was happening," I confided. "I drank from the jar completely ignorant of its power."

"How did it feel to be a jaguar?" he asked.

"No fear," I said, trying to remember. "I don't recall everything, and much is beyond my grasp. But I remember that I was not afraid." I let the words land and languish for a moment. "Not even when the dogs were chasing me toward the trap. Or when I could smell the men and their guns. I was very alert, but not afraid."

"You killed a man," he stated simply.

"I did," I said, searching for my emotions. I had forgotten.

"Have you asked yourself why?" He let the question hang in the air between us.

"The girl," I said.

"You killed to protect another," he observed, half asking.

"Yes."

"Did you hesitate to think about the moral implications of killing him?" he asked.

"No."

"Did you think at all?"

"No."

"A teacher might say that you acted solely at the behest of the moment. That the universe used you to set things right," he speculated. "Many believe that only the most powerful Shamans can change themselves. They believe that the Shaman will set things in order." He waited.

"Maybe you are the Shaman," he said.

I laughed at the absurdity of the thought.

"Then it was something else," he said and let that linger as a mystery to the moment. We sat in silence. The sound of the fire surrounded us, and the space opened like an umbrella in the trees.

I took in the sights: the gentle glow of the embers crackling and popping in the fire, the blackened and twisted branches against the sky, and the orange leaves of the trees as they stirred and danced in the wind. I remembered that feeling of being a jaguar. It swept over me again like a cool wave.

"Something else?" I asked, unsure.

"When we don't understand something, we look for a reason," he said. "Not all reasons are tangible, even if we want them to be." He looked at the wind blowing across the tops of the trees protecting us. "Humans want answers and reasons. The wind never asks why it blows."

I took the bowls back to the stream to rinse them out. The bits left in the bottom of the bowl floated in a cloud in the current. I could imagine downstream a beetle or rodent finding the morsel and being amazingly happy and grateful for the feast. I sat at the side of the bank and took my sandals off to soak my feet. The water carried the dirt caked between my toes downstream. The coolness of the water brought a shiver that subsided into resolve. My feet would have to get used to not living a more human life.

The sun would soon be setting below the ridgeline above us. The breeze still blanketing the hillside brought an added coolness to the water. My feet were not ready to carry me back to the clearing, so I sat. The heaviness of death weighed on me. I wanted to resist its reality. Resistance only made it heavier. So much death, and yet I was more alive than I had ever been. I hoped that by letting grief and guilt come, there would be a perceivable sense of order and purpose to death. There wasn't. I couldn't reconcile how Leah dying was somehow made better because I was alive. There was a sense of justice in the death of Roger and the unharmed release of his last victim. Justice rang hollow. Leah would not know justice.

"Life and death are the best of friends," I thought. Before, I had only been concerned with life. Death was an experience to be avoided or at least put off. In my ignorance, I missed that my life was predicated on death. Death was equated with suffering. Suffering was the scourge of existence. My life's work was to alleviate suffering so that people could live. I was awakening to the reality that what I thought was living was just a distraction. Somehow, I knew there had to be more. Leah handed me the key. I just needed to find the door.

My feet were going numb, so I stretched them out along the bank. The warmth from the setting sun gave me a heavy feeling. I thought about curling up right there in my sunny spot and taking a nap. I chuckled that it must be the jaguar in me who wanted to doze. At that moment, his quiet confidence wrapped itself around me. There was no need to figure it all out right now. The babbling of the stream and the rustling of the breeze called me to listen. I stopped listening like a human. I listened like a jaguar. The song on the breeze carried the weather. The stream couldn't cover the movement all around me. Nothing of concern, nothing to cause danger. My body completely rested beside the stream. My mind let go of any shadows of thought. To the ignorant observer, I was napping. Really, I was more alive than I had ever been before.

In the melody, the smell of flowers was followed by the familiar humming of wings visiting lovers. A splash of indescribable translucent color flooded my inner vision.

Then love. I listened to the sound of bees and butterflies — love. Flowers budding and bursting with nectar and buds waiting to be discovered — love. I took a deep breath — love. It was the first.

I remembered the seeds that I had gathered by the tree. I pulled one from my pocket and pushed it into the mud next to the stream. A sense of the continuity of life was real. The seed was inert and dead by all reasonable indications. Life would spring from it. Not just any life, but the lives of the seeds before it and the promise of life from seeds it would grow. They also carried the knowledge of death, that they someday would succumb to the elements and be reconciled to the earth.

The day was dimming. My feet would have to find comfort in my hammock. I walked back to find my friend sitting quietly by the small fire. Its light illuminated his face and cast a long shadow onto the stones behind him.

I sat on a stone near the fire and made myself comfortable. We watched the fire. I had questions — some I knew, some I didn't know yet. He was comfortable in silence, watching the fire. I wasn't.

"The last jar," I said finally.

"Yes," he responded.

"You seem to have a sense of it, not like the others," I said.

"When I held your last jar, it had the call of the ocean," he said. "Do you know what will happen?"

"No."

"That is why we are going to the ocean."

"Yes."

"After the last jar, what will happen?"

"Another door will open; it always does."

"Do you know what that door is?" I asked.

"No."

"Can I ask a personal question?" I asked, feeling like my window of opportunity was closing.

"Sure," he said.

"Did you go through this?"

"Different," he said.

"Different?" I echoed.

"And the same," he said. "Change is changing. A tadpole turns into a frog, and a caterpillar into a butterfly. Both change, but differently."

"You've watched others change?" I asked.

"Yes."

"Do you know if I will be a frog or a butterfly?" I asked jokingly.

"No, that's part of the mystery of it. But afterward, you will be different than when you started."

"I'm already different."

"But you could go back and forget."

"After the last jar?"

"I doubt it."

He put a few small pieces of wood on the fire and poked the coals. The fire sprang to life and fervently devoured the new fuel. He stared into the fire, lost in thought. Darkness was descending into the clearing. The breeze was now a whisper. I could hear the stream in the distance. I remembered how the tree sensed the change in the jungle when the sun went down. I began to listen carefully for the shift. It didn't take long before the birds went quiet, save for the sound of a few birds flying to safety. The shift came with a change in smells. Even the smoke had a noticeable shift in essence. The heat of the sun had cooked anything on the dirt. Evening brought a cool dampness that gently devoured what was dry. Insects looking for a host found us more easily. The hammock was a welcome refuge.

Before he went to his hammock, he pushed the coals of the fire around. He found a brilliant glowing charcoal that he moved over to the dirt. It was the size of a marble. He lifted a cord with a pendant from around his neck and carefully pried it into two halves. He lined each half with fresh moss and carefully seated the coal in the middle. He hung the pendant from a nub on the tree by his hammock, then settled in.

In a different world, the sounds of nightlife would have burdened the air. The evening would have been thick with voices, engines, and music. The smell of fried food would have pervasively overwhelmed anything else. Tonight, the air was unburdened. The only song was Life Around Us. In the simplicity of the moment, I looked for clarity. I realized the search was a distraction and settled, awaiting rest and sleep.

Movement in the night awoke me from my slumber. I waited silently, listening. There was much to listen to. The subtlest breeze in the darkness was filled with sound. The tree groaned when I shifted my weight. I decided to answer the call of nature and walked out past the stones that shielded us from the wind. He was lying there against the rim of the bowl, just looking at the stars. I headed off toward the cover of trees to do my business.

As I stood there, letting my bladder empty, I looked up. The sky was filled with stars. Away from the lights of the city, the brilliance was incredible. I could see the Milky Way banded across the sky.

Only hours ago, I had searched for clarity only to find it in the sky. Humility and awe were the only words I could use to describe the moment. If I had ears that could hear it, I was sure that the universe was singing. Not to me, but to the spectacle and marvel that it is. To say that I had a place in the universe was like a grain of sand proclaiming it owned the beach. I stood transfixed, looking up, moved by something so simple that it was casually forgotten. I took a deep breath. I felt alive in yet another and different way. I thought about staying there, staring into greatness. My body was still recovering from a long day, and anticipated another tomorrow. I said good night to the sky.

As I passed by, I could hear him breathing quietly. In reverence, I looked away as if that would provide him with privacy for his moment with the stars. I never heard him return to his hammock. In mine, I found clarity unexpectedly in silence. Clarity graced me with rest.

I woke to the crackle of the fire. He was sitting next to small flames. He had fashioned another pot out of a banana leaf, and it was full of water and warming by the fire. Like the night before, he turned it occasionally. He pulled open the leaf pot from the night before and set it beside the other. Overnight, the rice and beans had hydrated into breakfast. From his bag, he pulled some herbs and rubbed them between his hands. I could smell them release their aroma. He tossed them into the rice and beans. From yet another bag, he measured a powder into awaiting cups, then poured the warm water into each one.

I woke slowly, feeling each sense awaken to my surroundings. My stomach growled. I found a place on a stone near the fire and let my body take stock of what was needed. I held the cup in my hands. I blew across the top, anticipating its heat. I smelled it and it wasn't coffee. I had no idea, but it tasted smooth and bitterish. I felt a wash of heat and energy fill my body.

When I finally opened my eyes. I must have radiated my pleasure. He smiled and said, "You're welcome."

We sat and ate, drinking in the warmth of the morning. He carefully picked through the coals of the fire and found another charcoal bead. With precision, he prepared it and locked it into his locket, replacing it around his neck.

"For later," he said, tapping the locket.

We packed our bags. After checking to ensure the dry stash was ready for the next traveler, we extinguished the fire and stood at the rim.

"Do you know which way we are headed?" he asked.

I pointed in the general direction we had traveled. He smiled.

"We are heading toward that peak in the distance." It was a bit to the right of where I had pointed before. "There is a place to stay before we reach the mountain. That is where we'll spend the night."

I nodded in understanding. "You lead," he said.

"Is there anything I should know or be aware of?" I asked.

He was quiet for a moment. "Feel your way there," he replied. "Everything else will fall into place."

It is an entirely different mindset to lead rather than follow. Nothing inside me wanted to take the lead. I would

have been entirely happy to follow along. I was sure there
was a reason for this change.

Chapter Nineteen

The first hour or so was easy. We hugged close to the trees that climbed up the hill. Our path was unimpeded by undergrowth. There was a casual trail that made navigation simple, and it was easy to keep heading toward the mountain. We followed the groove set by animals, both feral and domestic. When we crested the top, everything changed. The roll of the hills gave way to ravines and small streams. I kept to the easier path until it was obvious that we had to head back down and into the trees.

I sat down to rest and weigh my options. He sat next to me, and we ate a mango that he had picked while we walked.

"Wisdom?" I asked.

He laughed. "What are you asking?"

"Which way to go?" I replied.

"Do you want to know which way I would go? Or which way we should go? Or which way is the right way?" he asked back.

"I'd take any," I laughed.

"Before I answer, which way are you considering?" I pointed to a break in the tree line ahead.

"Then let's go that way," he said.

"Which is it?" I looked at him, noticing a screw in his face. "I mean, is that the way you would go?"

"It is the way we should go; the rest doesn't matter," he said. I rolled my eyes, and he laughed.

"Oh," he said. "One more thing: there's no McDonald's at the end of the trail, so we'll need to gather as we go."

"Most of this is new to me; we may go hungry," I said.

"I'll help," he assured me. "It doesn't take long to get a feel for what you can eat."

In front of us was the jungle, its trees rising high off the ground and casting deep shadows, making passage simple. There was a barrier between us and the jungle. A violent tangle of barbs and bushes. Farmers and ranchers had worked diligently to hold back the depths of the jungle; they needed open spaces to grow grasses for grazing livestock. The demilitarized zone was manned by the most effective infantry imaginable. No shower of bullets could clear a path through. Small animals used the safety of the thicket to escape predators and scour low branches for sun-kissed morsels.

We walked the edge, looking for an access point. We eventually spotted a gathering of huge stones just inside the barrier. I surmised that if we could make it to the stones, we could either climb over or skirt around into the more forgiving older trees. I found some broken stems hanging. When I pushed them aside, I discovered a hole. It wasn't a hole that men would normally use; it was big enough that we could crawl toward the stones.

He looked in and then looked at me. "There isn't much room if something lands on you because you look tasty. I'm not sure you could fight off anything that wanted to devour you or parts of you."

It hadn't occurred to me that we might be a meal for something big and hungry. I sat down and closed my eyes. The jaguar would have listened first. The jungle could not conceal danger, nor did it promise safety. The jaguar would have smelled the earth and the breeze tasted its essence, and known whether to pass or enter.

I listened and heard only the march of ants carrying provisions harvested from the explosion of plant life at the edge. I could smell the sweetness of moss and water from inside, past the hole. I let the melody ring, and when the chorus passed by again, I smiled. It was safe. I was pretty sure he knew that already.

I looked up to find him standing and harvesting brightly colored orbs. He tossed several to put in my bag. He watched me bow down in front of the hole and push my bag in front of me. I made a loose knot in my hammock so that it wouldn't come undone and looped it around my foot. Progress was slow as I pushed the bag, waited, listened, then crawled up closer and did it again. And again, and again.

I was almost to the stones when I heard him start to maneuver through. I knew I was at the stones when I couldn't push the bag any further. I wiggled the bag beneath me and between my legs. Using my hand, I felt the rock and let it guide me to standing. The stone had a split running its length vertically, which allowed me to step up and observe my next steps. I put the bag strap over my shoulder and slung the hammock over the other. Using my hands and feet wedged into the crack, I lifted and crawled myself to the top of the formation. Using the rocks was a good call. I was able to scamper down the other side to the familiar smells of moss and leaves.

The ground was spongy. My steps left damp impressions that sprang to new shapes when my foot lifted.

I could hear him moving through the thickness of limbs and stems. I knew when he managed to scale the stones and waited until he found me on the other side. We were fortunate that the ferns and flowers on the ground yielded easily for us to pass. It would be easy to lose our bearings. I took note of the sun and which side of the trees was lit. The slant of the hill invited us to swing down deeper into the valley. I resisted and headed across the hill and up toward what I remembered was the direction of our destination.

The sounds of the jungle changed. It was a new song now, no longer whispering through the grasses and burbling along with a brook. This song had a reverence to it. The air felt thicker and smelled earthy. Our steps landed silently on the carpet of moss. If I stopped for even a second, I could feel the water from the moss spilling across my feet. Sound traveled further and faster. I could hear birds, the sound coming in waves of frantic verbal chattering, then silence. In between the waves, the rest of the jungle made itself known. Trees groaned under the weight of the vines clinging to them. The subtlest of movements translated to the snap of a stem or the crunch of a dried leaf. I patted trees as I passed by them, knowing that they could feel me when I touched them. I remembered how the roots would tremble between the trees and wondered if they could feel our footsteps. I took a deep breath and heard one from behind me.

We walked along, and I could feel him stop. I turned, and he was harvesting a few large leaves. He noticed I was watching. "Big leaves are good for when you need them," he said, making a wiping motion that made me laugh. I stepped back and grabbed a few for myself.

"Good to know," I said, feeling the urge build.

As we ascended toward the ridge above us, the ground became firmer and dryer. I started to see the tracks of animals that passed before me. Where the dirt gave way to undergrowth, well-worn paths gave us easy passage through but began to lead us back down the hill. I had to keep resetting, forging back up the hill. The higher we rose, the more sunlight speckled everything around us. Leaves became thinner, and flowers more abundant. Birdsongs changed. Butterflies surrounded us in abundance. I found a patch of sunshine like a spotlight on a stage. When I stood in the center, butterflies surrounded me so thickly that I could feel their wings. A snap of a twig in the distance broke the spell.

We both looked to see what was ahead. An anteater was foraging, unaware or undeterred by our presence. We stood and watched for a moment. When I started ahead again, he scrambled into the shadows to let us pass.

At the edge of the ridge, the trees became sparser, and we rested and ate before we would be exposed to the heat. From the ridge, I could see that we would have to course-correct through the next valley and hill. He seemed unconcerned. Looking out across the hills in front of us, it seemed to go on forever. Farther to the south, I knew that there were higher mountains. I knew our path was taking us to the coast, well past the populated portions of the coastline. The coast was still too far to see either the towns or the deserted beaches. I heard a whistle to my right. He was crouched among a bramble of bushes.

"Berries!" I heard him shout. I made my way over, and we ate our fill and then some. What we managed to save, I put in one of the empty jars we were using for water.

We walked the ridge to reset our course. The exposure to the sun brought sweat to my skin and face. Soon, I was dripping and could feel myself moving more slowly. Behind me, his footsteps kept pace with mine. When I looked back, he seemed impervious to the heat.

Brambles gave way to occasional plantains and mangos. The larger leaves made it more difficult to see where we were going and keep our course, but the shade was a welcome relief. I was building the habit of taking note of what was edible around me. He harvested a few leaves of the plantains, and I watched him carefully fold them for later. When I saw something that appeared ripe, I picked it. I watched and learned. He would feel its weight in his hands, smell the skin, then test its firmness before depositing it into his bag or taking a bite.

We found a path that wandered in the direction we were heading. It made passage into the deeper parts of the jungle more accessible. The hill rolled into deeper shade, and I began to smell water again. The ground became softer. The sweat from the heat made my clothes cling to my skin. The air of the denser jungle was warm and humid. Sweat still ran down my face. I gave up trying to wipe it away and just let the sweat run from my head and down my body.

The footpath guided us to a pool of clear, fresh water. Large smooth stones lined the bank, and a few stood silently in the middle. Water flowed from a spring on the high side of the hill and spilled into the pool. The canopy was unable to completely cover the water, so sunlight heated the stones and the water. On a stone near the spring was a circle with an "X" on it, similar to the one from the night before. This was a known safe place to stop.

I stood at the edge of the pool and set my bag and hammock down. I saturated the rag I had used to wipe the sweat from my face in the cool water. Instinctively, I put it on the back of my neck. The relief was immediate and welcomed. He was already unloaded, hanging his hammock and bag on the nub of a tree that must have seen countless bags over the years. Another tree welcomed my bag. I touched its trunk with gratitude.

By the time I turned, he was naked. He had his clothes in hand and was walking into the water. I did the same. At the edge, smooth stones welcomed my feet. The cool of the water sent a shockwave through my body. I paused. I stood there, my feet cool and my body still hot from the heat. I took a few more steps, and my legs both welcomed and resisted the extreme change in temperature. When the water reached the crucial point, I submerged myself rather than endure the complaints of my genitals. When I stood back up, he was smiling at me, having done the same.

At first, the coolness took my breath away. Then I took a deep breath with closed eyes. It was another first. I felt alive in yet another new way.

We put our clothes on a large rock in the middle of the pool. He motioned, and I followed him to the far shore. He scooped mud from the bank and rubbed it on his face. He massaged the mud into his hair and down his neck and torso. I did the same. The mud was cool and smelled earthy. It caked quickly to my skin. He pulled a huge handful and waded over to me, rubbing it down my back. The mud began to dry, pulling any soreness or fatigue out of my muscles. I returned the favor. Grabbing another double handful of mud, we waded back to the stones in the middle. The stones were warm from the sun, and we splashed water onto the exposed surfaces. Sitting on the stone, I finished the job with the mud, leaving no skin unprotected.

We turned to our clothes and soaked them in the water, alternately wringing them and then soaking them again. Eventually, I followed his lead and slapped the wet clothes against the rocks. Finally, we laid them out to dry. I laid back on the stone and let the sun warm the mud on my body. Sarms of flying bugs hovered above the water. They had no interest in either of us. I assumed the mud was a bug-repellent and rested back on the warm stone. My feet dangled in the water. Rest, let me listen to the music of nature. The water oozing from the earth and trickling into the pool created a murmur in the background of birds and bugs flying above us. My breathing was regular and shallow, keeping time with the water against the rock.

My mind drifted to my apartment a month or more ago in a city far away. A large-screen television was cycling through news that I would later forget. Its sound covered the mechanical sounds of the air conditioning unit, keeping the room at the perfect temperature. I looked out the glass of the balcony door to see gray. At this moment, the gray could have been the thick urban air or the stifling cold weather. It didn't matter. I rarely used the balcony because the smog burned my lungs, or the heat or cold was intolerable. I was upset and not paying attention to either the television or the gray skies. On the countertop that separated my kitchen from the modern living area were papers. Papers pilfered from the office showed just how similar my work was to the poison it was meant to remedy. They confirmed something I had suspected. Now I was sure.

The phone rang, and the smart TV reduced its volume when it heard the call come through. From a speaker on the counter came a woman's voice.

"We're all down at the bar celebrating. You okay?" asked the voice.

"Just checking a few things," I said.

"That's just like you," she replied. "The data is correct."

"That is what scares me," I thought to myself. "Just being sure," I said instead.

"You're a genius," she said. "Come have a drink with the team. The contracts are signed. The company is on board. We are moving to the next phase. This drug is going to be sent all over the world."

I looked at the glass with ice cubes in it next to me. Next to it was a bottle, half-empty. As I looked around, my apartment looked like a hospital. The colors were drab, and the lines were clean. The kitchen was barren of any signs of life. In my dream, my apartment was converted into a hospital room. My parents were in beds beside each other. The sounds from the TV turned into monitors that were hooked to them.

One line was the heartbeat, another blood pressure, another suffering. The pain was so great that they were sedated. The nurse came in and told me they were dying and nothing would help. I remembered a similar moment when I decided to go into research.

Sitting there with my dying parents, I realized it was my work that had caused their suffering. I poured another drink because I couldn't live with myself.

I woke weeping. I felt the mud caked to my body. It felt like it was sucking the last of the old life from my body. The sun was hot on the stone, but shadows were growing. My clothes were mostly dry. On the other stone, he had already gathered his clothes and was heading to the shore.

I heard the snap of a twig and the plunk of a foot landing in water. Something had come to drink. I couldn't see it; I could hear and feel it. It could be dangerous, and it may not be. At that moment, I realized that nobody cared. The dance of my life and death would play out regardless of any sacred plan or perceived purpose.

I waited. Whatever had joined us at the pool was small and wanted to remain invisible. I knew that it was watching to see what I would do. Still muddy, I carefully gathered my clothes. Stepping off the rock, my body was again reminded that it was still alive. The mud provided a thin barrier against the cold, but I felt myself brace against it. Satisfied that I was moving away, I could hear the movement of leaves and see the stems of plants shift as my company made its way away from the pool.

At the pool's edge, we hung our clothes close to the rest of our things. He sat on a stone at the edge and used water to re-wet the mud, then scrubbed his body. I did the same.

Eventually, we submerged ourselves. I scrubbed my hair underwater, and plumes of silt were suspended in the water. I swam to rinse the last remnants and emerged clean.

Near the circle and "X," I found a stash of dry fire-starting materials. There was an obvious ring where fires had been burned, and I made a nest. Dry wood was not hard to find, and I broke up small branches and twigs, stacking them nearby. From the locket he hung by his bag, he nurtured the ember in a small ball gathered from my nest. Carefully, he breathed life into the ember, and a flame began.

As the fire built, he folded the plantain leaves into a pot and filled it with water from the pool. He laid out another on an adjacent rock bordering the fire, and peeling the plantains, he set them to roast next to the fire. He tended the fire to build the coals so that it was hotter than just a flame. Leaving me to care for it, he disappeared into the trees. I heard some cracking and snapping, then some thumping noises before he returned with what looked like yams. He rinsed them in the pool and threw them right into the fire. He also had some greens that he lay on the coals. They let off a pleasant fruity smoke.

"Keeps the mosquitoes away," he said as he put them down.

Chapter Twenty

We turn the yams and plantains as they cook in the fire. He empties his bag next to him. I realize that I've been carrying the bag and am unsure of everything it holds. I carefully empty mine. I set the empty jar and lid next to me. Several more jars contain berries or water, along with the small wooden bowl and cup I've already used for breakfast. There is a mosquito net that I can hang above the hammock. A small flint and steel for making a fire are bundled with several small sachets of herbs. There are a few bags of rice and beans. Another bandana holds a toothbrush, comb, and a small knife. At the very bottom is the thin cord of hemp they made.

He watches me examine everything. He turns the tubers and plantains and stokes the fire. I look over everything I'm carrying. The hammock has clean clothes and a small blanket that can double as a large towel or weather covering. These are the items they felt I needed to make the trip. From his bag, he pulls a bundle wrapped in a bandana. It contains barber's shears and a razor. Using the comb, he begins trimming his facial hair methodically, using the comb as a guide. He goes to the water and uses a small bar of soap to lather. He uses the razor to clean up the edges. Using his fingers, he carefully trims his hair. Shortened locks of curls drop into the water and are carried downstream.

When he finishes, he looks at me and holds up the scissors. I try to use the comb on my face like he does. He starts laughing. He makes a few curious motions with his fingers before heading over to the pool of water. If I sit just right, I can see my reflection. I don't recognize myself at first. My face is gaunt, probably because of weight loss. I've never seen myself with facial hair. I sit and look at myself. I can't help but think that I am changing.

His method of comb and scissors takes some practice. Soon, I can comb and cut with ease. My head hair will have to wait for another time and place. The straight razor and soap create yet another comedy for his entertainment. Luckily, he shows me how to hold the razor.

He carefully cleans the scissors and razor with the bandana and rolls them up together. We take the plantains and mash them using a cleaned stick, then make them into small patties. The flat stone next to the fire is hot enough to char the flat edges. We slice the tubers and set them on the plantain leaves to keep warm.

Another set of greens on the fire makes more sweet-smelling smoke. We sit naked, eating by the fire. The depth of the jungle surrounds us. Water spills into the pool, gently obscuring the beautiful reflections of trees and flowers. The sun shares the space with the moon that will soon be rising and visible through the clearing above the pool.

I think about the meals I have eaten in my life. This is different in every possible way.

***

"Is this how you live your life?" I ask.

He thinks about it for a moment. "This is life."

I sit, waiting for more. He senses it. "Tomorrow will also be life. I think you are asking something different."

"Back in the States, almost every day is the same. Same people, same places, same food," I say. "Our lives are very predictable, you might say stable."

He nods gently, understanding. "And safe," he adds.

I think about it for a minute. "Safe?" I ask.

"You don't worry about being eaten by a jaguar or a bear, or being chased down by wild dogs," he says.

"Okay, I'm following," I say.

"Food comes from all over the world in boxes. There is no need to forage."

"Have you tried to shop at a grocery store on a weekend?" I chide him. "There is some serious foraging going on. Try taking the last frozen pizza on a Friday night. That's pretty dangerous." We laugh.

I smash a slice of tuber on a plantain patty and slide it into my mouth. It is amazing. I close my eyes as I chew.

"Would you prefer a frozen pizza?" he asks.

"No way, this is amazing," I say.

"Safety has a price," he says, smiling at me. His eyes narrow as his whole face beams. There is more behind the smile, I can tell.

I think about it for a while. "Fear," I say. "You don't have to be afraid of predators, starving, or being cold."

He purses his lips and waits. "Are you afraid now?" he asks.

His words give me pause. "No," I say, reflecting on the last few days.

"When I first met you, were you afraid?" he asks.

"Yes."

"What were you afraid of?" he asks.

I think about it. Our eyes meet. His gaze doesn't waver. Mine does. "Being wrong, doing the wrong thing."

He is quiet again. He is waiting for me. I am pretty sure he can wait as long as it takes for my words to sink in. They finally do. I haven't been afraid since I drank from the first jar. Up until that moment, I lived in fear.

"I had it backward," I say finally. "Safety doesn't alleviate fear."

His nod is subtle. He smashes another tuber into a plantain patty. "Freedom," I say. "Safety costs me my freedom."

"How so?" he asks.

"My life was full of obligations and expectations. I thought I was free, but I wasn't."

"Were you safer?"

I don't need to answer the question. We both know the answer. There is also the unspoken that burns in me like the coals of the fire. He doesn't need to ask. I am also alive now. That is the real cost of my perceived safety.

***

He floats his mosquito net over his hammock and arranges everything beneath him. I can tell this is a ritual he has done many times before. Being new, it takes me several attempts to get the netting to cover. We both retired to our hammocks. The light is dimming, and shadows chase the last speckles of sunlight past the edge of the pool. The song of the forest sounds sweet to me.

In my hammock, I reflect. I am changing. The thought of going back makes me uneasy. Scenes from my life play out the reality of my fears. There is the first bad report card. The uncoordinated young boy who wanted desperately to be on the team. The death of my parents dictated my education. The late nights working on the cure for an ailment that was unnecessary. The confrontation with my boss and the resulting decision to come here. Even now, fear lurks close. The choice is either to ride it out or revert back.

The sound of a mosquito finding the net breaks my daydream. It adds to the lull of the jungle song. For me, the lapping of the water and the bristle of the leaves invite me to rest. It reminds me that if I am in danger, the melody will change. Until then, like the jaguar, I can let my body rest and my soul recover. Somewhere in the dark, I can hear his breathing ease, and the night descends.

During the night, the melody changes. The breeze shifts, and even the pool changes to a staccato snap of water against stone. The grasses and leaves near the pool dance with the wind. I feel myself listening for footsteps. I am awake but not afraid. I think about our conversation earlier. It is only when I begin to imagine what could be hiding in the cloak of darkness that the familiar sense of dread bleeds into my gut. It distracts me from listening, causing another flood of anxiety and the quickening of my heartbeat.

I listen intently, quieting my fears by realizing that listening and watching are my best defenses against danger. I listen for his familiar regular breathing sounds. I can hear him breathing, but not deeply. He is awake, too, and listening. The hole in my gut starts to ease. There is a dampness in the air. The weather is changing. A cloud wanders in front of the moon, darkening our sanctuary. The sound of light rain pecks at the leaves above me. The occasional drizzle drop catches the hammock. I can feel the subtle tap and resulting spray of droplets on my skin.

The rain doesn't last long. His breathing deepens again, and I find my breaths following suit. Then sleep.

The crackle of the fire awoke me. He was watching parrots fly above the water, patrolling for danger and watching us carefully. Several landed on a branch just above him and squawked. When he turned, they would go silent and act like they didn't see him. When he turned, they'd start again. He'd turn again, and they spread their wings, strutting up and down the branch. It was obvious they were playing with him. Every time he turned, the screeching would start again. Then he'd turn, and somebody would do something silly. One waited for his back to be turned, dropped to the ground beside him, and took one of his sandals. It flew high into the tree, screeching and taunting him.

He smiled as he looked up. I started laughing hysterically. Almost immediately, the other parrots mimicked my laugh and laughed back. Soon, the laughter was overwhelming. He stood there watching the thief parrot while the rest of us laughed. The thief flew to another tree and then another as if to tempt him into climbing. Finally, as if surrendering, he peeled a plantain and held it above his head, extending his arm as high as he could.

Wings flapped, and the sandal dropped at his feet. In the same graceful motion, the parrot grabbed the plantain. A bevy of birds took flight after the thief with the plantain. The whole flock circled the sky above us and then dove in unison toward him. He stood motionless as the diving birds engulfed him and re-ascended to the trees.

"Birds like me," he said as if repeating it for the millionth time.

"No doubt," I replied. It was obvious he had spent time connected to birds.

***

For the next few moments, waves of birds flew through the clearing. The pool reflected a wash of green with the parrots, then specks of gray and black as smaller birds joined in. The flocks became so large that they engulfed me. I sat completely fascinated by the display. Whiffs of air from their wings caressed me gently as they flew around us.

The snap of a stick and the shuffle of leaves broke the spell. The birds ascended to the treetops. Silence descended. Ripplets floated across the pool from our guests, drinking. I looked into the shady recess by the rocks. I could only see eyes. With stealth, they retreated back into the cover of shade and foliage.

When I looked back, he was watching me.

"Do you remember which direction we were going?" he asked.

I pointed generally past the pool and up the hill. Near the place where the path entered the clearing was another path headed in the direction I was pointing.

"Good," he said, beginning to load up his things. "The birds say it's going to rain later, so we need to start to move." I started picking my things up, too.

"Today, why don't you go ahead? Follow the path, and when you get close to the top of the ridge, hug the tree line as you pass over the saddle. When you hear water, follow the sound, and you'll find shelter."

I nodded, understanding what he was saying.

"I'll follow behind and meet you there."

Again, I nodded. He paused as if thinking.

"If you find something edible, grab it."

I was almost finished packing my things.

"Make sure you are listening," he said. "It can make the difference between staying alive and being hurt or eaten."

I nodded. The gravity of his words was yet to land.

When I was ready, I raised my hand.

"I'm off," I said.

He was sitting on a stone near where our fire had been. Several birds were around him. He would toss a pebble, and they would chase it. The bird who succeeded would take flight and hurry back with other birds diving after him. They would drop the pebble at his feet while flying, and the circus would start again. Other parrots in the trees were still mimicking my laughter whenever he would toss the pebble again.

"Be safe," he said back.

***

As I headed up the path, the brightness of the clearing gave way to the darkness of shadows. The simple task of following the path took on a gravity instilled by his advice. My footsteps were now part of the song of the jungle. I could hear my steps adding to the melody. It occurred to me that something was probably listening and waiting for my steps to approach or pass. I was no longer a guarded visitor. My safety net was playing fetch with birds.

This wasn't an amusement park where everything had been painstakingly designed to give the appearance of danger with the reality of safety. The wrong step, the wrong turn, or a lapse in awareness could spell my demise. The possibility of death caused me to pause before I rounded past

226

the stones that sheltered the clearing. I saw my choice clearly. I could let fear drive me and distract me, or I could let my eyes and ears open. I chose the second, and within steps of the decision, I felt alive.

I realized I wasn't looking for danger; I was feeling everything. The smells weren't just to detect danger; smell could be a guide, an informant to food, water, or shelter. When you aren't listening for danger, you hear everything. Listening, I could still hear the parrots laughing and the burble of water and rocks. I could hear my footsteps, with mud barely clinging to the bottoms of my sandals. My hammock shifted as I walked, keeping time with my paces. The lull of walking dulled the enthusiasm of my start. About an hour into my walk, the realization that I was alone settled into my thoughts.

I remembered being the jaguar who moved solitary to everything around him. He never felt alone. He was part of the song. He was part of the jungle.

***

I walked past a mango tree and stopped. I turned around and marveled at how easily I missed it. It rewarded my return with several ripe yellow-orange mangos. I slid them into my bag and let the weight shift against my shoulder. In that

227

moment, gratitude filled me. Inasmuch as I thought I was alone, it was just my paranoid perspective. The jungle, all of the jungle, was a fantastic dance that played out into a perfect drama. To continue, I had to dance the dance of the melody and act out my part of the story. Even then, the script, though written, was invisible to the players. Anything could happen. Even trying not to be a part of the dance was itself a part of the dance.

Feeling a bit self-assured, maybe even cocky, I thought, "I've got this." Just then, a root caught my foot, sending me headfirst into a branch. I landed on my side in the mud. I was sure that I could hear parrots laughing.

"It only takes a moment," I thought. The fall brought me back to a healthy sense of awareness.

***

The path broke over a ridge and through the tree line, opening onto the side of a hill that had been cleared for agriculture. The sunlight was blinding until my eyes adjusted. Down the side of the hill were myriads of flowers, making a kaleidoscope of colors. This would be a cornucopia for the bees. I stopped to remember how the bees saw the flowers. In my mind, the colors transformed themselves into brilliance and translucence. What was red was now a shimmering burst of indescribable color. Yellows glowed and glimmered, changing colors and shapes like the aurora borealis. Blues melted into lavenders unseen to the human eye. The display made me wish I was a bee again, able to romance the jewels of the hill.

The path I was following dropped down into the valley, where I could see it wind toward a creek. Just before the creek was a gate. To each side of the gate, barbed wire. Posts made from trees held the wires off the ground, and metal posts occasionally reinforced them. On the gate was a shiny lock. I remembered his words and veered off the path, hugging close to the tree line that capped the ridge. At the top of the next rise, I could feel the earth vibrating with the sound of engines and motors. The smell of diesel whiffed past me.

Below me was a familiar valley. At the bottom was an abandoned farmhouse. Heavy equipment was moving dark earth into piles at either end of a long swath they were leveling. Survey stakes marked with fluorescent ribbons bordered the valley. There was a run of stakes and ribbon that rose up the hill toward the shack I had visited. A backhoe was digging a trench for a water line following the stakes.

My heart sank. I reached out to the tree beside me as I sank to the ground. Tears welled up and blurred my vision. I wiped them away, but it was useless. Months ago, this was what I worked for. This was our vision. Now, the gravity of that vision broke something inside of me. The guilt was overwhelming. I rested my back on the tree and wept.

Chapter Twenty-One

I felt the bark on my back, and it gave slightly under my weight. In my thoughts, I turned to the tree and confessed my arrogance. I told the tree that it would most likely be cut down and stacked alongside the other trees at the bottom of the hill. I admitted that I was responsible. There was no undoing what I had done.

Silence. The cool breeze from the dark clouds above rustled the grasses and leaves around me. I felt the rumble of earthmovers scaring the earth.

There was an invitation, like an embrace pulling me in. My eyes closed. The tree was listening. My mind exploded with memories explaining how this had happened. Silence. My memories gave way to a deep sadness.

***

"This is a ring," I felt more than heard. "It is an experience that will always be a part of us." A scar from a deep wound. A wound that I inflicted.

Within the tree, I could feel its rings. I touched a ring near its center and saw a once-vibrant forest below me. There was a connection to all the trees that surrounded us. The forest was vital and healthy. I touched another ring and felt the jolt of axes felling trees nearby. Huge, old-growth trunks fell to the ground. Fires burned away what was left. The forest gave way to burnt devastation.

Another ring felt the sunshine against the trunk and the grasses growing below us. Rings aren't like memories; they are the continuity of our experience, changing from moment to moment. The forest still lived in us. The axes were still swinging, and the fires were burning. Lush livestock meadows didn't replace the forest; the forest lived on as it was, as it is, and as it will be. The rings of the tree continued to grow. They didn't abandon the past; they carried it forward. There were rings yet to be experienced. The tree already knew it would eventually succumb. There was no fear. There was no blame. We sat together as droplets signaled the beginning of rain.

When the rain began to fall in earnest, I could feel the tree's relief. Perhaps from the heat, or maybe it had been dry for a long time. The rain soothed and nurtured the tree. Birds flew seeking refuge, resting in the branches below the huge leaves. The crack of thunder and flash of lightning brought a heavier downpour. I pulled my bag close and covered it with a part of the hammock.

Work in the valley never stopped. Windshield wipers and lights came on so that men in protected cabs could continue. The exposed dark earth drank in the rain. Streams of dark, liquid mud oozed into the tracks the equipment made. It was like watching the earth bleed. An old tree fell to its demise. The loader carried it to a stack where other trees awaited chainsaws and trucks to haul them away.

The tree sensed my anxiety. My tears mixed with the rain and fell to the ground. I wished I could die rather than see the destruction. A part of me died with each tree, each vine, each cut into the hillside. Still, the tree supported me. My body shook. The tree stood fast.

Forgiveness is a humbling pill to swallow. It would have been easier to be rebuked or physically punished. Instead, the whole valley watched the devastation without condemnation.

***

A hand touched my shoulder. I knew it was him without looking. He sat beside me in the rain. He was silent like a tree. I opened my eyes and caught his. His eyes held nothing but gentleness. I tried to speak but shook instead.

233

The rain began to ease. The earth drank in the fluid. Birds greeted the sun with songs. I turned to him again and looked him in the eye.

"This is my fault," I said.

He watched as my face contorted. My body broke down and shook again.

"I want to die," I said.

He stood up and took my bag and hammock, then stretched out his hand. I looked at the outstretched offering like a murderer given undeserved parole. Only through humility does grace reveal its essence. The depth of its essence has a pull, like gravity. At this moment, the weight was beyond my ability to bear. At my feet were seed pods from the tree. I took several and put them in my bag.

His hand was an offer to help carry the load, if only for a short time. I took his hand and felt both deep shame and incredible gratitude. My legs were unsteady. He put a hand on my shoulder, and we walked together along the tree line. I knew that down the ravine a short distance was a shack and a pristine pool. We headed that way.

***

He had already been to the shack. The necessities for a fire were carefully set on the dirt floor in the center of the shack. A rusted vent pipe rose through the roof. As he lit the fire, the smoke lifted to the vent and escaped. Air drew in from the floor and sides of the shack, keeping the air fresh. He hung my hammock and bag to dry. I sat on the floor, now shivering, saying nothing.

The fire brought light and heat as it grew. The flames lit an idea inside of me. Maybe I could sneak down to the tractors and cut their tires, steal spark plug wires. Maybe I could set fire to the old farmhouse and somehow turn the tide of progress.

I looked over. He was cutting the mangos I found and adding what he foraged.

"I could go down and break the machines," I said. "I could take your knife and damage the tires, maybe set fire to the gas tanks."

He listened.

"I have to do something," I said.

He stopped and set everything he was working on aside.

"It won't make any difference," he said.

"It will slow them down," I said. "Maybe they will stop."

"Even if you slow them down, they won't stop," he said. "Too much money, too many people."

"I have to do something," I said again.

"Like what?" he asked.

"I don't know," I confided.

He took a deep breath and met my gaze.

"Listen," he said. "Every time humans try to make something better, they generally make things worse."

"But," I retorted, "I have to do something. The guilt is too much."

"Have you asked yourself why you feel guilty now and not before?"

"No," I said.

"What's changed?" he asked.

The fire popped as if in agreement. He returned to preparing the food and sat quietly. Water was heating in a folded plantain leaf, and plantains steamed in others. There was more to be done, but I became lost in thought.

***

The rain had almost stopped. He looked up from his work, listening to the occasional drops hitting the tin roof.

"Come with me," he said, standing up.

I stood, still unsteady, and followed him out the door. We headed toward the hillside, crawling over and under rocks, trees, and roots. He stopped when we reached the edge of the jungle.

From our vantage point, we could see the farmhouse and the earthmovers.

"Look," he said, pointing to the top of the adjacent hill.

At first, I didn't see anything. Then, a flash from the reflection of sunlight hitting glass caught my eye. There was a man with a gun sitting on the hill. He pointed to the other side of the valley, near where I had sat with the tree, where another armed man stood watching the machinery below.

Four black SUVs and an old pickup truck pulled up to the farmhouse. Men in slacks, golf shirts, and sunglasses got out of the SUVs. Among them was a giant of a man with long curly hair. I recognized him instantly. It was Ben.

A thin man in a cowboy hat and a scruffy gray dog emerged from the pickup truck. The cowboy holstered a gun and held a rifle in his other hand. The businessmen shook his hand as Ben introduced him to the group. As they talked, the cowboy pointed to the man on the hillside. The cowboy raised his rifle, and the man on the hill did the same. Then he pointed to another spot, revealing two more men we hadn't seen.

"They have it guarded," he said. "Even if you tried, chances are good they'd stop you."

My heart sank again. There would be no redemption for me.

"I know one of the men by the house," I said.

"The big one," he nodded.

"Yes, how did you know?"

"The rest look the same," he said. "Except the cowboy."

"Eh, the big one seemed more likely," he smiled.

"He said that you were who I was looking for." I caught his gaze.

"It wasn't me you were looking for," he corrected. "You were searching for a door to pass through. I had nothing to do with it."

Ben was pointing and gesturing broadly across an imaginary canvas. They looked in our direction and pointed. I instinctively flinched.

"Hold still," he put his hand on my back. "They can't see us while we're in the trees. If they could, we'd already be dead."

"The fire," I said. "They'll see the fire."

"Probably not," he said. "The wind is blowing in our favor, and the rain has brought the clouds down."

He was right. Wisps of fog hovered just below the ridge.

"When it gets dark, the smoke will be invisible," he said.

The cowboy walked back to his truck and pulled a mason jar from under the seat. He unscrewed the top and took a swig, then took the jar back to the group. He handed it to one of the men in golf shirts, who took a drink, gagging as he swallowed. The rest of the group laughed, passing the jar around before walking to the farmhouse.

The cowboy and his dog headed for the pickup. Before he opened the door, he raised his rifle, and the other guards mirrored his action. The truck rattled to life and headed down the dirt driveway. The others watched him leave from the porch. A driver from one of the SUVs brought out a tray with a bottle and tumblers. Several of the men pulled cigars from their pockets and lit them. The whole party sat on the porch overlooking the valley. I could hear laughter when the earthmovers quieted down.

We watched it a while longer. The backhoe digging a trench toward us was making steady progress but would still take days to reach the edge. Now, we could see each of the gunmen. Most sat down, some lighting cigarettes, watching the machinery. There's something hypnotizing about watching dirt being moved from one place to another.

***

Raindrops intruded on the moment. They were heavy and sporadic, a warning of what was coming. The men on the porch looked up at the sky turning grayer by the second. Another man emerged onto the porch, dressed in work clothes and a hard hat. He spoke into a walkie-talkie, glancing at the sky. The machines began moving toward a cleared area near the farmhouse, where fuel tanks and temporary buildings lined the side. Next to the farmhouse, RV trailers were parked, with a few tents and portable toilets set at a respectable distance. The men from the tractors, donning hard hats, ran for cover on the porch. The gunmen made their way slowly down the hill, while the black SUVs pulled closer to the farmhouse so the VIPs could get in without getting wet.

In moments, the operation shut down. A crack of lightning flashed across the sky, and the rumble echoed down the hill. The last of the gunmen were still navigating the muddy hillside when the deluge began.

***

We retreated back to the shack. The fire had laid down a healthy set of coals, and he added another log to revive the flames. The sound of rain on the roof grew louder, droplets sizzling as they struck the smoke pipe. I sat quietly and pulled into a ball in front of the fire. He gathered the plantains, mangoes, and other items, placing them into bowls. He set a bowl in front of me and sat down himself. He ate. My body was famished, but I couldn't bring myself to eat.

"I've changed," I whispered. I knew he heard me as he gave a hint of a smile and a familiar, unconscious nod.

"How have you changed?" he asked. "You look pretty much the same, maybe a little wear and tear."

"I see things differently," I replied.

He continued to savor his meal. "I am changing," I said quietly.

He finished chewing a piece of mango. "How are you changing?" he asked.

"What I saw affects me differently. What I thought was a great achievement is now the source of my guilt."

"And tomorrow?" he asked.

"Tomorrow?" I echoed.

"Maybe you'll see things differently tomorrow," he said gently.

"I can't imagine how," I said. "My work set all of this in motion."

"Maybe tomorrow you'll learn something new that will change your perspective, change how you feel."

"I can't imagine how," I repeated.

"That's sort of the point. If you knew, then how you feel now would be different."

He sat quietly, staring into the fire. The rain eased to a tolerable volume. I looked around the shack, noticing things I hadn't before: old nails and iron stains from where tools had hung, water from the pool dissolving the wood at the base of the walls, moss growing on most of the beams, and the remains of a rusted electrical box, with white glass insulators barely hanging from old nails.

He shifted his position and then looked at me.

"Do you feel more or less human now?" he asked.

The question caught me off guard. I stared into the fire, silent. He waited.

"I'm not sure," I finally replied. "I feel more alive. I feel awake. Maybe that's what it means to be human."

"Then, are you becoming what you didn't want to be?"

"No, definitely not," I said, realizing the conundrum his question posed.

He smiled and chuckled as he stood up and stretched his arms.

"Maybe you should eat something," he said.

I reached for the bowl and sat cross-legged in front of the fire. As soon as I tasted the plantain, my hunger reawakened. My thoughts dissipated, replaced by the simple act of eating. I devoured the bowl, and he handed me half a mango. I ate it with relish, feeling warmth return to my body. I closed my eyes and took a deep breath. It was a new sensation.

I walked to the door and pulled it open. Darkness had fallen. I took a deliberate breath; the air was heavy and earthy, with a familiar feel to it. I saw water spilling over the broken wheel alongside the building. The water cascaded from bucket to bucket, spilling onto the rocks below.

"We will leave early tomorrow," he said.

I nodded… it made sense. I turned back to the room.

The rice and beans were already set to soak for the night. He was folding the clothes we'd hung by the fire to dry in preparation for the morning. I closed the door and found my hammock, hung diagonally between two walls, while his was suspended from the other two. It drooped deeply, swaying slightly as I surrendered to its shape. The room was quiet, with only the crackle of the fire and the gentle thrum of water on the roof.

As I drifted off, I let go of the images I'd seen on the hillside.

I expected the conundrum of humanity to keep me occupied and awake, but sleep found me. I drifted, pulled along by a feeling of continuity. My dreams took on the colors of my memories, painting a massive explosion of sensations. Then, everything imploded into a singularity, growing smaller and smaller. I was reaching to grasp it before it disappeared… and I awoke.

In those first moments of being awake, there was no connection to my surroundings. I had no immediate recollection of the day before. I was in a dark shack, with splinters of sunlight shooting through cracks in the wooden walls. The last of the fire's smoke rolled and turned in the shards of light. It was eerie. I saw him gathering his things and dividing the rice and beans. He was a shadow in the shadows. Then, the previous day started rushing back.

Birds, path, tractors, the tree, guns, Ben, the shack.

"We need to leave," I thought. Then, blank.

My body took over the task of eating and packing. When I grabbed my bag, the spell was broken. I reached into the bag and took out the last jar. Stepping out of the shack, I scrambled to the pool above us. I stood there like I had weeks before, filled the jar, and secured the lid. At that moment, I thought of nothing else. There was clarity of focus and a distinct feeling of connection. He came to my side, my hammock and bag in tow. He set them down next to me and squatted, waiting.

"What is happening to me?" I asked, looking over at him.

"What do you feel?" he asked.

"I don't know."

"Is it bad?" he asked.

"I don't know. I don't think so."

The sounds of earthmovers coming to life and the beeping as they backed up fell on me like a ton of bricks. The wave of emotions that started the day before returned. I dropped to my knees and hung my head. Tears. Sobs.

I wasn't sure how long I wept, but he sat beside me the entire time. When the heaves of emotion stopped, he stood and slung his hammock and bag across his shoulder. I did the same.

***

"This way," he said, walking toward the pool and away from the shack. I followed.

At the edge of the rock face that held the water back, we were able to step across to the other side. The hillside was thick with trees and brush. I watched him move. It was starting to make sense. I mimicked his movements, and my steps became the rhythm of the jungle's song. Listening to the song kept me aware and focused. His pace conveyed a sense of urgency. I did my best to keep up.

246

We headed down and across the hill. The sounds of destruction gave way to birds and monkeys conversing about our approach. The ground was still soft from the rain. Drops clung to the edges of the leaves. Leaves lying on the ground slid under my steps. The air was humid. As I brushed against bushes, branches, and trunks, I became wetter. My shirt stuck to my skin, hanging heavily across my body. He was the same, yet undaunted, he continued swiftly.

We crested the side of the hill, where there was an open space to look back. I could see the tractors moving, thick bursts of diesel exhaust billowing up. Trees carpeted the vista between us. There was no sign of the shack, the fence, or the pool. He was looking in the other direction, likely charting our course. I saw him look to the sky. Clouds were moving quickly.

"A good chance for rain," I thought to myself. He seemed to nod as if he'd heard me.

We dropped down the side of the hill, moving across and down. Soon, we emerged onto the next ranch, where trees had been cleared for cattle to graze. I expected to hug the edge of the cleared area as we had before. This time, he headed straight across — faster but far more exposed. Below us, I could see dots of cows and maybe some white dots of sheep or goats. Between us and the livestock, an old fence held its position proudly.

***

We crested another hill, and then another, before encountering a dirt road. We walked along it downhill, weaving around gullies and through stands of trees until it met another road. We continued, crossing other roads until shacks appeared with driveways and rusted debris. Eventually, we saw cows grazing alongside the shacks, followed by chickens, cows, and abandoned trucks next to hastily built homes.

When houses, yards, and gardens appeared, I knew we were nearing a town. Old men sat on the porches of older homes, watching us pass. Children ran from yard to yard, oblivious to our presence. Dirt roads became improved dirt roads. The sides of the streets were mowed, so we didn't have to walk in the street. Fences created privacy not afforded by the proximity of the homes.

The familiar hum of air conditioning mixed with the sound of a car coming up behind us. We transitioned from the song of the jungle to the sounds of civilization. The clouds had gathered behind us, shading us from the sun — a welcome relief. It also signaled the probability of rain. We needed to find shelter.

***

We came to a main street with a paved road. Trucks rumbled past the intersection. To either side, stucco buildings lined the street. Gravel driveways and parking areas led off the side of the road. He turned to the main street and walked along until we found the square.

It was a humble common area with a stand of trees and a few old cannons thoughtfully placed to leave room for farmers and street merchants to sell their wares. At one end of the square was likely the town's only bar. Alongside the square was a modest restaurant with a covered patio where people were sitting. There was a post office, a government building, and a few stores selling necessities.

As we passed the restaurant, a voice called out in perfect Texan, "Y'all lookin' for somethin' to eat?"

A stout woman with black hair stood in the doorway with her hands on her hips.

"If you came lookin' for a job up at that factory, they ain't hirin' yet. If you ain't got no money, there's some soup in the back. Ain't much, but it'll fill your belly."

He looked at me. We hadn't gathered much on the trip down. I shrugged.

"Gracious," he said.

She smiled and nodded around the side.

"When you boys get rich, you remember old Kat," she said, following us around the corner. "They make you work for a couple of weeks before they give you any money. God put me here to help you poor souls from the jungle."

Around the side was a tent with several tables. Several others were sitting, having soup. A serving table was housed under a tin-covered roof next to the tent. At the far side, partially protected by the building, was a small podium and makeshift altar. A cross was nailed to the podium, and candles surrounded the altar.

"We do church on Wednesdays and Sundays. Those days, we serve up special dishes," she said, repeating her practiced invitation. "You boys know about Jesus, right?"

He smiled and nodded. I was relieved.

We sat down under the tent beneath building gray skies. She returned with two bowls of soup and some deep-fried plantains. Setting the bowls down in front of us, she stopped and bowed her head.

"Dear God, watch over these boys who are truly grateful to you for this meal. Bless and watch over them and bring them to your son. In Jesus' name."

I said, "Amen," completely out of habit. I wasn't sure if my grandparents would have been proud or turned over in their graves.

As abruptly as she finished, she turned. "That was some rainstorm we had last night. You boys get caught up in the hills?"

We both nodded.

"Fixin' to do the same tonight, I reckon. You boys gotta place to stay?"

He shook his head no.

"Police won't let you stay here. Up the way, there's trees and a toilet. Might be able to find a dry spot there."

"Gracious," he said again.

A bell above the door to the street rang out. She looked to see several men enter the restaurant.

"Got more souls to feed. You boys take care."

Chapter Twenty-Two

Before we could finish our soup, the rain started. Thunder clapped a warning, and the wind picked up, tugging at the sides of the tent. We sat, watching water pour from the sky. Our only choice was to wait it out. Others joined us in the tent, and we all watched rivers of rain run past us.

We gathered our plates and bowls, found the bussing station, and washed our dishes along with what was already in the sink. We left them on the rack to dry. When the rain lulled, we moved to a wooden bench in the covered space between the street and the restaurant door. The building afforded us some protection from the wind. Water poured off the tin porch roof and down the street.

We watched as people dashed to cars or from cars to the bar or another door. A cowboy exited the bar, obviously drunk. He pulled his hat down tight on his head, walking under the cover of the bar's overhanging roof. He made his way up the street, ducking under the porch where we were sitting. He stopped just in front of us.

"You boys want a dry place to sleep tonight?" he asked. "You drive me home, and I'll let you stay in the barn." He glanced up the street where an officer sat in an SUV, watching us. He nodded toward the police. "Bastards just waitin' to bust me." He spit into the water, running past the porch. "Girls in the bar used to drive me home. Paid 'em good too. Then I got frisky with one of 'em, and they won't drive me no more."

He looked at us again. "Bitches screwed up a good thing. Now ol' Pablo over there wants to run me in 'cause I kilt his brother." His balance wavered, and he steadied himself on the post holding the roof. "One of you boys can drive, can't you?"

I nodded.

He looked at me, giving a subtle nod. We picked up our bags and followed him up the street, keeping under the cover of roofs whenever possible. The pickup truck was hastily parked, straddling a stream of rainwater pouring from a downspout. In the cab sat a small gray, short-haired dog with a patch of white on his chest between his tiny legs. His tail beat against the seat as soon as he saw us.

The cowboy slid into the passenger seat, and the dog jumped to the seat behind him. We got in on the driver's side. I took the wheel, and he sat behind me with the dog. Sitting next to the cowboy, I could smell the alcohol.

He handed me a handful of keys on a large ring. A claw from a small alligator dangled, affixed like a rabbit's foot.

"Use the square key," he said.

I put the key in the ignition, and the dash lit up. I turned it, and the motor growled to a start, then rumbled as it idled.

"Made some improvements," he said. "Bitches in this country don't know that a truck needs a real mutherfuckin' motor." He pulled a mason jar from under the seat. I checked the mirror. From the back seat, both he and the dog watched me negotiate the controls.

I found the windshield wipers while the cowboy took a healthy swig from the jar. Just before I released the emergency brake and dropped it into drive, the police SUV pulled alongside the car. The cowboy cranked the window down and smiled at the officer. The officer looked past him at me, rolling the toothpick that stuck out of his mouth. He looked back at the cowboy.

"I ain't your bitch tonight," the cowboy said, laughing and slapping his knee, almost spilling the mason jar he held between his thighs. The officer smiled and nodded at me, saying nothing, then rolled ahead, parking up the street with his running lights still on.

We pulled past him, and I made sure to use my blinker when I turned onto the paved main street. I guessed that it was a right turn; he didn't make any complaints.

"Keep drivin' until you come to train tracks and turn on the road after 'em," he directed.

The windshield wipers flapped back at a furious pace to keep up. The dog curled into a ball next to my friend.

"Yep, ol' Pablo's got an ax to grind. Back where I come from, we call it a feud. I ain't got no family here for him to kill, so he just waits and busts my balls. Too bad those bitches at the bar won't drive me no more. Had a good thing goin', them bitches."

I checked the rearview mirror to see if Pablo was following us. I had to look past the camo-painted rifle to confirm the coast was clear.

"Back in the States, I met Maria. We had some fun." He took another swig from the jar. "We started livin' together. Pretty soon, she spent all my money. She was always talking about home and how it was prettier here, how the food was better. She was always talkin'. Bitch never shut up."

"One day, she was jabberin' about back home and talked about these shamans. She said these guys could turn into a jaguar whenever they wanted. She said they were real men, not some pussy like me." The memory called for another swig.

"So I came up with a plan. We'd come down and find us a shaman and learn how to turn into a jaguar. Then we'd go back and charge people to watch. We'd make a killin', I reckoned. Think of all the church folk that would pay to see a goddam jaguar straight from Lucifer."

The rain let up a little, and I slowed the wipers down. I fumbled to find the defrost and ended up wiping my sleeve on the windshield and opening the window.

"I sold the house and anything someone would pay for. We packed our shit and drug it down here to this hellhole. She found us a shaman. He talked all sorts of shit about letting go of fear and only eating meat. He'd take me deep into the jungle and make me swim naked with snakes and shit to prove I wasn't afraid. Mutherfucker didn't know I grew up with Crocs. That claw's from the first croc I kilt as a boy. Crocs ain't stupid; they can smell a croc killer like me a mile away."

"The next day, he brings a bloody piece of meat. He asks for more money and says that I need to eat the heart of a jaguar before I can become one." He rolled down the window and spat. "He must've thought I was too pussy to eat it. But I did. Maria nearly spewed her shit."

"He starts saying I'm ready. I need to capture the spirit of a jaguar; then, I can be one whenever I want. He tells me a story about how he hid in the jungle pretending to be a jaguar, sensed the jaguar spirit float by the tree, and grabbed it. He said he fought the spirit until the sun came up, and now he owns it. He says I'm ready. Maria says I should do it. She says when we go back, we'll be rich. She says to do what he says."

"The mutherfucker shaman takes me into the jungle. He handcuffs me to a tree and tells me to wear the skin of a jaguar he kilt. He says the jaguar spirit will be attracted to the skin. I ask him why the handcuffs. He says the jaguar spirit might drag me into the water to get free. He says this keeps me from drowning." He took another swig, this one seeming to slow him down a bit.

"He leaves me there, naked with a jaguar skin handcuffed to a tree. Let me tell you, I smelt a rat. What he don't know is that southern boys like me been handcuffed since we could walk. There ain't no chains we can't pick. So I pick the lock and climb into the tree. I put the skin on a bush underneath me."

"Mutherfucking shaman hired five local boys to go and shoot a jaguar. He gave 'em guns and told them where I was. Sure enough, these boys show up and try to shoot the skin. When they came over to see if they kilt it, I dropped. The first one dropped his gun when I landed on him. He shit his pants, and I broke his neck like they do in the movies. He had a knife stuck in his belt, and I pulled it. I gutted the next fucker and shot the other three with his pistol."

"They left the keys in their car. I took the knife and guns and drove back to the shaman's place. When I got there, I could hear Maria screaming and moaning. I stepped in the door, the place smelled like a dive bar. The two of them were drunk, and he was buried in her thighs, banging her stupid. She screamed when she saw me. He jumped up. I grabbed his pecker and cut it off with the knife. Maria was still screaming when her boy came running into the room. I pointed the pecker at him and said, 'Heel boy' and he turned into that welp of a dog that's in the back seat."

He took another swig. I half hoped he'd pass the jar. He looked back at the dog.

"Didn't know Maria had a son. Found out later from her brother. Back home, nobody would believe me. Down here it's different. They told me the dog would turn back into a man and hunt me down for killin' his ma. I took the welp straight to the vet and had his balls cut off. I figured that if he turned back into a boy, he'd have no balls."

He looked out the window; the rain was now a drizzle.

"With no balls, the boy has no reason to live, I reckon. No reason to bite the hand that feeds him."

We crossed the tracks and I turned on a dark dirt road.

"I nailed the pecker to my door so that any other mutherfucking shaman would know I was a shaman killer. Next day I went down to the church and found the padre. I told him about the shaman and the boys I kilt. I confessed my sins. He told me that Jesus was proud of me for killin' a shaman. He said the shamans were keeping people from going to church. He said that now that the shaman was gone people could be saved. Turns out one of the boys I kilt was Pablo's brother. He don't care if it were self-defense or not. He don't care that the shaman was bangin' my girl and takin' my money."

***

The road was barely wide enough for the truck to pass. Leaves from low-hanging branches brushed the roof of the cab.

"My place is up ahead," he said. "Downriver are the groves. Good place to shoot Crocs. Gotta boat down there just for huntin' em."

We pulled up to a dark structure.

"Leave the lights on for a minute," he said as he got out and walked up to the door. He pulled a key hidden beside the door frame and unlocked the door. As soon as he entered, I could see him flip a switch, and the house lit up. He came back to the truck to retrieve his jar, now almost empty. I turned off the truck and pulled the brake. We followed him to the house.

"Barn's in the back," he said. I handed him the ring of keys, and he hung them next to the door. Other keys hung beside. Each was neatly labeled.

He grabbed the key marked "barn," and we followed him around the side of the house.

"Live off grid," he explained. "Keeps people from asking questions. Keeps the bills down too," he laughed. "There's an outhouse over yonder. Just follow the path. You fall into water, and you've gone too far." He laughed. The barn was some tin covering a few sheets of plywood nailed to some posts. It was dry underneath, and there was room for our hammocks. He pointed to a dark spot between the barn and the outhouse.

"Over there's a jaguar," he said, motioning. "Caught her a few weeks ago. Got called by folks in the city. Said a jaguar killed a woman and a man. They told me it was a shaman terrorizing the city. They knew I kill mutherfucking shamans. So I went to the city and tracked the shaman with dogs. Mutherfucker jumped the city wall before I could get him into the trap. This bitch somehow took the bait. I've been holding her till I find a buyer." He stopped for a minute and steadied himself against the barn.

"I got called by this big man from the city. He said he needed protection. He said the shaman that kilt the man knew about the factory being built. The workers at the site were afraid that a shaman who could change into a jaguar would kill them too. The big man said if I kilt the shaman jaguar, I could have his pecker to nail to the door. He would pay me when I gave him the pelt from the jaguar shaman. He said there were important people in the states that wanted the shaman pelt."

He emptied the jar. It proved to be a movement that caused him to stumble.

"I found some boys with guns and showed em how to guard the hill. I set them up and promised big money when we kill the shaman. Them boys are eatin' it up. I gave 'em guns." He paused, turning back toward the house. "Been thinking I could skin this bitch and pass her off as a male. But then I wouldn't have a pecker to nail to the door." When he made it to the door, the dog at his feet waiting to get in, he shouted, "Flashlights inside the door." He and the dog disappeared.

We stood in front of the barn. It was too late to look for another place to stay. I found the flashlights and we hooked the hammocks to the posts holding the roof. We tested them before we got in. He was quiet.

He knew that I had much to digest. Ben had called the cowboy to catch me. Ben had to be acting on behalf of the company. The company wanted me dead. As I thought about it, I realized that I could never return to my apartment or my old life. No doubt that the men in golf shirts were here to protect their investment. Most likely they had already been to my apartment. There was no phone, no wallet, no computer, and no passport to return to. Somebody wanted proof that I was dead. Fear.

There had always been the safety net of going back. The chance that I could discover by some miracle a way to save humanity and the forest and retain my life. Like the tree at the edge of the forest, there was no returning to what was. I could only stand and face what was coming.

Outside was a jaguar in a cage. She had taken my place and was destined to die or be caged for the rest of her life. The lights from the house went dark. I waited. I heard the song of the jungle call. It was sweet and inviting. The moon had crested and was about to hide behind the hill. For now, I could see the path to the outhouse past the cage.

I slipped out of the hammock and made my way to the cage. As I approached, the smell of death, decay, and feces caught me off guard. At the back of the darkness, caged in the bars were two eyes staring back. The eyes looked at me, then in the direction of the house. I knew instantly.

I silently crept to the front door where the shaman's pecker hung like a withered green bean from the frame. The door slipped quietly open, and I saw the key marked "cage." When I closed the door, the dog appeared and watched me silently. He neither alerted nor welcomed me. I went back to the cage and slid the key into the lock. The tumblers fell, and the key rotated. I felt the door release.

I opened the door and sat. A shadow with eyes sniffed the frame and stepped out of the cage. She was a magnificent creature. I closed the door behind her quietly. She stepped up to me. We sat face to face. She smelled me. Her eyes locked onto mine. She moved in closer and rubbed her head against my head. Then she rubbed her body against mine, finishing the motion with her tail. She turned and looked me in the eye again before disappearing into the darkness.

I locked the cage back up and returned the key to its hook. The dog had settled in the doorway. He didn't stir. When I got back to my hammock, I knew he was awake. I assumed he knew what I did.

"We should be gone before he gets up," I whispered.

"Agreed," came from the darkness.

I settled into the hammock. I remembered her eyes. I remembered what her fur felt like. I remembered watching her disappear into the darkness. I felt relief. I knew the trap was meant for me. I felt horrible that she suffered. At least now she was free. I felt like I set things right. It was the comfort I needed to fall asleep.

***

She slipped into the darkness. The moon had settled behind the hill, casting gray shadows against the trunks of the trees. For days, she had watched him stumble to the outhouse in the middle of the night. She had seen the tree branch that hung over the worn path. She climbed the tree and waited. She was hungry. She patiently awaited the familiar click from the door.

The cowboy was still drunk. He headed to the outhouse in just his briefs. He stumbled up the path, leaning on each tree as he made his way to the next. He didn't see the branch above the path or what awaited him there. He stumbled to find the tree, and darkness dropped on him. His body collapsed under the weight. He felt the grip on the back of his neck. Blood spurted where her long teeth penetrated his skin. It ran down his neck and pooled in his collarbone before dripping to the earth.

The dog was at the door when he saw her drop onto him. He immediately bolted toward them. She heard him coming, and when he leapt, she swatted him off his feet, and he flew into a tree. He fell motionless to the ground. She watched as he stood back up and shook his head. She had a firm grip and control of the body. She lifted and twisted the neck until she felt it snap. His arms and feet jolted and kicked. The dog leaped again and was met by a paw once more. This time, the claws tore at his flesh, and he landed stunned on the ground a few feet away. She felt the body go limp. Blood stopped spurting and just drained down his body. She left the body in a shallow pool of rainwater and turned to the dog. He would be an easier meal to carry into the jungle.

He was just waking up when she closed her jaws around his head. He didn't stand a chance. Her jaws were a vice around his neck, and she shook the body like a plaything. The dog's body went heavy, and she dropped it to the ground. It didn't move. She picked it up and disappeared into the trees to the safety of the jungle.

We must have an unknown sense that feels when death is close. Before I even woke, I knew she dropped him and he was dead. When I woke, I could hear the last of the struggle. Waves of life penetrated the quiet melody that had lulled us to sleep. Ripples of the passing of life resonated against the quiet when she disappeared into the jungle. The stillness could have been mistaken for reverence. It was simply the pause between waves. Soon, before the visible eye could see it, light would cast itself onto the scene.

His body shuffled in his hammock. I knew he was awake too. Once again, my actions instigated actions beyond my control. Another man was dead. I didn't need to see to know. We waited silently for first light.

When just the glimmer of light revealed itself, we both quietly packed up our hammocks and bags. Neither of us went to investigate. As we walked past the house, he stopped. I could see him mulling thoughts. He went through the door to where the keys were hanging. He picked one from its hook and slid it into his pocket. We walked silently in the shadows of the morning.

In the burgeoning light, the house took form. To say it was modest would have been polite. He was probably squatting on the property. There wasn't a house number, and the driveway was an unimproved set of tracks. The building was stout, meaning it could withstand winds and rain, but the foundation looked dubious at best. Windows that had been pilfered were hastily cut into the walls. The siding was painted the color of mud, making it almost imperceptible from a distance. A row of solar panels was bolted to the tin roof, and wires hung down the side wall and ran into the house to where batteries must have been stored. There were 55-gallon drums discreetly placed to be hidden that most likely held drinking water. The trash container held empty liquor bottles covered by empty dog food bags. The "barn" where we stayed may have been the better of the accommodations.

***

We followed the parallel tracks down to a dirt road. When we met up with the paved road, trucks were already passing by. We walked along the edge of the road, feeling the gusts and pebbles from the dump trucks. When we met a bridge, we slipped down the side of the embankment and followed the creek. Livestock and wildlife left us a modest path alongside the water. Fencelines became less frequent. The modest path all but disappeared as the jungle took back its foothold. We walked along the bank of the stream when the path disappeared. The stream met up with other streams until we had to decide which side of the growing river to walk on. He kept us moving. Our progress was slowed by the water and the jungle.

Only occasionally did he stop to pick up a mango or other fruits. He was silent. I couldn't tell if he was trying to distance us from the shack or if his urgency was prompted by the possibility of weather. I worked hard to keep up. Sweat dripped from my body. Hunger found its way into all of my muscles. When we came to a waterfall, we stopped. Standing by the crashing water, we each ate a mango.

He squatted next to the water and looked at the sky. It was clear blue now, but we both knew that it could change quickly. He washed his face and then his arms in the water. He retrieved a cup from his bag and dipped it to take a drink.

***

The waterfall was magnificent. The rains of the last few days had fueled its flow. The water raged from the cliffs above us. A bow formed in the mist of the crashing water. I had never seen anything like it before. More than just the visual spectacle, I could feel its power. The sound was deafening, making any conversation impossible. He pointed to the rocks beside the falls. There was a familiar X and circle. This was a safe place. He walked toward the symbol, stepped to his left, and disappeared. I followed, unsure what I would find.

There was an entrance hidden that led to a room behind the falls. A cavern that had taken eons to form twisted behind massive stones into a dry room. It was dark. It took a moment for my eyes to adjust. Just enough light was able to beam its way through holes in the cliff to lightly illuminate the room. There was a ring where a fire could be lit and evidence of smoke rising to escape from the same holes that let light enter. It was a marvel a million years in the making.

To my surprise, it was quiet. I could hear the falls, but we could also speak. He sat, and the same gentle eyes that saw the first time we met caught mine.

"If there is any hesitation, this may be the last chance to turn back," he said.

Gravity. I closed my eyes and took a deep breath, another first.

"There are things that cannot be undone," he said. "It's important that you know this."

"People have died, I know," I said.

"Death is a part of being alive," he said. "Something dies so that another can live."

"Are you saying that they died for me?"

He sat quietly for a moment. "No," he said finally. "Their deaths had nothing to do with you."

His words stopped me. Of course, they died because of my actions. "Leah, Roger, and the cowboy would all be alive if I hadn't come here."

"Really? How do you know?" he asked.

Now I sat quietly. He let me sit.

He disappeared behind the stone that blocked the sound of the waterfall. His hammock rested where he had been. Time passed. I found that I couldn't move. Images from the past crowded their way into my mind. I saw myself when I lost my parents, and I devoted myself to finding a cure for what killed them. I saw myself at the university working fervently to make the necessary grades to be noticed and hired by the company. I saw the moment I realized I was working for the same people who were responsible for my parents' deaths. I remembered saying, "I don't want to be human." Until this moment, I hadn't realized how much I was what I had come to hate — self-involved and self-important.

Chapter Twenty-Three

He returned with his bag full of roots, leaves, fruits, and an armful of firewood. Close to the wall was a recess with the necessary dry tinder to start a fire. The ember he carried around his neck had gone cold. He pulled the flint and struck it close to a nest of hair and shavings. Sparks led to smoke that turned into a weak flame. The flame caught, and he nurtured the fire until it could sustain itself. Smoke meandered around the chamber before finding a way out. As the fire grew, the smoke in the room cleared, and he went about preparing a meal.

The crack of thunder startled me. We were safe and dry; this would be home for the night. The light of the fire revealed where to hang our hammocks to stay dry and warm. He busied himself hanging both our hammocks and making sure that our things were dry.

I sat.

Despite his warnings, there was no turning back. When I realized it, it sank into my gut. Then came the fear.

"How will I live?" I blurted out. "I have nothing."

He rotated the plantain leaf pot like I'd seen him do many times already.

"You are alive," he said. It seemed an odd response.

"I don't know how to survive in the jungle," I said.

"Who says you have to live in the jungle? People have lived all over the world and for centuries," he said.

"I'll die," I said.

"Eventually, we all die," he said. "Now you have a chance to live."

His words hung in the air like the smoke before it found its escape. But there was no escape from his words. They both stung and liberated me.

"You learned how to survive in the human world. You will learn how to live in the rest of the world." He made it sound simple.

It was true; I knew how to earn a paycheck and pay my bills. I knew how to buy food from the market and drive a car home. As nice as my apartment was, it was nothing like sleeping behind a waterfall sitting by a fire. No store-bought meal was as satisfying as roots and plantains roasted by the fire.

"You communed with birds," I said, changing the subject. He nodded.

"What did you learn?" I asked.

He thought about it for a while.

"Joy," he said. "Scientists have studied how birds fly, and man has marveled and mimicked them. The secret is joy. Joy is what lifts a bird to heights. Joy is what makes them sing and laugh and play." He sat quietly, perhaps remembering, perhaps feeling the joy of being a bird.

I remembered the bees.

I juggled the logs on the fire and put a new one on. Flames sprang to life. He watched.

"What did you learn from the jaguar?" he asked.

I was hesitant. "No fear," I said. "But that doesn't really explain it." He waited as I struggled for words. "The forest was musical; I listened to the music." I expected him to laugh at me. Instead, he listened without speaking. "The music spoke to me without words; I just had to listen."

"You didn't have to learn to be a jaguar?" he asked pointedly, smiling. "Nobody taught you to listen?"

"No, it was natural," I said. "As I think about it, the listening took away my fear."

"And now?"

"My thoughts keep me from listening," I replied.

"And afraid," he pointed out. He turned the plantain pot again; water was steaming. He added the rice and beans to soak for the night. There was the familiar pinch of herbs that came from his bag. He closed the pot carefully and slid it away from the fire.

"I see what you are getting at," I said. He smiled gently.

I got up from the fire and found the blanket that had been stowed in my hammock. I went past the big rock and stood looking at the waterfall from behind. When I stepped to the side, I could watch rain disrupting the surface of the pool. I closed my eyes to listen. I could hear a distinct difference between the waterfall and the rain. The sound became two parts to a melody that wove itself together. Thunder rumbled, adding to the song. If I listened with my whole being, I could hear the rain on the leaves of the trees and the dripping droplets settling to the muddy ground.

I thought about Leah. She was the first glimmer of life that I encountered. She taught me to breathe. I took a deep breath. My breath added to the melody. It invited me to become lost in its magic. I closed my eyes and leaned against the stones behind me. Now the sounds became even more pronounced.

Water ran down the vines that hung to the sides of the waterfall. The rain ran down them, accumulating in pools where the vines clung to the rocks. When the pools filled, they overflowed, spilling with yet a new sound. The stone I leaned against carried the vibrations of the rain and water. Near my shoulders, the hum was pitched high with the plink, plink, plink of raindrops. At my feet, I felt the growl of the water crashing on stones and into the pool. I listened more closely. Birds chirped in the distance, their voices nearly concealed by the water. The experience took me out of my body. I resonated. The beating of my heart and the cadence of my breath made the experience complete. Every moment brought a new subtle change to the song. I fought the urge to open my eyes.

When I finally did, the world awakened. It took effort to keep the feeling of being immersed in the vibration of the moment. When I wavered, I closed my eyes again until the melody called me back. I let my eyes softly open, not looking, not seeing but giving my sight over to the accumulated experience. I took a deep breath again. It was a first.

The light of the day was dimming. I didn't know how long I stood by the falls. There would be no stars tonight; the clouds held back their brilliance.

***

In the protection of our secret room, he had divided out dinner and was sitting in his hammock. His feet dangled on either side, and he held his dinner bowl between his thighs. He ate silently, undisturbed by my return. It occurred to me that he'd sat and eaten this way many times. He savored every bite slowly. There was nothing to distract him from being completely in the moment. I moved quietly, "like a jaguar," I thought to myself.

I sat in my hammock and ate. The fire crackled and cast shadows onto the stone walls. I wouldn't have been surprised to see glyphs or graffiti, but the walls were pristine. It gave the room a sacred feel. The shadows moved as the flames danced. It was mesmerizing. I felt myself being pulled again toward an unknown part of my psyche. Light and darkness mingled.

I let my eyes soften. The movement between light and dark became a randomness that let my mind soften too.

My body relaxed back into the hammock. I felt something welling up inside. As it rose in me, I saw my parents and then my team. Grief. Leah. The hillside that would become a factory. Grief. Finally, I grieved the life I was walking away from. The safety of a predictable life was gone. The emptiness of not knowing was familiar; I had felt it with the death of my parents. I had pushed it away by filling my life with school and then with work and research. It was an ache that rose in me. I curled into a ball and let the waves of emotion waft over me. My body contorted and shook. For a moment, it felt like I was fighting for my life.

Part of me wanted the darkness of death to free me from the ache of emptiness. Another part was prepared for a battle. Then the question, "What am I fighting against? Who am I fighting?" I didn't have an answer. I listened to the sound of the fire, his breathing, and the distant growl of the waterfall, hoping to hear an answer. Instead, the ache became a part of the song. I could feel the beating of my heart in my head. It kept time. The volume rose and diminished. Images appeared in the dancing shadows, and I had to let go. I tried to understand, tried to grasp the meaning. I finally submitted to the idea that maybe there was none, or no meaning that I could understand. I let the grief swallow me. I invited it, hoping it would take the last of my ache.

***

I heard him moving. I remained motionless in the hammock as he prepared a meal and packed his few things. He made sure the dry place was stocked for the next traveler.

When he was organized, he took his bowl and stepped out beside the waterfall.

I didn't want to move. My body still ached from the emotional upheaval of the night before. My mind wanted a plan, trying to devise a way to keep what I already knew was gone. It was useless. I rolled out of the hammock, packed my things, and joined him with my bowl.

He had found a spot on the other side of the pool. Mist rose from the water as he sat, watching birds dart across the clearing. Other birds perched in the trees, calling. Monkeys descended from the branches to scavenge fruit that the rain had knocked down. They would capture one or two pieces, then dash back to safety, chased by diving birds. He seemed content to watch.

***

When we were ready to leave, I retrieved a seed pod from my bag, holding it in my palm. There was something satisfying about planting a seed and letting new life thrive after so much death. I drove it deep into the mud by the pool. Behind us lay the path. He looked at me, asking with his eyes if I was ready or planned to turn back.

"Forward," I said.

He nodded.

We rose from the pool's edge to an overlook above the valley below. When we crested, we stopped to look. The waterfall dropped several more times before a river snaked through the jungle below. Stone cliffs hemmed in the dense trees, and off-white stones emerged from the canopy like the walls of a castle.

Our path took us around the rim to a gentler descent into the valley. Smoke drifted in the breeze, faint but present. He turned to me before we descended.

"They're clearing parts of the jungle for the factory. What they can't bury, they burn."

***

Guilt rose within me. I'd have to plant a lot of seeds to make up for this devastation. As we rounded a corner back toward the paved road, I heard a familiar sound—a humming that called to me.

"I need a minute," I said.

He stopped and watched as I stepped off the path, moving deeper into the jungle. The smell of smoke thickened. When I found the hive, it was cloaked in smoke. The bees were confused, hovering near the hive, unable to navigate their way out. My heart broke, knowing this swarm might not survive. Clearing the jungle for roads, housing, and stores would eventually displace or eradicate them.

As I approached, the bees landed on me, tasting the sweat on my skin. Their confusion resonated with me. They sang a lament, a call for help. I sat at the base of the tree. A hum grew in my throat, and I began to hum a melody. It calmed the swarm, and they rested on my body. When the air momentarily cleared, they would flap their wings and begin to hover, only to be met with smoke and confusion again.

I could hear the queen's sweet voice as I hummed. She sang back, and our songs merged. My song became my breath, filling my heart with love. The bees went still in my palms and on my shoulders, listening to the queen's love song. Their confusion quieted, and we found a stillness.

****

I sang to her about the factory. I confided my part, confessing my guilt. She sang sweetly to my soul, offering only love and acceptance. I sang of progress and the danger to the hive. Men would stop at nothing to claim this part of the forest for profit. I remembered the pass above the factory, filled with flowers, the old trees and forest we had passed through. As I did, the bees began to dance on my chest, following along.

She asked how I came to be here. I remembered the hill where earthmovers tore down old-growth trees. I remembered the stream next to the old shack, the path to town, the ride to the barn, and the trail to the waterfall. The bees danced.

They knew the waterfall; they were sure they had been to the town. Safety wasn't far. I revealed that the smoke was thick, floating between the trees. Above us, the sky was clear, free of smoke and danger. The dance quickened, and all the bees moved in unison, learning the steps. I heard her voice rise, a sweet request for the swarm's safety. A contingent of brave-hearted bees rose, broke through the smoke, and flew to investigate. They returned, reporting clear air above the trees.

***

I wept. She continued singing, her voice now a song of hope. There would be a new hive. She urged them to gorge themselves on honey and fly to build a new nest. Her song shifted, now one of possibility and empowerment. I knew she would stay until the end, awaiting the last of the swarm who might not understand. She would nurture the birth of new bees so they could make the journey, knowing she might not be able to leave. Still, there was only love.

It broke my heart, yet my heart soared at the same time.

Tears ran down my face, and the bees moved to let them spill. I wanted to find her and carry her to safety. She knew. She heard my heart. She sang to me like a lover who was leaving, telling me I must go—not back, but forward. She sang that, when the time came, I too needed to fly.

***

The song became the buzzing of the swarm. Smoke began to clear, and the air around the tree grew lighter. The bees swarmed me, their dance now a mission. As much as I wanted to stay and protect them, they bid me farewell.

I found him back on the path where we had parted. I wasn't sure if he had watched or knew; it didn't matter. He looked me in the eyes and held my gaze. I was sure that the tears that had fallen moments before began again. It made no difference.

I don't know what he saw. He put his hand on my shoulder. I wrapped my arms around him and wept, my body shaking against his thin frame. His arms held me until the shaking stopped. When I loosened my grip and stepped back, he met my gaze again. There was nothing to be said.

He nodded. I nodded back, took a deep breath, and he turned, leading us back down the path.

***

The path took us down into the valley. The rain from the night before made our progress slow. Tree limbs hung heavy, drunk with water clinging to their leaves. The dirt was muddy and slick, and even his movements seemed like slow motion.

The sun brought heat, and our clothes stuck to our skin. Small, residual streams from the rain ran down and across our path. Only the birds seemed impervious to the humidity and mud. Fruit hung low, making it easy to pick a few mangos and papayas.

Eventually, the path led us to what might be considered a parking area that connected to a dirt road. The road was much easier to follow than the jungle trail. It wound itself in and through the trees, occasionally opening into clearings where cows grazed on wild grasses. Sometimes, we had to cross a fence. The parallel stripes of muddy dirt grew wider until they became a single, wide road. Mud still pooled where the road dipped, while trees bowed over us, shading our progress.

The road merged with another, wide enough for two cars to pass, graded to allow water to flow on either side. The first shack, nestled in the trees, surprised me. It resembled a pile of wood and tin. As we passed, bags of trash and a huge jug of water hinted that someone had been there recently.

***

Soon, whenever we saw that someone had cut the fence along the road to create a path into the trees, we knew what it meant. Abandoned cars started appearing, trees growing through their windows, with little evidence left of where rubber had once been tires. The shacks became more frequent and substantial.

It wasn't until the space on either side of the road opened up that we saw other people. I smelled the fumes from a generator before I heard it—a constant hum. A group of buildings stood at the end of a gravel road. Children ran naked in the mud, howling with laughter. Several old men and women sat in plastic chairs the legs sinking into the mud, watching the children. Most of them held a cigarette in one hand and a bottle in the other, laughing and chatting about the children. Behind them, open doors led to dark rooms. Cardboard served as makeshift porches, and trash piled up between the structures. Skinny dogs yipped and ran with the children.

One building stood out. Freshly painted, it had liquor signs nailed to the walls. An LED sign blinked in the window. Three doors were perfectly spaced across a cement entry: one led to a bar, another to a liquor store, and the last to a bodega. The generator powered this operation, keeping the lights on and making ice. The ice kept beer cold in giant coolers.

Several cars were parked in front of the bar, but one stood out—a white, clean vehicle with an official logo on the door. Inside the bar, a man in a clean, starched white shirt barely containing his belly sat with a cold beer bottle in front of him, condensation dripping down to a pool at the base. Beside him, a doe-eyed young woman pretended to savor every word he spoke.

We remained mostly unnoticed until the far edge. A woman sat in the doorway of a dirt-floored shack, linens hanging from a laundry line behind her. She smiled and made a come-hither motion with her hand. Her dress hung loosely on her small frame, ready to be abandoned if the opportunity arose. I smiled politely back. After we passed, I heard her tap a cigarette out of the pack beside her.

***

We followed the road to a cement building with a parking area nearby. Beyond the building was water. The streams we had followed had become a river. It looked almost still, but the water moved deceptively fast. Boats rested on the bank beside the river. Most were plywood rowboats, painted to help keep them watertight, but there were a few motorized boats on trailers. They sat in a colorful row, and we walked past them slowly. When he reached the end, he looked perplexed and glanced up and down the riverbank.

"This is where most people store their boats and put them into the river. I don't see…" he paused and started walking toward the jungle at the far side of the lot.

I didn't see what caught his eye until we were almost on top of it. A metal skiff was hidden behind some bushes, secured by a giant chain and lock to a nearby tree. He squatted next to the boat and carefully moved a couple of heart-shaped leaves away from it, then gently let them fall back into place.

I stood watching, confused at first. He walked over to the tree where the chain was wrapped around the trunk and lifted a few more leaves. A large padlock held the chain to the tree. He put the leaves back and looked around. Moving to a nearby tree, he pulled back the leaves to reveal an arrow with a steel tip pointed directly at the boat, held in place by a trip line. Any movement to the line would have released the arrow with devastating consequences for the intruder. We marveled at the ingenuity and simplicity of the trap— either the thief would be wounded, or the boat would have a hole to repair.

"Stand back," he motioned, and I moved. He grabbed the shaft of the arrow and carefully released the tension. He ensured there was no other arrow or obstacle before letting it go, and the slack line allowed the arrow to fall a few feet past the boat. The perimeter line went slack.

***

He was still careful as he reached for the lock. The key turned, and the shackle lifted. The chain slumped to the ground. A motor and oars were neatly tucked under the seats. When we slid the boat out from under the bushes, the key fit a second lock that released the motor and oars, revealing a long box bolted to the boat's floor. A combination lock protected its contents.

We stood back, looking at the conundrum. We took a moment to ensure the boat looked watertight. It was newer aluminum, with registration stickers on the back. For all his complaints about Pablo, he had ensured the boat was legal for the river. He grabbed the bow, and I took the stern. We carried it closer to the water. Using the year of the oldest-looking registration sticker, I tried the combination on the box.

Inside, alongside a couple of lifejackets, were a rifle and pistol, both carefully wrapped in waterproof sleeves. A watertight ammo box sat neatly beside them. He looked at the cache, unfazed. The boat was big enough that, if he shot a crocodile, it would fit inside—small enough to negotiate narrow passages.

He went to the cement building and filled our jars with water from a spigot that jutted out from the wall.

We placed our bags and hammocks in the skiff and pushed it into the water. The motor could have been mounted to the back of the boat, but instead, he pulled out the oars and slid them into the hooks on either side. He sat in the middle and began to row. It was clear this was his first attempt at rowing with two oars.

Sitting at the front, facing him, I could tell that my watching him made him nervous, so I turned around. The boat veered left, then right, then left again.

"Have you ever done this before?" he asked, frustration in his voice.

"When I was in summer camp, I did some rowing across a lake," I said.

"Good. Why don't you try?"

We carefully changed seats, gripping the sides of the boat as it rocked. This would have been the perfect time for the parrots to laugh, but instead, the boat drifted and rotated so that we were looking where we'd been, not where we were going. I started to laugh. He did too. The oars hung loosely in the water, floating uselessly as we spun aimlessly downstream.

When I finally got a hold of the oars, I lifted them out of the water and composed myself. As the rotation brought us in the right direction, I dropped the oars back in and pulled us straight. I took a few practice strokes to move the boat downstream. After a few missteps, I managed to keep us more or less steady.

He pointed to our right.

"Stay close to the banks on this side in case we have to get out."

I maneuvered the skiff, and soon we were floating with the river's flow. I used the oars to adjust our direction and kept an eye out for obstacles jutting or lingering near the banks.

Initially, the river was narrow and shallow enough that I could have swum across easily. Other streams joined, widening it to the point that reaching the opposite bank would take effort, whether by swimming or rowing. The water started clear but grew murky with sediment from the rain-fed streams. Jungle encroached on both sides, with limbs arching over the river to provide shade from the sun's heat.

I was sure the motor would have propelled us faster, but after my experience with rowing—and with no cash for gas—I was content to drift. I watched the banks, grateful to avoid hacking through the dense brush. Occasionally, we'd pass a boat or canoe tied to a tree. The song of the jungle mingled with the song of the river. The dip of the oars created ripples, and birds watched from branches above, some squawking, others swooping closer to observe us. Swarms of insects hovered along the banks, and occasionally, we'd glide through them, briefly disturbing their cloud.

He sat at the front, occasionally pointing out obstacles. I could tell the river was deepening, although the banks stayed consistent. The river's depth dictated our speed; shallow areas sped us up, while deeper stretches slowed our pace. We approached a makeshift platform stretching from the bank into the water. He motioned me over. When we neared, a few men in shorts and t-shirts tossed him a rope, and we pulled ourselves to the dock. He had closed the box in the boat and covered it with our bags. I stowed the oars along the boat's sides and tied it off.

He stood uneasily in the boat's center, and one of the young men extended an arm. The boat rocked as he steadied himself and climbed onto the dock, laughter marking our inexperience. I let the boat drift closer, grabbed an outstretched hand, planted a foot on the dock, and made the transition smoothly.

The hand belonged to a young man with dark eyes, cinnamon skin, and a disarming smile. His dark hair was pulled back in a tail, and he motioned toward a plankway leading to the bank. The rough, weathered boards shifted underfoot as we walked. A few steps up the damp earth, the jungle opened into a village of huts.

Chapter Twenty-Four

As we approached the central structure, children ran to greet us. They pointed at our linen clothes and beards, chattering words I couldn't understand. An older man, accompanied by several others, met us in the communal area. He extended his hand to my companion, and they greeted each other warmly, chatting briefly before both pointed back toward the boat. Together, they walked to the dock, talking quietly. When they returned, he turned to me.

"They've invited us to stay the night. Can you get the mangos from our bags?"

I nodded and, accompanied by the young man who had helped me, returned to the boat. I carefully stepped to the center and retrieved a few ripe mangos from the bag, tossing them to him. Now surrounded by children, he handed them the mangos, and they ran off laughing.

***

We ate communally with the villagers. They shared stories of increased river traffic. He explained that more people were coming to work on a large building upriver, near the mountains. The villagers exchanged glances, and the old man made a few comments. He translated for me, explaining that the building was in the mountains and that the villagers had lived here by the river since it first made its way from the mountains. The old man was unconcerned. The young men listened intently. They had seen fiberglass motorboats blaring music; some had even shared cigarettes and heard about life in the city. The promises of progress could tempt some of them. The old man knew this, and like the tree on the hill, he could do little to prevent the changes that the factory would bring. I held my words, letting my heart grow heavy.

Later, in the hut where we hung our hammocks, he took a moment to explain. We sat quietly, as he told me that the villagers recognized the boat. He had offered it as a trade, but they were afraid of the cowboy who owned it. Even though he assured them the cowboy was dead, they still refused. We would leave in the morning, but we were invited to gather what we needed from the forest. The old man believed it was good for the village to see us traveling without motors or phones. He held out hope that the jungle's wisdom would eventually outweigh the appeal of an easy life.

***

In the morning, we ate with the community, and I followed the young man I had met into the jungle. We wove through the forest along a worn path. As we walked, he would point to plants, and I'd nod, though I had no idea what I was looking at. Soon, he understood I was a novice and began gathering leaves and fruit himself, adding them to my bag. Sometimes, he'd stop to dig or pull up roots. I began to recognize some of our harvest, and eventually, I started to point things out, earning approving nods. We filled my bag and a smaller one of his.

We stopped beside a sunlit stream. Digging into my bag, I pulled out a seed pod I'd collected from the tree on the hill. I carefully chose a spot where sun and water met, used a stick to make a hole, and planted the seed. The young man watched closely. I dug out another pod and handed it to him. He examined it, unfamiliar with its kind.

Back in the village, he sought out my friend, showing him the seed and speaking in rapid words. My friend called me over.

"He'd like to know why you planted the seed," he said.

I thought for a moment. "The tree where I found the seed is a friend," I said. "My friend might be cut down for the big building. I'm planting parts of him where he'll be safe."

He translated, and the young man listened carefully. "How do you know the tree was your friend?" he asked.

I smiled. Both of them waited for my answer. I placed a hand over my heart.

"In a moment of darkness, I leaned against the tree. The tree touched my heart."

The young man nodded in understanding and tucked the seed into his pocket.

"He says he has another spot for his seed. He'll plant it deep in the jungle where there's a clearing and tall trees."

I placed my hand over my heart again and bowed in thanks.

***

Our harvest brought a smile to my friend's face. My guide handed over his bag, beaming with pride, and received a warm thank-you. Our hosts helped us back to the boat. I got in first to steady it for my friend as he prepared to step in, surrounded by discussion on the best way to board. He finally stepped into the center, grasping a strong, outstretched arm.

We pushed away and into the current on our side of the river. It propelled us quickly enough that I only used the oars to keep us headed the right way downstream. The sun sparkled on the water, and birds called and soared above us.

Parrots chattered from high in the branches that overhung the bank. I waited to hear them laugh; instead, they screeched.

He seemed to be listening to the birds. Occasionally, when the screeching was loud enough, he watched the bank to see what had caught their attention. Other times, I could tell he simply closed his eyes to listen. When we came to a fork in the river, he would point, and I would row us into the proper current. The river would meet up with its fork, with others adding to the flow.

I began to notice and recognize where the occasional path would stray from the water and head into dense trees. Then I could see where canoes were pulled and stowed next to the path. A ribbon or metal sign with bullet holes would mark and perhaps identify who lived there. The first sign, nailed to a board anchored to two posts, caught me by surprise. It had a picture of a beer bottle and a large arrow pointing downriver. The next sign had a picture of a jaguar holding a beer with a big arrow. The next showed a steak on a plate with fried plantains and tortillas folded neatly beside it.

I heard a motor before I saw the boat that was headed upriver. Its bright red hull sparkled with metallic paint. Men in caps sat on padded cushions, holding beer bottles. A shirtless young man manned the wheel. He guided his boat to the other side of the river, but still, the wake rocked us when it reached our skiff. They watched us floating and waved as they motored by.

***

The bullet-holed markers gave way to simple docks that led to the bank and up into the trees. A few had skiffs or motorboats tied off. A few had people watching us pass, and most waved. More boats and more wakes to negotiate before a pier jutted its way into the river. It stood several feet above the water and had steps leading down to floating platforms. The sign above the pier showed a jaguar roaring, its tail turning into an arrow that pointed to a group of buildings above the banks.

He pointed to the pier, and I rowed us close. There were several other boats, all equipped with motors, some with platforms on top and sophisticated electronic antennas. A worker tossed us a rope, and we pulled ourselves to an empty spot near the shore. The floating platform was stable enough for him to get out without capsizing the boat. Pulled to the shore were several canoes, and music thumped from one of the buildings.

Several storefronts were adjacent to the pier, and an old church stood at the far end of the clearing. Trucks with muddy tires were parked in a makeshift lot beside the church. Neon lights blinked in the windows of a bar. As I looked at the church, I saw a single power line hanging between poles that lined the muddy road, like a leash keeping the last bastion of civilization connected to the outer world.

We stood in front of the church.

"You might like this story," he said. "Years ago, the church decided that the natives in this area needed to be saved. They sent a missionary who convinced the tribe here that they should have a church. He brought tools and food, talked about God and Hell, and soon they were helping him build the church." He paused, glancing at the shops to see if anyone was listening.

"When the church was almost finished, the local shaman got upset and tried to get the people to abandon it and move deeper into the jungle. The priest convinced the tribe that the shaman was evil, so they banished him. Later, one night, a jaguar ventured into the church. The priest was inside praying and was startled by the jaguar. The jaguar was startled too, and when the priest tried yelling and charging, the cat leapt and killed him. It left him on the floor of the church, and they claim you can still see the stains from his blood. The jaguar fled into the jungle.

"The next morning, when they found the priest's body, they knew he had been killed by a jaguar. Someone speculated that the shaman had turned into the jaguar to kill the priest. The tribe had a big meeting, decided the shaman was right, and abandoned the church and the village to go search for him."

I shook my head, and we both chuckled a little.

"A businessman who was hunting in the area decided to buy it. The church suspected something had happened to the priest and sent some men to check. They found his decomposed body in the church, and the village was abandoned. The bishop back in the city had bigger problems and sold the property to the businessman. Now people come to fish the waters and hunt. Lots of money flows through here. Smugglers have long used this as a place to stock up before they head to their bigger boats waiting on the coast."

***

We stood in the middle, where the communal hut must have been before it was torn down for trucks and buildings. Near the pier, modern-looking structures gave wealthy

300

visitors a sense of civilization. There was a bar and liquor store, a grocery store, a gas station, and a small hotel. Though they were not connected, it was obvious they were owned by a single entity.

"I'm going over there," he said, pointing to the storefronts. "It might be best if you wait here or by the boat." I nodded in understanding as he walked off.

I found a spot in the shade near the church where I could watch what was happening. Younger men in collared polo shirts emblazoned with a jaguar followed older men in expensive boots and sunglasses. The older men would point, and the younger men would nod and follow instructions. After most interactions, the younger men tended to boats and gear, while the older men ended up in the bar.

Soon, he emerged from one of the doors, followed by two men in polo shirts. One was older, with a toothpick sticking from the side of his mouth. The younger followed behind, listening intently. They went to the pier and looked at the boat. The younger one jumped into the boat like he'd done it a thousand times before. He moved our bags to reveal the case, lifted the rifle and pistol, and handed them to the older man. He checked the modest motor still sitting unused beneath the seat, pulled it out, and bolted it to the back of the boat. He flipped a switch, pulled on the handle with a rope attached, and the engine sputtered, then purred. Satisfied, he gave a thumbs-up to the older man.

The older man checked the rifle and pistol to be sure they weren't loaded—something neither of us had thought to do. Satisfied they were safe, he handed them back to the young man, who was now on the pier beside him. The young man checked the rifle's scope, smiling, and then tested the pistol's weight at arm's length, smiling again.

He took both weapons back to the row of storefronts. My friend and the older man strolled over to the canoes, with the older man rolling the toothpick to the other side of his mouth. They passed several canoes before stopping beside a larger one. It had an outrigger affixed to the side, making it look more substantial. The two talked for quite a while, the older man shrugging and pointing, then glancing around. My friend shook his head occasionally, pointing again at the canoe.

The older man pulled a cigar from a leather case on his belt, bit off the end, and spat it out. He drew a match across the case, scarred from previous use. The flame pulled into the cigar as he took a deep draw. He puffed, arms crossed, kicking at his boots, and waited. My friend squatted like the men at the last village. It was a waiting game: the old man standing, my friend sitting silently.

Finally, the old man went back to the boat, returned, and nodded. He and my friend shook hands. The old man headed back to the store, and my friend looked over at me, smiling as he motioned me to come.

We took our bags from the boat and put them in the canoe. Two other men retrieved the boat, carrying it up onto the bank and flipping it to rest on some carpeted sawhorses. They immediately started peeling the registration stickers from the boat. Carefully, they inspected the bottom, then the inside, and finally one crawled under to check beneath the seats. With the registration stickers gone, there was nothing to identify the boat; it was anonymous.

We picked up the canoe and carried it closer to the river, letting it rest partially floating and partially settled on the muddy bank. The younger man came down to the canoe with a bag hoisted over his shoulder. It hit the ground with a thud. He smiled, then went back to get another. I lifted the bag; it was heavy. I set it in the middle of the canoe. We loaded rice, beans, corn, and flour, along with several smaller bags of salt and sugar. We pushed the canoe further into the water. Already barefoot, I waded in, holding it steady as he climbed aboard. The water was cool, and the mud squished between my toes. The current was already pulling us downstream as I stepped in. He looked up at the sky. It was clear, for now.

For all our failings at rowing, he was adept at paddling and guiding a canoe. It didn't take long for me to fall into his rhythm. I understood why he wanted to trade the boat; he was much more comfortable in the canoe. I looked at the bags, then at him. He smiled. It was enough food to sustain us for a long time, even if we didn't forage.

The river pulled us past the sign with the jaguar, and soon the sounds of classic rock and commerce faded behind us. A few boats passed us, some headed downriver, others up.

"He wasn't sure he wanted to trade," he said finally. "They knew the boat, and they knew the cowboy. Nobody wanted to cross him."

"Did you tell them he was killed by a jaguar?" I asked.

"No," he laughed. "It wouldn't have helped. They'd never believe it." He was watching the side of the water closely. "Ahead, we'll make a turn and head upriver where this river meets another."

***

When the two rivers met, we pulled to the side where the current was much slower. Two long poles rested on the seat beside me. We stood up, using them to push our way up the river close to the shore. It was hard work. We stopped several times, using the poles to hold our position. Our progress seemed slow, but soon we couldn't see where we had turned.

This river was less traveled. Gone were the makeshift docks and markers with bullet holes. The water moved slower, and my pole disappeared into the murkiness. After a while, it was easier to paddle. He guided the canoe along the bank, keeping us in the slow current. We slid through the water quietly, the rhythmic sounds of our paddles tracking our progress. I was lulled in my fatigue, moving without thinking, and I found myself listening to the sounds around me. I could feel his paddle pulling the canoe to one side or the other, and I followed his lead without thinking.

The sky was growing darker, and the river narrowed. Trees bowed over on either side, covering us like an arch. Vines hung from branches, dipping their roots into the water below. I could hear a new song from the jungle—our paddles dipping and dripping, our small wake lapping against the banks where old branches and twigs buoyantly kept time. There was a silence to the melody, an earthy smell filling my breath. It was the familiar smell of leaves and moss transforming, nurturing what was yet to come. This scent was thicker, almost tangible, capturing any anomalous sounds that interrupted the stillness.

I could hear raindrops, though few made it past the canopy above us. Alcoves of gentle eddies invited us into private, secluded pools beside the river. We drifted into one of these alcoves. He maneuvered us next to a log that bordered the bank. Beside the log, several large stones allowed us to pull our bags of supplies out of the canoe. He mounted the log barefoot, finding his footing with one foot on the log, the other on the flat stones. I hoisted each bag up to him, letting it rest first on the log, then sliding it to the stone. With the canoe lightened, he motioned to a sandy area where we could pull it ashore.

***

He met me at the sandy area, and together we pulled the canoe out of the water. A path hidden behind the stones led further up the bank. We dragged the canoe up behind the stones and flipped it to keep the rain out. It seemed like few ventured here. Barefoot, we followed the path, leaving our bags and supplies behind. The path was familiar to him. I looked around; everything here was different from the higher rainforests we'd come from. The leaves were larger and striped. Vines hung on vines, clinging to giant trees. Moss draped from branches and vines. High above us, branches held clusters of leaves to catch the sunlight. The path was clear but narrow, as the jungle reclaimed every centimeter not consistently cleared.

Smoke hung between us and the sky, billowing softly through the trees. Not far ahead, on a rise, stood a hut. Smoke was rising from a metal pipe darkened from years of use. He approached without hesitation, and I stayed just behind him. As we drew near the door, it opened. I could sense him smiling.

An older man with long, dark hair stepped into the doorway. When he saw us, he smiled and opened his arms. They embraced like old friends. He stood taller than the older man, who seemed to disappear into his friend's thin frame as they embraced.

When their arms loosened, the older man held his friend's biceps and turned to look at me. He seemed like a younger version of himself, his dark eyes soft yet piercing. His smile was welcoming as he stepped slowly toward me. It was only now that his age showed. He held his right hand up, palm toward me. Unsure of what to do, I stood motionless, watching him. Despite his slow approach, he seemed to float gracefully. When he reached me, he placed his hand on my heart and looked into my eyes. I couldn't blink or look away; my thoughts went silent, I experienced absolute clarity.

He lifted his hand from my chest. Though I could see it drawing back toward his own heart, I could still feel its warmth, coupled with a heaviness. As the weight lifted, my mind returned. I was still looking into his face when he turned to my friend. Their gaze locked for a long moment before he turned back to me, placing his hand on his heart and inclining his head.

"Welcome, friend," he said. His voice was quiet yet powerful, carrying the tones and character of experience.

"Thank you," I replied, placing my hand over the still-warm spot on my chest.

My friend smiled. "The door has opened yet again," he said. "Let's get the bags and bring them in before the weather hits." His words broke the spell.

***

We stood in a clearing in front of the hut. The open space was bordered by old trees, their bark gray from years of sun and rain. The ground was clear, allowing sunlight to reach it. Stones lined the edge of the clearing, forming a perfect circle. Several paths branched off into the jungle. I recognized the one we had come in on.

I made my way back down the path, picking up our bags. With the hammocks slung over my shoulder, I could still carry one of the big bags. They were still standing in the circle when I returned. I set the bags just inside the hut's door. It took several trips to bring everything inside. When I set down the last bag, I hesitated. They were still outside.

Instead of joining them, I took a moment to look around the hut. It was simple, with two windows on either side of the door. One faced the clearing; the other looked toward the river. A narrow door at the back likely led to a cooking area, judging by the smoke and the stack rising from the roof. The doors and windows were the only modern elements in an otherwise traditional hut. The walls were woven and fitted between sturdy poles. The roof was meticulously thatched with palm fronds. The walls were bare, except for a shelf toward the back, which held jars like the one I was carrying. The floor was earthen, though immaculately swept. A center post provided a place to hang a hammock, allowing the hut to sleep several people.

A single hammock hung from the center to the back of the hut. Beneath the shelf of jars was a bag much like ours.

A change of clothes sat neatly below the bag. Near the back door was a bin. I looked around to see if there was the X symbol anywhere. The room was simple enough; it could have been a place where travelers would rest.

They came in together behind me. I could hear the rain starting outside. He took the large bags of staples and put them in the bin by the back door. Then he disappeared out the back. The older man stood in the doorway watching the rain. Then I noticed his eyes were closed. I balanced myself against the center pole and did the same. The image of rain made me think about mud and being cold. The sound of the rain had a different effect. Something was life-affirming about hearing the water. The thickness of the roof dulled the sound of drops landing. It had a droning effect that lulled me. I heard the back door open and close. It added to the sounds. The shuffle of the older man as he turned was the first indication of his age. Then I smelled the smoke from the cookstove. It gave way to the smell of something that would taste good. I opened my eyes and turned. He was holding a pot of soup in one hand and three bowls in the other.

He set the pot on the bin by the door. It had a top that acted as a table when it was closed. There was plenty of soup. Its aroma was new to my palate. He portioned out a bowl for each of us, and we sat on the floor. Each of us took a moment to savor the first spoonful. There was a thickness and bite to its warmth—chunks that felt and tasted like potatoes. A few spoonful's in, I paused.

I turned to the older man and asked, "Did you know we were coming?"

The two of them looked at each other and smiled.

"No," he said. "I didn't need to."

"But you made just enough for the three of us."

"Did you show up because you knew I made enough for visitors?" he asked.

"No," I said. "I followed him." I looked over at my friend. "Did you know?" I asked. He shook his head no without looking up from his bowl.

"Then how?" I asked.

"You have lots of questions," said the older man. "I do," I said, thinking of all the things that I wondered over the last few days. "Would you like to know a secret?" he asked. I nodded.

"If you aren't satisfied with the answer, then you've asked the wrong question." He looked over at my friend, who was trying to eat while smiling.

"What is the right question?" I asked.

"You seem pretty concerned about how much soup I made," he said. "I would guess you have a bigger question. Are you brave enough to ask it?"

Confusion crossed my face. They saw it without looking at me.

"Little questions and little answers are an easy way to hide from the bigger questions and the real answers."

I felt a bit like a dog who'd been swatted. I was looking for a retreat, a distraction. I had no idea what the bigger question was.

"Why don't you want to be human?" he asked, putting his bowl down beside him. "That's a bigger question."

Suddenly I had no escape.

"Humans care for nothing but themselves."

"Did you start this journey for someone else?" he asked. "No."

"So you are doing this for yourself," he said.

"I didn't think about it that way, but in a way I am," I said.

Chapter Twenty-Five

We sat quietly for a minute. It was clear he was willing to wait.

"I didn't want to be someone who exploits weakness for money," I said.

"So money is the problem," he said.

I thought about it for a while.

"If all the money was gone, then everything would be perfect," he observed.

"No, not necessarily."

The rain had stopped. The sun was peeking through the door. He carefully stood up and walked to the door. He looked back at me. I took it as an invitation to follow him. Outside the hut, the ground was moist. The clouds were rolling past the tops of the trees. He walked along the edge of the clearing where stones demarcated the clearing from the jungle. I had thought the stones were simply decoration, but they served as a perfect path. I followed him to where the stones segmented, opening to another path. It was well covered by trees and vines shielding us from rain. Up the path was a pool that fit perfectly below a steep hill with giant stones. Water oozed from moss between the stones and trickled into the pool. Somebody had meticulously placed stones at its sides to make it more accessible. Like the pool by the city wall, herbs were strategically planted between the rocks. A downed tree doubled as a bench where we sat.

Our bench was succumbing to the moss and insects at one end. The bark and roots disintegrated into sawdust when touched. At the base, broadleaf plants poked around for sunlight and filled the hole where the roots and trunk had once stood. At the other end, vines were already looking for a new tree to climb. Bromeliads that had hung from the canopy stretched hard to find the light they had lost. In the middle, the tree was worn where it was used for a bench.

The older man sat and looked at the pool. I settled in beside him. Instinctively, I took a deep breath. I felt him do the same.

"Many feel that something is amiss in the life they are leading. They come to reconnect. Some come looking to regain power over their own lives. Some have left the jungle or the mountains and family where they grew up. They come to regain a sense of what they lost." He looked around at the trees and vines that surrounded us.

"We are never not connected," he sighed. "There is no magic that will give you what you want. Do you understand?"

"I'm not sure," I said.

"Good," he said. "Keep looking."

"Since I drank the first jar, things have been pretty wild," I said. He smiled and nodded his head.

"Very few know what they really want. When it finds them, they are rarely ready."

"Then what?" I asked.

He smiled and looked me in the face. His dark eyes had a softness.

"Something dies," he said. He didn't bother to explain. His body took on a heaviness. A bird landed beside him, instantly lifting his spirits.

He held out his hand; there were some small seeds in his palm. The bird hopped to his thumb and took a seed before flying off. Another saw and landed beside us. He looked at the open palm with seeds and cocked his head. He looked at the old man's face and hopped to the thumb to retrieve his reward too.

My friend made his way up the path to the pool. He dipped a bucket in the water and filled it. He stopped to watch the birds circling in the trees. He pulled some seeds from his pocket and handed them to me.

"Sit very still," he said. "They will come when they feel safe."

I held my hand out with several seeds in my palm. A small bird landed on my arm and inspected my fare. He stepped lightly to my thumb pad and took a seed. He pushed off my hand, causing it to drop slightly as he took flight. Several birds decided to simply sit on the log next to us. They chirped, and when they felt brave enough, they would snag a seed and fly back to the trees.

He left down the path again with the bucket in tow. The old man looked toward the sky.

"Would you like to see more?" he asked.

"Sure," I agreed.

We took the path beyond the pool. Much like at the city wall, stones were placed strategically to allow us to pass without sinking into the mud left by the rain. Up the hill, just far enough that the sounds of the water trickling into the pool evaporated, we stopped next to a massive tree. The grayed bark glowed. Moss hung wispy from the branches and vines. Ants made their way up the trunk carrying bits of leaves. They found their way around thorns and into the flowers. The flowers shared the water they gathered from the rain.

"You see the tree," he said. "We think we are like the tree." He put his hand on its trunk. Ants started to gather around and attack his hand.

"The tree is a whole community," he said, pulling his hand back to safety. "The tree might survive somewhere else, but it would be incomplete."

I put my hand on the tree and instantly felt the invitation. He watched as my knees started to buckle. He caught my arm. Clarity, like before. The tree felt us. There was a barely perceivable vibration that pulsed to the upper limb and into the roots. I knew the other trees felt it. The ants responded by ignoring my hand, no longer seeing it as a threat. Birds landed closer to see what caused the shift. Even the vines responded. I was the tree, and the tree was me. This time, though, we were the tree, and the tree was us. The us that was the older man, the tree and me became others.

Before, I had sensed only the tree. Now we were the forest. The gratitude of the flowers in the canopy fueled our strength. The embrace of the vines became lovers as we intertwined our bodies and lives together. We were welcomed. A secret melody took my thoughts and lifted my heart. As my heart soared, I found more clarity.

A crack of lightning broke the moment. Pulling my hand away felt like losing Leah once again. I looked up into the branches towering above me and saw so much more than the tree. Rain began to fall. I could not move. I closed my eyes and raised my face to the sky. Rain collected in the leaves and moss. It ran down the vines and spilled onto my head. The water was cool, and it saturated my clothing.

I don't know why or what the catalyst was, but I started to weep. Tears mingled with water and ran down my body. The pool at my feet found its way to a pocket at the base of the tree. Another flash, a crack of lightning and thunder, and I began to laugh uncontrollably. My head dropped back, and my heart lifted. My body rhythmically shook with laughter. I felt cleansed.

The older man watched, water soaking his tangled mess of hair. His eyes never left me. I bent over to catch my breath and began to weep again. I dropped to my knees in the mud and heaved emotions until there was nothing left. For the first time, I felt empty. I took a deep breath; it was my first.

The rain did not give us a reprieve. He held my elbow for stability as we walked back down to the hut. My friend was already inside. We stopped at the door and stripped off our wet, muddy clothes. We dried ourselves using the light blanket that was stowed neatly in the hammocks. I found my clean clothes, as did the older man.

Fading light fell through the windows, cast gray by the rain. We sat on the floor and mixed some of the masa we had brought with water in an earthen bowl. One of us mixed while the other flattened and rolled out fist-sized balls. The other stepped out to the cooking area. The tortillas grilled on the iron stovetop. Water sizzled as it hit the smoke stack.

We feasted on homemade tortillas and avocados until it was dark in the hut. The rain decided to sprinkle, and the moon illuminated the clouds, casting an eerie light on everything outside. Each of us retreated to our hammocks. My body was ready for sleep. I tried to recount the day and couldn't. The hammock was a loving nest that carried me into deep sleep.

***

I dreamt of Leah. In my dream, she didn't die; she disappeared. I spent hours, then days, then years looking for her. Eventually, I abandoned the search. Then, one day years later, I chanced to meet a woman. She was standing on a pier that jutted into the ocean. She was watching the waves and the gulls. She seemed very somber. I stood next to the woman and watched a storm gathering on the horizon.

"I've been waiting for you," she said. Her hand found mine. I looked into her face. Gone was the fire of youth; it was replaced by the glow of experience. Her hand felt familiar, and we walked to the end of the pier together. My heart soared.

"I am so very sorry to keep you waiting," I said. She smiled.

***

We were alerted to the first light of morning by the birds and monkeys hailing the rising sun. The residue of the rain rose in wispy clouds. I didn't realize where I was at first. The sounds were new; the hut was still dark, and the hammock held me in between wakefulness and sleep.

Sounds and smells from the cooking area proved too much to ignore. Outside, the older man was sitting in the sunshine. His eyes were closed, and he sat enraptured by the sun. He heard me moving and made room on the bench next to him. We sat quietly. Behind us, pans rattled, and the familiar smell of cooking smoke hung in the air.

After breakfast, the older man pulled his bag and readied it as if he were leaving. He emerged from the hut with our muddy clothes from the night before. He looked at me, and I followed him. Behind the hut, by the old wood-fired cooking stove, there were several buckets. We each grabbed a bucket and headed off to the pool. We spent the first part of our morning plunging our clothes into the buckets and wringing them out until they were clean. We hung them in the sunshine off a low vine.

My friend showed up after with a long pointed stick and several buckets. We walked into the jungle where the outhouse sat. Together, we moved the structure off the hole and started another pit. He used the pointed stick to loosen the dirt and stones. We used a large tin coffee can to scoop up what couldn't be grabbed and filled the buckets. We salvaged the large stones and used the dirt to fill the old latrine hole. The first few inches were muddy and thick. I pulled off my shirt and pants to keep them clean. He did the same.

We dug, working together to create a hole that was big enough for a man to stand in. We would break up the bottom, and one of us would jump down to scrape the dirt and lift the stones to the surface. It was hard work. The older man joined us and moved the buckets of earth to the old hole. I made sure not to overfill the buckets so he could carry them.

After several hours, the pit was deep enough that I had to climb a makeshift ladder to get in and out of the hole. Nobody proclaimed the job done. The three of us stood looking into the hole. We were all covered with dirt and sweat. We pulled up the log we used as a ladder and replaced the outhouse over the new hole. The old pit had a heap of dirt that we stacked the stones on top of.

***

The older man motioned to me. He had a smile and a jar in his hand. We walked further up the path, past the massive tree and even higher up the hill. There was an old tree that had been struck by lightning. The center of the tree had burned out, but the outside was still intact. I heard buzzing before we saw the tree. There was a rusted sheet of corrugated metal bent to protect the hole left by the fire.

Bees greeted us. They flew and landed on our bodies, drinking up the sweat.

"They like the salt," he said, watching me.

He didn't seem at all surprised to see the bees greeting me. I was surprised that he was also enjoying their company. Beside the tree was a perfect sitting stone. He sat down and closed his eyes. Bees rested on his shoulder, while others investigated the tangle of hair on his head. I sat beside him, leaning against the tree. It took only moments before I heard the queen singing. The hive vibrated with the excitement of two visiting.

The queen sang the song of the hive. Years ago, after a devastating storm, the swarm was forced to find a new home. The queen was visited by the older man when he was younger. He told her about the hollow log deep in the jungle above the water. When the bees started to arrive, he constructed the roof to protect them from the rain. The swarm thrived. So much love and gratitude. Tears welled up in my eyes. The bees drank them as they rolled down my cheeks and onto my bare chest.

The queen heard my heart. A sweetness resonated through the hive. I inquired about the swarm and how it was where they found nectar. The swarm began to dance, and lines of dancing bees formed on the trunk. A single bee landed on my forehead and danced. When she took off, my mind's eye went with her. She flew to the heights of the canopy where flowers budded and blossomed in the sunshine. The flowers shimmered and called to us. It was exhilarating. We visited each bloom before returning to the hive.

At the base of the tree, next to the rock where the older man sat, a hole dripped honey. There was a half-full jar waiting there. The older man saw that I discovered the honey. He smiled and swapped the half-full jar for the empty one he was carrying. I could feel him say thank you, and the queen sang back.

We both stood. I took a moment to observe the tree and the swarm. The bees flew off and let us wander back. We met my friend at the pool. He was bathing at the edge of the water, rubbing mud on his skin and in his hair. We joined him in the water. The mud felt good on my skin. I rubbed and scrubbed sweat off my body. The water was cool, but in the heat of the day, it felt refreshing.

The older man sat at the side of the pool, and my friend pulled out his scissors. He went to work trimming his hair. He used his hands to measure and snipped away. Hair fell to the ground. He moved around him, trimming eyebrows and the few beard hairs that grew errantly from his chin. When they finished, he returned to the pool and scrubbed his head and face with fine silt from the bottom of the pool.

After we bathed and checked the clothes we had washed, we made a flatbread from the flour and cooked it on the wood stove until it ballooned. We used honey on the flatbread and sat together silently in the shade, enjoying the bread and honey. Everything else drifted away. There was nothing but the pleasure of simple bread and honey. I felt a peace unknown until this moment. I stopped eating, not because I was full, but to savor the moment.

I closed my eyes and just sat.

I heard them get up, which roused me from my silent contemplation. I quickly finished my bread and honey. My friend retrieved a machete from the cooking area, and we set off up the hill. We found trees and branches that had fallen and not yet succumbed to the process of decomposition. We used the machete to cut the wood into pieces that would fit in the cookstove. As we cut and split what we found, we stacked it on the path. The older man took bundles back to the hut and stacked them so they would dry. We helped him bundle and stack the last of our work. While we worked, we foraged for what the jungle had to offer.

***

As soon as we finished, we started dinner, hoping to eat before the rain started again. While he was cooking, my friend folded his extra clothes that were finally dry and packed them alongside the hammock bundle. He distributed some of the rice and beans into our bags. He showed me which herbs to harvest from around the pool, and we mixed them into cloth bags to be added to our own. It was clear he was preparing to leave in the morning. The older man did the same.

We ate in the clearing in front of the hut, watching the clouds build.

It occurred to me that I had no idea what day it was or even the date. Details that had held my life together were slipping.

"I don't know what day it is," I said aloud.

"Is it important?" asked the older man.

"It used to be very important," I said.

"Why?" he asked.

"So I would know what to do," I replied.

The older man sat quietly. "Do you know when you are hungry?" he asked.

"Yes," I said.

"You know when it is dark and when the sun comes up?" he asked.

"Yes," I replied.

"You're not stupid; it seems like you already know what to do," he observed.

"The world is different there," I said.

"The sun doesn't come up in the morning?" He chided me.

A drop of rain landed on my forehead. He looked at me and smiled. "Rain will make you wet; maybe we should go inside," he said. I caught the joke, and we laughed.

***

We retreated to the hut and listened to the muffled sounds of the rain. The three of us found our hammocks and sat so that we could lean back. We were silent. It made me slightly uncomfortable. The other two seemed completely at ease, sitting without small talk.

My mind tried to think of something to say. I thought about asking where they came from, if they had family, and what happened when they drank from the jar. I dismissed each topic. The older man sensed my discomfort. He caught my eye and smiled.

"You do realize that all three of us opened a door to be here," he said. I knew my friend was listening too. It hadn't occurred to me that without our visit to the cowboy, we wouldn't be here now. The older man watched as the wheels turned in my head. "Some people try to make it cosmic," he shot me a questioning glance, and I nodded. "It isn't," he finished.

Now the wheels in my head turned even harder. I wanted to question what he said but had no idea what to ask. Suddenly, our silence was much more comfortable than the questions that just exploded into my mind. He was grinning when I looked over at him.

"You are looking for meaning," he observed. His suggestion summed up the buzz in my head.

"I think so," I said.

"What do you think this all means?" he asked.

"I don't know," I replied.

He was still grinning. He let my words hang in the air between us. I wanted to ask what this all meant and instantly knew his answer. I asked anyway.

"I don't know," he said.

We laughed. I knew that I was asking about something that should be obvious, and I was completely oblivious. I tried to weave everything together as I remembered it. I wanted to believe there was a continuity inspired by some divine orchestration. The closer I looked, the more I was drawn further back in my memories. There was an overwhelming sense that everything had led me here. Somehow, life distilled itself into this intoxicating moment. I waited for some sacred revelation, some insight, something that would tie all of this together. I listened. I expected something magical. I heard the soft rain on the roof and the dripping of it running off.

At some point, I stopped listening for divine insight and just listened to the rain. I had my eyes closed and didn't notice that the sun had set. I began to smell the world around me. The wet thatch of the roof had a distinct woodiness. The smell of cooking smoke lingered on the walls. The dampness of the air made it earthy. I was completely at ease. I remembered this from when I was a jaguar. My body was limp and resting while I listened and smelled.

Chapter Twenty-Six

I thought about the song of the jungle. I was hearing another verse to its song. I thought about how easily I lose the music and how comforting it is when I find it again. When I was a jaguar, I heard the jungle all the time. It was never lost. I took a deep breath. Sleep found me.

In the morning, we made breakfast and sat in the sun. There was a breeze that carried the rain clouds away from us. It rolled the smoke from the cookstove along the tips of the trees in the clearing before lifting it to the sky. A piece of paper found itself dancing in the wind. It circled the space in front of the hut before dropping to the ground at my feet.

I turned it over and read it. It was a flier advertising jobs at the factory being built. Concrete hadn't been poured, and already the company was looking for cheap, uneducated labor. The paper had a rendering of what the factory was supposed to look like. It had clean lines and neat rows of bushes lining the walkway to the front door. Rows of brand-new cars sat parked in the lot next to the building. Below the factory was another rendering of the housing that would be built for the workers—modern-looking, multi-floor boxes with windows and balconies. Cars were parked in the lot around the building, and quaint shops bordered the property.

A playground with children's playsets and a pool were surrounded by manicured lawns.

I knew that it was a lie. The factory and housing would be built, but they wouldn't look like the image on the paper. For a young man or woman who was already contemplating leaving rural life, it was just the sort of image they hoped for.

My heart sank. The older man watched me and took the paper to look at the pictures.

"This is my fault," I said to him. "The factory will make poison, and it will make the drugs used to treat the poison." Anger and shame were building inside of me. "This isn't right." I took the paper back and stared at the rendering.

The older man stood and walked to the edge of the circle. At the base of a plantain tree, he found a plantain that had been freed by the storms of the last few days. Off the stalk, the plantain was past ripe and putrid from sitting in the sun. He came back and sat next to me.

I began again. "Lives will be ruined. The jungle will be cleared for parking lots and bars." The older man carefully peeled back the plantain and took a bite. I could smell its rot, and the thought of eating it turned my stomach. "The whole thing is a trap," I said as he took another bite.

The more I railed against the factory and lamented my part, the more he ate. Finally, I asked why he was eating rotten fruit.

He smiled. "I was just joining you," he said. "I didn't have rotten words to shout, so I ate a rotten plantain." My face twisted. "Everything you say is rotting inside you. The more you chew on it, the more it festers."

"It's not right," I said.

"You used to think it was right," he said.

"I was wrong and stupid," I replied.

"How do you know that you are right and smart now?" he asked.

"I can see how wrong it is now," I said.

He sat for a while, tossing what was left of the plantain back into the forest. No doubt it landed where the jungle could absorb it back.

"Have you ever watched a fire burn?" he asked.

"I have lately," I said.

"Is the flame bad?" he asked.

It seemed like a silly question. "The flame is what gives off heat; it's how we cook."

"The fire consumes everything," he said. "It consumes everything until it starves itself out and dies."

"Okay," I said, not sure where he was going.

"Some trees need the fire to sprout and grow."

"I've heard that," I said.

"Because of fire, trees and plants will be consumed and die, but others will sprout and live." He let his words hang. I was content to listen.

"Do you think the flame thinks it should hold back or feel guilty about burning?" he asked.

"No," I replied.

"Then why do you?" he asked.

My friend had joined us and was listening. The three of us sat in silence as the implications of his words settled in my belly.

I couldn't help but shake the feeling that I was missing the obvious. The older man put his hand on my shoulder in a way that made me feel like everything was going to be okay. His whole face had a smile that did the same.

My friend had his bag and hammock sitting on a rock outside the door to the hut. It was clear we were heading out soon. The older man went inside and gathered his things too. He brought them out to the stones where we were sitting and set them down. He took a deep breath and closed his eyes. His face lifted to the sky, and he stood motionless for a moment. In the distance, a flock of birds took flight. Shadows caused by the clouds crept along the ground until they found him. A breeze blew gently.

***

This is how he started every day. He was ready, willing, and able to answer the call. He would listen with his whole body to the melody of the jungle. He listened to where his voice was needed and where it was best to be silent. By the way his body gently swayed, I could tell it was a love song. He brought his hands to his heart and bowed his head.

"I am here today," he said. "I wish you a safe journey."

His words brought tears to my eyes. My heart grew sad at the prospect of leaving him. For a moment, I wanted nothing more than to become his student, to stay and absorb all his wisdom. Then I realized that I was on a quest to learn the obvious, and all the wisdom in the world is useless without it.

He looked into my face and smiled the most loving smile. Love, like the queen, like the swarm, buzzed in my heart. He embraced me as a friend and as a father would embrace his son. I wanted this moment to last and end at the same time.

My friend stepped up, and the two hugged, then separated. Holding each other's hands, they let their foreheads touch like I'd seen him do with the woman at the city wall. This time, I could feel the pause and the movement in the trees. Even the breeze paused in seeming reverence. I didn't feel like I was outside looking in. I felt strangely like an inclusive part of the ripple of energies.

There were no lengthy goodbyes or platitudes. The older man returned his things to the hut and made his way to a path I hadn't yet explored. We returned to our canoe. In the sand near the bow were distinct jaguar tracks. The prints were heavier next to the canoe where he had stopped before leaving again. I didn't need to point them out; I knew he saw them too. Without discussion, we loaded our bags, hammocks, and some fruit.

We pushed off into the eddy that made the alcove like something we did every morning. I wanted to watch the shore where we left, remembering it like an emotional postcard. It was a useless endeavor. The river pulled us into the current, leaving no time for memories.

It was still early in the day, and the sun cast morning shadows across the water. The flowers and leaves created a canvas of watercolors that followed in our wake. Birds sat strategically on logs that guarded the banks of the river. They watched for insects or small fish for breakfast. In the canopy above us, the familiar calls of the parrots heralded our passage. Other calls from birds and animals added to the din with cinematic flair. The sound intensified and subdued, as if orchestrated for our passage.

For the most part, the current was sufficient to keep us moving, and only minor course corrections were needed. It was much easier than negotiating the jungle. The river continued to grow in size and speed. Leaves and small branches floated along with us. The rains had dislodged and purged the buildup on the banks.

We cut up a mango and papaya and shared them as we floated. I watched as the trees took different shapes. Later in the day, the river split, and we veered off to the smaller branch. It slowed until we had to paddle to move. We made our way into mangroves. Birds stood in shallow water fishing. The brackish water was pungent, and swarms of small bugs hung between the trees. We negotiated a maze of narrow pathways through the trees. The outrigger on our canoe made some places impossible, causing us to backtrack.

I thought about getting out of the canoe to pull back roots or branches until I saw a crocodile slide into the water and follow us. The crocodilian escort increased my sense of awareness. I began to notice other crocodiles that were inadvertently concealed by roots and the banks. It was the first time I felt like prey. It gave me a somber feeling. The reality of death was now a bit heavier.

All of this didn't seem to phase him. He would steer to pull new round fruits from low-hanging branches. A few he grabbed a bite of before handing them over to me. My mouth was unsure what to do with the new flavors and textures. Had he not first bitten into them, I would have surely passed or spit out what was unfamiliar.

The mangroves stretched on endlessly. The air was humid and hot, brackish and heavy. Our progress was a chaotic movement back and forth. He showed me how to lean to lift the outrigger past close roots. Just when we found a passage through, it disappeared, and we would have to forge ahead on a new trajectory. It was a long day paddling in the heat. The sun was flirting with the horizon when I first heard the gulls.

The trees became sparser, and it was easier to navigate. The smell of the sea was a welcome change from the dank mangroves. We had to step out to pull the canoe over a sandbar that marked the start of waves. Once past the sandbar, we paddled out far enough to skirt the coast to a beach. We pulled the canoe up close to the tree line, where the sand met the jungle.

Chapter Twenty-Seven

We found a couple of stout trees to hang the hammocks and went out to the beach. The sky was turning. The waves were softly rolling onto the sand. Birds followed the waves as they receded. We sat at the line between the wet sand and the dry. Down the beach, the vestiges of an ancient lava flow created a natural barrier. Further down, cliffs hung over the churning waves, blasting themselves against the blackened stones.

The dry sand was warm. It clung to my skin anywhere it touched. I stretched out and watched the clouds building and floating across the sky. The waves sang the song of the ocean. The water gurgled with the sound of stones being rolled in the surf. It was a moment. The thought of Leah came to me. I took a deep breath; it was the first.

He sat next to me, silent like always, but it felt like he was distant, even distracted by something. I didn't question it. It made me a bit uneasy. I realized that his presence was enough to allay my fears. He was a safety blanket. That queasy feeling of wondering how I was going to live started to grow in my gut.

There was nothing to go back to. No life to pick back up. I wasn't even sure if I could get to the money safely digitally secured by the bank. The spiral started. I saw it. I knew I had to stop before it ate me alive.

I thought about being the jaguar when the dogs started hunting me. I was never afraid. I listened, smelled, and was alive. The jungle sang to me, warned me, and opened the door for me. All I had to do was listen.

I listened. The waves stopped being mundane and became unique. The sound of the breeze through the thick tree leaves next to the shore was different than in the mountains. There was a constantly changing rhythm to the breaking of waves against the far rocks. I heard his breathing. I heard my breathing.

The buzzing of a mosquito was the signal to retreat to the hammocks and the mosquito nets. As we stood up, he looked down the coast toward the outcropping of lava and rocks. He hesitated and looked at the waves again.

"Tomorrow, we will leave early," he said.

I looked down the coast and wondered what he was seeing, what he was concerned about.

***

The hammock had become a private sanctuary. I let it engulf me. I started to realize that this part of the adventure was about to end. He had asked if I wanted to go to the sea. We were at the sea. I wondered if another door would open. What would happen to me? It was a question that hung close whenever I looked ahead.

There was no way to know. He was quieter than usual in his hammock. I could either worry or become okay with not knowing. I thought of the older man and how he listened in the morning, not knowing what was next. Silently, I let myself hope that I could live like that too.

***

The night was restless. My body was weary from paddling and the heat. My mind was anxious. The two kept sleep at bay. I woke to the sound of the waves being very close. The tide had risen through the night, and the waves were now discovering new territory with each pass. Thankfully, the canoe was nestled safely beside us in the brush. He was already making preparations. I quickly packed my things in the hammock and joined him for some flatbread and honey. We split some mango and loaded the boat.

Our timing couldn't have been better. We pushed out into the water as the tide noticeably changed. The current helped us pass the break into deeper water. We paddled parallel to the beach. We were far enough out that the swell of waves gently undulated the canoe. We paddled hard to move past the massive volcanic formations closer to the shore. We were far enough out to appreciate the power of the waves but not be thrown into the rocks. The tide was to our advantage, keeping us safe.

***

We passed several arches and caves. The waves continued to carve their way through toward the cliffs holding the land back. Idyllic beaches populated coves between volcanic marvels. There was always the pounding sound of waves against rock.

Curious porpoises rose to investigate and swim alongside the canoe. They swam in a pod that remained close. I was careful with my paddle, though they anticipated our every move. They were a welcome distraction from the work of paddling.

The color of the water changed, and the undulation of the waves diminished as we found a deep-water channel. It followed the coast like an underwater river. When I looked over the side, I couldn't see the bottom; it was like a deep abyss. Ahead, next to a beach with a river running through it, was a massive stone that looked like a whale breaching the surface. As we came closer, he pointed the bow of the canoe toward the beach and rested his paddle on his lap. We had gone long enough; the tide was shifting back in. Its natural current carried us to shore.

***

We pulled the canoe up on the beach, close to the demarcation of the jungle. We wandered close to the river that was spilling itself into the waves. There, on the shore, was a natural outcropping of stones that formed a small cave. In front, a small ring of stones served as a fire pit. I went back to the canoe and retrieved our bags and hammocks. He disappeared into the tangle of branches and leaves. While he was gone, I scoured the beach for dry wood for a fire. I stacked more than enough near the fire pit. He was still gone.

I dug through my bag and found the flint, deciding to try my hand at making the fire. I found dried shreds of palm bark and worked to free the threads. It took a couple of tries to get a spark and quite a few more to get the spark to fly into the dry bark. When it started to smoke, I cradled it in my hands and gently blew life into it. The dry bark proved to be a very good kindling, and soon my smoke had the weakest of flames that were hungry for more wood.

344

I built the fire in the ring, remembering to keep it closer to the flat stones where we could cook. With the fire now building, I looked around at our accommodations. I could tell that others had stayed here. I looked for the familiar hooks or ropes to hang the hammocks. I found hooks driven into the stone where we could sleep safe from the weather. I found the empty water jars and filled them from the river.

He returned with an abundance of foraged greens and roots. He quickly set about cleaning and prepping next to the fire. I could tell he was happy with the fire, though he was silent about it. While the roots cooked, he made the familiar leaf pot and set it on the flat stone near the coals to heat.

***

Sitting next to the fire, we watched the waves. He went over to my bag and pulled out the jar of pure water.

"Tomorrow, the last jar," he said.

My body came to attention.

"That is whale rock," he said, pointing to the huge breached whale formation past the wave break.

"Tomorrow, we will paddle out to it. See that ledge that hangs out past the rocks?" he asked.

I looked, and there was a small ledge that looked like a whale fin hanging over the rocks.

"You'll climb up there, put this cord on your ankle, and drink the jar."

"What then?" I asked.

"Jump." Instant terror.

My heart didn't skip a beat; it pounded in my chest.

"Really?" I asked.

"You can always choose to climb back down," he said.

"And if I do?"

"We will come back to the beach. If you walk far enough, there is a road that will meet the highway that will take you back to the city. Or you can go wherever you want," he said matter-of-factly.

"Did you jump?" I asked.

"Yes."

"Can you tell me about it?" I asked.

He pursed his lips and looked into the fire.

"It would be like telling you about sleep; until you experience sleep, no amount of description will reveal what it is."

"You could try," I said.

He smiled. "You should find out for yourself."

"Is it safe?" I asked.

He laughed instead of smiling this time. "You opened the cage for a hungry jaguar, and you're worried about jumping into the ocean?"

"I might die!" I said.

He laughed even harder.

"You might live," he chuckled.

Dinner was ready. I took my warmed roots and greens down closer to the water's edge. For the first time since we left the city, I wanted to be alone. Deep inside me, there lived the reality of death. It had held its peace until now. Now it raged.

There was a sort of accounting going on—a measure of what possible value there could be in jumping into the sea from a rock ledge with a string tied to my ankle. There was no measure. There was no foreseeable value; there was only the possibility of death.

My father fought death his whole life, and it killed him. He suffered. As I sat on the beach, I wondered what he would say in this moment. Would he encourage me to run back to safety, or would he have me jump? Was the suffering worth the safety it promised to provide?

I took a deep breath. I could hear the waves. They took on his voice.

"We all die, we all die, even the lies."

***

I went back and watched the embers of the fire. I remembered the older man talking about the flames. I watched them consume every stick of driftwood and ask for more. The warmth of the coals was a welcome relief from the damp cool air coming off the sea. The coals became a radiant reminder that consumption would eventually lead to the fire's death - its warmth a radiant aliveness I could feel on my skin.

I waited until the stars came out. I lay on the beach, marveling at the Milky Way. The indigenous had believed it was a cosmic snake. They attached stories and ways of living to the sacred snake. I saw it as stars—just stars. Who was correct, I wondered. For a moment, I envied their belief in something greater, even if it was just a story about stars.

I slept on the beach. Sometime during the night, I woke, put another log on the fire, and found my hammock. I took the time to note that the Milky Way had shifted. It was slithering across the sky.

***

In the morning, we wrapped what was left of last night's dinner in the last of the flatbread tortillas. He busied himself checking the hemp rope and tying a loop that slipped in the end. He stoked the fire so that it would continue to burn while we were gone. I picked up my jar, and we headed for the boat.

The waves close to shore were difficult to paddle past. We made it past the break and rode the surge, paddling when it was to our advantage and waiting when it wasn't. Soon enough, we were close to the rock. I couldn't appreciate its size until we were in its shadow. Vines and small trees hung from the sheer sides. Near the outcropping was an obvious landing spot. He maneuvered us close.

I took off my clothes and slipped the loop around my ankle. I looped the rest around my shoulder. I grabbed the jar and looked up.

"Do you see the way up?" he asked.

I nodded. I could see small foot placements in the rock. I took a deep breath and climbed out of the canoe.

***

I stepped off onto a flat stone and grabbed a vine to steady myself. I had to transition from the motion of the canoe to the solid stability of stone. My legs were already feeling unsteady.

He paddled off and around to a calm space near where he expected me to enter the water. I began to climb, looking only at the rock and the next handhold. I let my toes explore the rock face for safe places to lift myself up. I moved slowly and held tight to the stone. When I finally found the ledge, it was much bigger and higher than it looked from shore. I realized how far I had come. The ocean stretched endlessly before me. I felt both small and immense, just like the landscape.

My hands were shaking. My legs were jello. I looked down at the canoe. A dime floating in a swimming pool. I carefully unscrewed the lid from the jar. It slipped. I lost my grip on the jar. I instinctively grabbed and missed. It fell. It fell down the cliffs into the water below me. The jar floated briefly and then sank. I looked at him for guidance. I hoped for something. Then I heard the queen: "When the time comes, you will have to fly." I jumped.

The second my feet left the cold hard stone, my fear disappeared. There was absolute stillness until I hit the water.

It was cold. Bubbles surrounded me, tickling my skin. It tasted salty. My lungs let go of some air, and my throat closed to preserve what was left. I could barely see in the salty water. Below me was something dark. It moved. It was massive. It was a whale. I reached out to touch it.

A tug on my leg. It was the hemp twine. My body was pulled to the surface. I remained, watching. The body was limp. He maneuvered it between the canoe and the outrigger. He lifted the body into the boat. I remained with the whale.

In the boat, he took the body and rolled it on its side. He slapped it on the back, and it released water. The lungs drew in a breath. It coughed and whispered, "I am the sea, and I am not the sea." Satisfied the body was still alive, he began to paddle back to shore.

The whale floated to the surface, and I followed. The surge lifted us; seawater spilled over the whale, and I was carried in the wake to the waves just cresting.

The body whispered, "I am the wave, and I am not the wave."

I followed the whale into a garden of corals, brilliantly alive with color. I meandered among the tendrils and was pulled into the anemones. Little translucent shrimps jetted about.

The body whispered, "I am the reef, and I am not the reef."

The whale turned toward the deep, and I followed. The temperature of the water changed. The body began to shiver. The whale met up with others and they floated themselves vertically. One began to sing. I felt the song. I became the song.

The body coughed as it shivered. "I am the song, and I am not the song." Watching the body shiver, he paddled faster toward the shore.

It seemed like one of the whales sensed me and moved closer. I touched it and instantly became the whale.

The body in the canoe raised its hand. "I am the whale, and I am not the whale."

The whale rose to the surface and blew out its blowhole. I was expelled into the air. The air was warm from the sun. The body in the canoe stopped shivering. As I rose above the sea, I could see the whale taking a breath before returning to the deep. I could see the canoe getting closer to the shore. Waves rolled in behind the canoe, pressing it forward. I could see the body and the man paddling. I rose higher. I was engulfed in a cloud.

The body stretched out. "I am the cloud, but I am not the cloud."

The cloud was building, and I rose higher and higher. I saw the sun. I felt its heat. "I am heat, but I am not heat." The sun consumed me. The continuous explosion of brilliance consumes itself. I became the sun.

"I am the sun, but I am not the sun." The canoe reached the shore. He jumped out and pulled it onto the sand. He lifted the body from the canoe and carried it toward the shelter and the fire.

From the sun, I could see a billion other radiant explosions. The brilliance of the cosmos called to me. It sang a song that cannot be heard. Its melody was stillness. The stillness wrapped itself into the violence of creation and destruction. The beauty was both incredible and terrifying.

"I am the stars, but I am not the stars," the body wept. He set the body in the shade of the rock where we slept. When the body landed, I felt it. It called out.

I could see the earth. It pulled me back. I became the wind. I blew like a hurricane across the sky.

"I am the wind, but I am not the wind."

I flew in the wind past mountains. I buffeted against buildings. I became a breeze. Birds floated in me. I became a bird.

"I am a bird, but I am not a bird," the body moaned. He stoked the fire and sat quietly next to the body.

As a bird, I landed in the canopy of the jungle. I became the tree. I became the fruit. I became the insect that ate the fruit. When the fruit hit the ground, I fell with it. A lizard foraged in the rotten fruit and found me. I became the lizard.

The lizard scampered through fallen leaves and dirt. The body twitched and moved. The lizard concealed itself on a fallen log covered with moss. It hunkered down next to an orchid. I became the orchid.

"I am a flower, but I am not a flower," the body repeated.

I held nectar in the belly of my bloom. I let my color radiate in the sun. A hummingbird found me and drank my nectar. I became the hummingbird.

"I am the bird, but I am not the bird." The sun was drifting across the sky. He stoked the fire to keep the body warm.

I flew down the river, stopping and drinking nectar as I went. I landed on a branch near where the river and the sea meet. There was a leaf at the end of the branch where I was sitting. It wavered in the breeze. I became the leaf. As I fell toward the ground, I became the breeze.

I was inhaled by a body.

"I am the breath, but I am not the breath," the body confirmed. "I am the body, but I am not the body," it whispered.

"I am the man, but I am not the man." My eyes shot open.

The body sat straight up. Our eyes met. There was instant recognition. In that moment, neither of us existed separate from each other. "I am you, but I am not you," barely audible.

I looked around, and it was too much. My body began to shake. I felt everything. I could feel the waves, the sun, the birds, the insects, the fire, and the sand. My eyes rolled back into their sockets. He reached for me and caught me as I fell back.

"Breathe," he said.

It was my first breath.

"Close your eyes and listen to your breathing," he said. I did. "Listen only to your breath, nothing else." I'm not sure how long I just listened to my breathing. It could have been moments; it could have been hours.

"Let your mind find stillness," he said.

Everything fell away. My body went limp. My mind was completely blank. "Watch and see what thought comes into your mind."

Stars, brilliant explosions of life surrounded by nothingness. Life enveloped in stillness. "Listen to one thing at a time," he said. Breath. Waves. Water. Air. Birds.

He let me sit on my own. I kept my eyes closed. When I opened my eyes, I awoke to a new world.

I sat.

I didn't notice another outrigger pull up onto the beach. A woman and two men stepped out. The men pulled the boat further up the sand. She walked toward us.

He stood and waited. I sat naked with a blanket draped over my shoulders. My eyes were open, but nothing was registering. I didn't move. I couldn't.

They smiled at each other as she came to stand in the circle of our fire. They spoke. I heard sounds. I heard words, but nothing made any sense. Their conversation was just part of the sounds that whirled around me.

They stopped talking and watched me.

Everything was new when I started to look around. Even the woman in a simple skirt and the familiar bag felt proper in my new world. Her hair was pulled back, and wisps of gray strands moved with the breeze. She had a gentle face and soft eyes.

"She asked if you were the one swimming with the whales," he said. "I told her you were." She smiled at me. Her companions stood safely a good distance behind her.

"She asked if you spoke the language," he added. "I told her that you now knew the language of life. The language of love, and nothing else." She nodded at me.

I didn't understand what was happening. He saw the confusion on my face. "This is the door opening," he said.

They spoke a few more words. They stepped close and embraced, then let their foreheads touch. I felt it. Everything felt it with a resonant hum.

He looked at me and motioned for me to stand up. My legs complained. My body took a moment to find balance. For the first time, he embraced me. It was like being held by a loved one. He pulled back and let our foreheads touch.

Stars, brilliant stars. Life. Trees. The river, the sea, and the whales all came rushing in. The jaguar, the older man, the parrots, the queen were alive in the moment. My body shook. My legs collapsed. He helped me back to the sand and stood back. He nodded to our guests and gathered his bag. He didn't look back as he disappeared into the jungle. She watched him leave, then looked at me. She made a motion asking if it was okay to sit down. I gestured with an open palm. Her companions took a seat next to us. We sat. It was all I could do. They sat with me.

She held her palm out. I looked into her palm. A moment of recognition briefly held the essence of Leah when she did the same to me. She placed her hand on my chest. I felt warmth. My heart slowed. I looked into her eyes and found a familiarity. Heard a voice inside my heart. It was like the voice of the queen, full of love. "I have been waiting," not words. Acceptance. Her eyes held steady.

I looked past her to the waves still caressing the beach. They wordlessly whispered, home. I looked to the sky, seeing it for the first time. Wordlessly "home."

I had no words. I wept.

I felt movement above me. An eagle flew from the jungle and glided over our heads. It dipped its wings into the waves. It soared to the whale rock and landed on the ledge.